College English
Integrated Course

大學
英語綜合

梁 虹、王 洋 主編

崧燁文化

前言

　　外語是人生成功的一個重要工具。從曾經的「學會數理化，走遍天下都不怕」，到現在21世紀的人才必要的兩項「本領」和基本素質———外語能力和計算機技能，外語的重要性日益凸顯；進一步深入和經濟發展的全球化，使外語尤其是已成為一種國際語言的英語的重要性日益突出。

　　《大學英語綜合》的編寫思路是，既注意打好語言基礎，又注重培養應用能力，特別是實際使用英語進行涉外交際的能力。在培養閱讀能力的同時，加強聽、說、寫、譯等語言技能的綜合訓練，尤其注重口頭和書面實用表達能力的訓練與培養，以適應中國入世以後對外交往的需要。

　　本書共有十個單元，每單元都由 Get Started、Read and Explore、Practical Translation 和 Focused Writing 四個部分組成，重點訓練學生的說、讀、寫、譯能力，提高學生實際使用英語進行涉外交際的能力，較好地體現了大學英語教學要全面培養、提高學生的英語綜合應用能力的大方向。

　　由於學識所限，謬誤差錯在所難免，我們歡迎專家學者以及使用教材的教師和學生提出寶貴意見，以便及時修正。

編者

目錄

Unit 1　Men and Women ………………（1）

　　1.1　Get Started ……………………（1）

　　1.2　Read and Explore ……………（1）

　　1.3　Practical Translation …………（15）

　　1.4　Focused Writing ………………（19）

Unit 2　Man and Nature ………………（25）

　　2.1　Get Started ……………………（25）

　　2.2　Read and Explore ……………（27）

　　2.3　Practical Translation …………（51）

　　2.4　Focused Writing ………………（54）

Unit 3　Man and Technology …………（58）

　　3.1　Get Started ……………………（58）

　　3.2　Read and Explore ……………（59）

　　3.3　Practical Translation …………（76）

　　3.4　Focused Writing ………………（79）

Unit 4　Education ……………………………………………… (82)

　4.1　Get Started ……………………………………………… (82)

　4.2　Read and Explore ……………………………………… (82)

　4.3　Practical Translation …………………………………… (97)

　4.4　Focused Writing ………………………………………… (99)

Unit 5　Work and Career ……………………………………… (104)

　5.1　Get Started ……………………………………………… (104)

　5.2　Read and Explore ……………………………………… (105)

　5.3　Practical Translation …………………………………… (123)

　5.4　Focused Writing ………………………………………… (127)

Unit 6　Attitudes to Life ……………………………………… (132)

　6.1　Get Started ……………………………………………… (132)

　6.2　Read and Explore ……………………………………… (133)

　6.3　Practical Translation …………………………………… (151)

　6.4　Focused Writing ………………………………………… (154)

Unit 7　Travel Around the the World ……………………… (160)

　7.1　Get Started ……………………………………………… (160)

　7.2　Read and Explore ……………………………………… (162)

　7.3　Practical Translation …………………………………… (180)

　7.4　Focused Writing ………………………………………… (184)

Unit 8　Living a Full Life ……………………………（188）

　　8.1　Get Started ……………………………………（188）

　　8.2　Read and Explore ……………………………（189）

　　8.3　Practical Translation …………………………（206）

　　8.4　Focused Writing ………………………………（209）

Unit 9　Psychological Health ……………………（211）

　　9.1　Get Started ……………………………………（211）

　　9.2　Read and Explore ……………………………（211）

　　9.3　Practical Translation …………………………（226）

　　9.4　Focused Writing ………………………………（230）

Unit 10　Conflicts in the World …………………（235）

　　10.1　Get Started …………………………………（235）

　　10.2　Read and Explore …………………………（237）

　　10.3　Practical Translation ………………………（254）

　　10.4　Focused Writing ……………………………（257）

Unit 1  Men and Women

1.1 Get Started

Ⅰ. Prepare as many questions as possible about the role of the father in the family and interview your classmates with the help of the tips given below.

1. Are you very close to your father? How close?

Are you and your father buddies? In what way?

2. Does your father take good care of you? Give an example.

Do you get gifts from your father? Which do you like best?

3. Does your father play games with you? How often?

Does your father encourage you? In what case?

4. Is your father an at-home dad? Explain.

Or a working dad? Explain.

Ⅱ. Discuss in groups the following questions.

1. Do you think fathers are as important to children as mothers are? Why or why not?

2. What's the image of a 「good family man」?

3. A 「working father」 as a family breadwinner is often too busy to take care of his family. Now people have a negative image of the 「working father」. What do you think of the 「working father」?

1.2 Read and Explore

Text A

The Unsung Heroes: What About Working Dads?

On our first 「date」 after our twin daughters were born, my husband and

I went to see the movie *Toy Story*. We enjoyed it, but afterward my husband asked, 「Where was the dad?」 At first, it seemed petty to criticize an entertaining family movie because of one small point. The more I thought about it, however, the more glaring an omission it seemed. Not only was dad not around, he wasn't even mentioned—despite the fact that there was a baby in the family, so dad couldn't have been that long gone. It was as if the presence—or absence—of a father is a minor detail, not even requiring an explanation.

This is only one example of the media trend toward marginalizing fathers, which mirrors enormous social changes in the United States. David Blankenhorn, in his book *Fatherless America*, refers to this trend as the 「unnecessary father」 concept.

We are bombarded by stories about the struggles of working mothers (as opposed to non-working mothers, I suppose). Meanwhile, a high proportion of media stories about fathers focus on abusive husbands or deadbeat dads. It seems that the only time fathers merit attention is when they are criticized for not helping enough with the housework (a claim that I find dubious anyway, because the definition of 「housework」 rarely includes cleaning the gutters, changing the oil in the car or other jobs typically done by men) or when they die. When Mr Blankenhorn surveyed fathers about the meaning of the term 「good family man」, many responded that it was a phrase they only heard at funerals.

One exception to the 「unnecessary father」 syndrome is the glowing media attention that at-home dads have received. I do not mean to imply that at-home dads do not deserve support for making this commitment. I only mean to point out the double standard at work when at-home dads are applauded while at-home mothers and breadwinner fathers are given little, if any, cultural recognition.

The very language we use to discuss men's roles (i.e., deadbeat dads) shows a lack of appreciation for the majority of men who quietly yet proudly fulfill their family responsibilities. We almost never hear the term 「working father」, and it is rare that calls for more workplace flexibility are considered to be for men as much as for women. Our society acts as if family obligations are not as important to fathers as they are to mothers—as if career satisfaction is what a man's life is all about.

Even more insulting is the recent media trend of regarding at-home wives as 「status symbols」—like an expensive car—flaunted by the supposedly few men who can afford such a luxury. The implication is that men with at-home wives have it easier than those whose wives work outside the home because they have the 「luxury」 of a full-time housekeeper. In reality, however, the men who are the sole wage earners for their families suffer a lot of stresses. The loss of a job—or even the threat of that happening—is obviously much more difficult when that job is the sole source of income for a family. By the same token, sole wage earners have less flexibility when it comes to leaving unsatisfying careers because of the loss of income such a job change entails. In addition, many husbands work overtime or second jobs to make more money needed for their families. For these men, it is the family that the job supports that makes it all worthwhile. It is the belief that having a mother at home is important to the children, which makes so many men gladly take on the burden of being a sole wage earner.

Today, there is widespread agreement among researchers that the absence of fathers from households causes serious problems for children and, consequently, for society at large. Yet, rather than holding up 「ordinary」 fathers as positive role models for the dads of tomorrow, too often society has thrown up its hands and decided that traditional fatherhood is at best obsolete and at worst dangerously reactionary. This has left many men questioning the value of their role as fathers.

As a society, we need to realize that fathers are just as important to children as mothers are—not only for financial support, but for emotional support, education and discipline as well. It is not enough for us merely to recognize that fatherlessness is a problem—to stand beside the grave and mourn the loss of the 「good family man」 and then try to find someone to replace him (ask anyone who has lost a father to death if that is possible). We must acknowledge how we have devalued fatherhood and work to show men how necessary, and how important they are in their children's lives.

Those fathers who strive to be good family men by being there every day to love and support their families—those unsung heroes—need our recognition and our thanks for all they do. Because they deserve it.

Words

1. omission n. 遺漏；疏忽
2. marginalize vt. 忽視；排斥
3. enormous adj. 巨大的；龐大的；極惡的
4. bombard vt. 炮擊；轟炸
5. deadbeat n. 賴債不還的人；遊手好閒者
6. abusive adj. 虐待的；濫用的；罵人的
7. syndrome n. 綜合徵；綜合症狀；典型表現
8. obligation n. 債務；義務；責任；恩惠
9. flaunt vt. 炫耀；輕蔑；蔑視 vi. 炫耀；誇張 n. 誇耀；招搖；飄揚；招展
10. implication n. 含義；含蓄，含意，言外之意；捲入，牽連，牽涉，糾纏
11. deserve vt. 值得；應得；應受 vi. 應受報答；應得報酬；應得賠償；應受懲罰

Notes

1. *Toy Story* (1995): In this first full-length computer-animated movie, a little boy's toys are thrown into chaos when a new Space Ranger arrives to vie for supremacy with the boy's old favorite (a wooden cowboy). When the feuding toys become lost, they are forced to set aside their differences to try and get home. This extremely popular and successful film features the voice talents of Tom Hanks, Tim Alien, Don Rickles, Wallace Shawn, Laurie Metcalf, and others. Academy Award Nominations: 3, including Best Original Screenplay. Director John Lasseter also won a Special Achievement Academy Award for the film.

2. David Blankenhorn: Founder and president of the Institute for American Values, a private, nonpartisan organization devoted to contributing intellectually to the renewal of marriage and family life and the sources of competence, character, and citizenship in the United States.

3. *Fatherless America*: Published in 1996, the book presents a compelling and controversial exploration of absentee fathers and their impact on the United States. Fatherlessness is now approaching a rough parity with fatherhood as a defining feature of American childhood.

Content Awareness

Ⅰ. Discuss with your partner and try to figure out the answers to the following questions. Share your thoughts and responses with the class.

1. What's the main idea of this passage?
2. What's the author's attitude toward working dads?
3. What evidence does the author use to illustrate that the importance of fathers is being diminished by American media?
4. Do you agree with the author in saying that 「the absence of fathers from households causes serious problems for children and, consequently, for society at large」? Can you list some of the problems?
5. What's the author's purpose in writing this article?

Ⅱ. Read the passage more carefully and fill in the following table with information from the passage.

Different Media Attitudes Towards Fathers and Mothers

	Father	Mother	Key words
Father Vs. Mother			abusive deadbeat struggles
			at-home dads breadwinner fathers at-home mothers
			rare workplace flexibility
			family obligation career satisfaction
			luxury full-time housekeepers

Ⅲ. Fill in each of the blanks with an appropriate word.

Nowadays there is a media trend toward diminishing the importance of fathers in the United States. On the one hand, we have easy access to m_____ stories about the struggles of working mothers. On the other, the i_____ of fathers presented in the media are always a_____ or irresponsible. Fathers are usually blamed for not helping much with the housework. Compared with working mothers and at-home dads, working fathers have received less media attention, although most are quietly yet proudly f_____ their family duties. Our society has given little cultural r_____ to those breadwinner fathers. Recently, there is another media trend of regarding at-home wives as 「s_____ symbols」—a luxury not many men can afford to have. In fact, men as sole wage earners suffer many s_____. They have to work extra hours to make more money to support their families. It would be wise for us to be a_____ of the importance of fathers to their children. It would also be advisable for us to recognize the great efforts that fathers make to support their families. They, the unsung heroes, d_____ our recognition and our thanks for what they do.

Language Focus

Ⅰ. Fill in the blanks with the words given below. Change the form where necessary.

applaud   mirror   entail   strive   consequently
supposedly   devalue   flexibility   obligation   fulfill

1. Taxes are a (n) _____ which may, fall on everybody.

2. We _____ the authority's decision not to close the hospital.

3. The doctor's instructions must be _____ exactly; the sick man's life depends on it.

4. Do these opinion polls really _____ what people are thinking?

5. I prefer to think of memorization as a stepping-stone to _____ in use of words and phrases.

6. In her office memos she tended to _____ the work done by her staff.

7. The history of railroad transport has partly been a history of

_____ for greater efficiency and profit.

8. He took on the new post without having the faintest idea of what it _____.

9. He is _____ one of the greatest experts in that field.

10. Absolute secrecy is essential. _____, the fewer who are aware of the project the better.

II. Complete the following sentences with words or expressions from the passage. Change the form where necessary.

1. This period is usually _____ the postwar period.

2. It would be a setback _____ if we were denied the use of their software.

3. We make people mentally old by retiring them, and we may even _____ make them physically old.

4. I know that the public _____ aren't interested in this issue.

5. My sister was always _____ to me _____ a model child.

III. Each of the verbs and nouns in the following lists occurs in Passage A. Choose the noun that you think collocates with the verb and write it down in the blank.

Verbs	Nouns
1. suffer _____	a family
2. support _____	luxury
3. take on _____	recognition
4. fulfill _____	attention
5. deserve _____	a burden
6. afford _____	responsibility
7. merit _____	a commitment
8. make _____	appreciation
9. give _____	support
10. show _____	stress

Ⅳ. Translate the following sentences into English.

1. 隨著職務的提升，他擔負的責任也更大了。(take on)

2. 他感到沒有必要再一次對約翰承擔這樣的責任了。(make a commitment)

3. 閒暇時瑪麗喜歡外出購物。與她相反，露茜喜歡待在家裡看書。(as opposed to)

4. 說得好聽一些，可以說他有抱負；用最糟糕的話來說，他是一個沒有良心且沒有資格的權力追求者。(conscience, at best... at worse)

5. 我們已盡全力想說服他，但是卻毫無進展。(strive, make no headway)

Text B

A Manifesto for Men

As men, we know we could get a better deal. We look at women and see modernity: expansive people exploring new roles, conquering the world. Quietly, secretly, we admire the gathering pace of their achievement. And we say to ourselves: what about us? Isn't this how we are supposed to be: bright and confident, going places?

So what's getting in our way? There is no point in blaming women, stoking up a sex war. This remains, after all, a man's world. If we knew what we wanted, we could enact it. No, the problem is our lack of imagination. Ask women what they, as women, want and they'll tell you: equality. Men? We haven't a clue. And the reason is simple. We have failed to understand the opportunities of this century's greatest and most enduring social movement, the collapse of the sexual division of labor.

We're making a mistake. The past ill-served our real needs. It forced us into a narrow sense of ourselves as workers, which fell apart when we were sacked, retired or fell ill. It drove us out of our homes and made us strangers to our children. It meant we subcontracted our physical, emotional, and practical needs to women. They fed us, nurtured us, gave us access to our feelings, mediated a social world for us. They did our private labor, just as we did their public work.

For all the adult behavior we demonstrated outside the home. we remained children within it. It left us, particularly the elderly, half-dead, living sad, limited lives, often stuck in soured relationships.

We can change all this. And it isn't just wishful thinking. A fair wind was behind women's liberation: in a few decades they gained control of their own fertility, while the economy demanded a vast expansion in the labor force. Even conservative men couldn't stop them.

The first step must be for us to break our silence. Hence this manifesto.

Just imagine how we might be

When the sexual division of labor underpinned notions of being a man, we defined ourselves in three ways: as bread-winning workers, as the opposite of women, and as fathers who did what mothers did not do. Each notion rules out a vast sphere of activity and stifles men. We must rewrite these definitions.

Work is not the promised land

When people ask me what I am, I say I'm a journalist. Not a man, not a father, not a husband , not a son, not a brother, not a citizen, not even a combination of these; a journalist. Like many men, I am my work. When work's OK, I'm OK. Everything else might be falling apart, but success at work sustains a man. It provides status, power and a means to be a bread-winning father. The women's movement has only further emphasized the paramount status of work and that, by implication, domesticity and child-rearing is drudgery.

Yet expecting work to support our sense of self so fundamentally is a mistake. Many self-definitions survive the passage of time. Job isn't one of them. It's too insecure. One day we know we'll get fired, sick or retire. For those who are young and can't get a job or are dumped on the scrap heap at an early age, failure at work leads to depression, crime, violence and, in some cases, suicide. Must a man go mad before he discovers a sounder way of valuing himself? We have to realize that putting faith in work is a con.

Man is not the opposite of woman

When women were seen as weak, we had to be strong. We did what women didn't do, but now there's hardly anything women won't do. They play sports, earn money, attend football matches, fly RAF fighters and initiate sex. Yet we persist in thinking of ourselves as the 「opposite」 of women. At this rate, we'll end up defined as the people who do the few activities women don't want to do: rape, murder and abuse.

Fathers, too, can fulfill all a child's needs

We remain limited by the traditional image of fathers as providing income, discipline and, in some cases, a playmate for a child. Physical and emotional intimacy with children have been the prerogative of women and largely continue to be so. Today many men want to be closer to their children and are active fathers. We enjoy it and are competent. But some women refuse to treat us as equals.

Equality begins at home

In many homes men are passive, allowing women to organize our personal lives, letting them act as gatekeepers of the home, determining which friendships are maintained, how involved the couple is with family. Many of us find it difficult to take the initiative or to say no to women at home, because we never learned how to say no to our mothers.

Men must start doing it for themselves

Successful men must take up a leadership role. Too often they stay quiet because they have least to gain from rethinking their roles. Their jobs are relatively secure, with high status and power over women. They have some control over their working hours, can often work from home and afford child care. They can still have it all.

So they hang on to what can be salvaged from the old order, and close their minds to reshaping the world in a way that better suits all of us. The men's movement is thus often inhabited by angry, inarticulate men who lack an intellectual framework for understanding their dilemmas. Intelligent, educated men could lead the way. We need them to start thinking, fast.

Words

1. modernity n. 現代性
2. subcontract vt. 轉包，分包（將大工程）；制定（履行）轉包 n. 轉包契約
3. mediate vt. 經調解解決；斡旋促成 vi. 調停，調解，斡旋
4. demonstrate vt. 論證；證明，證實；顯示，展示；演示，說明 vi. 示威遊行
5. liberation n. 解放；釋放，逸出
6. fertility n. 肥力；肥沃（土地的）；豐產；<生>繁殖力
7. conservative n. 保守的人；保守黨黨員，保守黨支持者（英國）
8. underpin vt. 用磚石結構等從下面支撐（牆等）；加固（牆等）的基礎；加強……的基礎
9. stifle vt. & vi. 扼殺；窒息（使）；窒悶（使）vt. 扼殺；遏制；鎮壓；藏匿 n. 後腿膝關節；後膝關節病
10. sustain vt. 維持；供養；支撐，支持；遭受，忍受
11. paramount adj. 最高的，至上的；最重要的，主要的；卓越的；有最高權力的 n. 最高，至上；有最高權力的人；元首，首長
12. drudgery n. 苦工，賤役，單調沉悶的工作
13. fundamentally adv. 從根本上；基礎地；根本地
14. initiate vt. 開始，發起；傳授；創始，開闢；接納新成員 n. 新加入某組織（或機構、宗教）的人，新入會的人；被傳授初步知識的人 adj. 被傳授初步知識的；新入會的
15. intimacy n. 親密；親近；親昵的言行；性行為
16. prerogative n. 特權，君權，天賦的特權（能力等）；特性，特點，顯著的優點；優先投票權；<美史>總督委任組成的法庭
17. salvage n. 海上營救；搶救出的財產；救援費；經加工後重新利用的廢物 vt.（從火災、海難等中）搶救（某物）；回收利用（某物）
18. dilemma n. 進退兩難；窘境，困境
19. inarticulate adj. 不善辭令的；笨口拙舌；嘴笨

Notes

1. RAF：Royal Air Force 英國皇家空軍

Content Awareness

I. Choose the best answer to each question with information from the passage.

1. In the author's opinion. men are not sure of what they actually want because _____.

　　A. women are getting in men's way in their life and work

　　B. there is no equality for men in the family

　　C. the world today is controlled mainly by women

　　D. this is the men's world and they take their social status for granted

2. By saying「we subcontracted our physical, emotional, and practical needs to women」(para. 3), the author implies that _____.

　　A. women are too dominant in family life

　　B. men are very dependent on women to look after them

　　C. men are too busy with work to cater for their own needs

　　D. men prefer to do public work rather than domestic labor

3. According to the passage, the author is likely to agree that _____.

　　A. men's devotion to work does not necessarily mean a sense of accomplishment

　　B. men should be valued primarily by their success at work

　　C. men should spare no efforts to be successful at work

　　D. men should do as much work as they can to maintain their status

4. The author's purpose in writing this article is to _____.

　　A. criticize women's liberation movement

　　B. persuade men to give up their career

　　C. argue for a movement for male equality

　　D. call on men to take actions to control the world

5. The tone of the passage is _____.

　　A. sarcastic

　　B. serious

　　C. matter-of-fact

　　D. humorous

II. Fill in the blanks with information from the passage.

As a manifesto for men, this article urges men to support a movement for male equality. To start with. the notion of being a man needs to be _____, because the stereotyped notions seem to have confined men to a limited _____ of activity and have placed too heavy a burden on men. Secondly, men's devotion to work does not necessarily mean a sense of _____. Thirdly, in view of women's predominant status in all social activities, men should not consider themselves as the _____ of women. Fourthly, men are not just breadwinners or _____ for children, instead, they can also be close to children both physically and _____. Fifthly, the starting point for men's _____ is at home. Men should take the _____ in trying to manage every aspect of the domestic life. Finally, men should not feel conceited about their _____ and power over women. It will be beneficial for men to _____ their stereotyped roles.

Language Focus

I. Fill in the blanks with the words given below. Change the form where necessary.

sack   expansiveness   sphere   sustain   sour

clue   define   depression   division   equality

1. Some people do, and some people do not, believe in _____ of opportunity.

2. He bravely _____ a great loss from the death of his father.

3. Police have still found no _____ as to the whereabouts of the missing woman.

4. In designing a bridge, one must allow for _____ in hot weather.

5. One of the workmen was _____ for his always being drunk.

6. When boundaries between countries are not clearly _____, there is usually trouble.

7. Gardening is outside the _____ of my activities.

8. She said that the hat made me look silly, but perhaps that was _____ grapes.

9. The newspapers are full of such _____ news nowadays as crime,

natural disasters, and rising prices.

10. The _____ of the world into developed and underdeveloped nations is a gross simplification.

II. Complete the following sentences with words or expressions from the passage. Change the form where necessary.

1. Too much social life got _____ of her studies.

2. Ann did what she could to keep the marriage from _____.

3. Police _____ murder but are still holding several people for questioning.

4. If you go on burning yourself out _____, you'll injure your health.

5. As a result of his grandfather's influence, John _____ art while at school.

III. The following words occur in Passage B. Find 6 pairs of near synonyms and 7 pairs of near antonyms, and write them down.

intellectual   active   public   feeling   feed   physical
sack   emotion   intelligent   fire   passive   private
dump   expansive   secretly   sick   bright   quietly
traditional   ill   failure   emotional   weak   nurture
modern   strong   success   narrow

Synonyms

1. _____ is similar in meaning to _____.
2. _____ is similar in meaning to _____.
3. _____ is similar in meaning to _____.
4. _____ is similar in meaning to _____.
5. _____ is similar in meaning to _____.
6. _____ is similar in meaning to _____.

Antonyms

1. _____ is nearly opposite in meaning to _____.
2. _____ is nearly opposite in meaning to _____.
3. _____ is nearly opposite in meaning to _____.
4. _____ is nearly opposite in meaning to _____.
5. _____ is nearly opposite in meaning to _____.

6. _____ is nearly opposite in meaning to _____.
7. _____ is nearly opposite in meaning to _____.

Ⅳ. Translate the following paragraphs into Chinese.

Mounting evidence suggests that men and women think differently, and this seems to hold true in the unfortunate case of prejudice. New research by evolutionary psychologists at Michigan State University suggests that prejudice in men tends to be linked to aggression, while prejudice in women tends to be linked to fear. These researchers propose a「male warrior hypothesis」in order to explain how our history of group conflict may have shaped male and female psychologies in distinct ways.

Essentially, men are more likely to start wars and to defend their own group, sometimes in very risky and self-sacrificial ways. Attacking other groups represents an opportunity to offset these costs by gaining access to mates, territory, resources and increased status. Women, meanwhile, live under the threat of sexual coercion by foreign aggressors, and are apt to display a「tend-and-befriend response」toward members of their own group, while maintaining a fear of strangers in order to protect themselves and their offspring.

1.3　Practical Translation

語篇層次的翻譯——連貫

　　一個完整的語篇應該銜接得當，連貫性好。在翻譯過程中，我們應該注意翻譯不是以單個詞或句為轉換單位，而是以語篇為單位進行轉換，而語篇要注重整體性和一致性，也就是語篇的連貫性，語篇的連貫性決定了語篇的整體質量。為了實現語篇的連貫，有效的詞彙和語法銜接手段必不可少，但銜接手段是實現語篇連貫的必要但不充分條件。除此之外，我們還應注重語篇邏輯順序的調整和視角的轉換。

　一、邏輯順序的調整

　　在邏輯關係的敘述上，英語常先總結後分析、先結果後原因，句子重心取前置式。而漢語句子則恰恰相反，先原因後結果、先條件後推

論、先分析後總結，句子重心取後置式。因此在英譯漢過程中，為使漢語語篇連貫，有必要根據漢語的邏輯關係進行合理的調整。

例1：We should not be surprised that increasing numbers of people choose to live entirely indoors, leaving buildings only to ride in airplanes or cars, viewing the great outside, if they view it at all, through sealed windows, but more often gazing into screens, listening to human chatter, cut off from「the realities of earth and water and the growing seed.」(Scott Russel Sanders, *A Few Earthly Words*)

譯文：越來越多的人們選擇完全足不出戶的生活，離開樓群也只是為了開汽車或者乘飛機，透過密封的窗戶去看一看外面的大千世界，假設他們去看的話，也不過如此。但是，在更多的時候，他們凝視著屏幕，傾聽人們的閒聊，與「土地、水和正在生長的種子的現實世界」隔絕開來。這一切我們都不必大驚小怪。（範守義譯）

解析：原句是一個完整的「形合」英語長句，採用了各種語法手段，如賓語從句、獨立主格結構、狀語從句等來進行銜接，而且在邏輯關係上也體現了英語句子先下結論後分析說明的特點，句子重心取前置式。在翻譯過程中，為了符合漢語「意合」的表達習慣，原語中顯性的語法和詞彙手段被隱去，整個句子被切分成漢語中靠隱性的意義和邏輯關係銜接的三個單句。而且譯文充分考慮漢語先分析後下結論的特點，對整個句子結構進行了大調整，原語中表示結論的句子 We should not be surprised 在目標語中被放到最後，形成了一個自然的結論，句子重心取後置式。譯文銜接順暢、邏輯性強，讀來非常連貫和通順。

例2：It is a curious fact, of which I can think of no satisfactory explanation, that enthusiasm for country life and love of natural scenery are strongest and most widely diffused in those European countries which have the worst climate and where the search for the picturesque involves the greatest discomfort.

譯文：歐洲有些國家，天氣糟透，要找到景色如畫的所在，這裡的人們得辛苦一番。奇怪，他們就喜歡過鄉村生活，也最愛欣賞自然美景，而且這種情形在這裡是普遍現象。這是實情，可我怎麼也想不出令人滿意的原因。

解析：原句是一個典型的英語「形合」的句子，採用了各種語法手段，如定語從句、同位語從句等，而在邏輯關係上也符合英語先下結論後分析說明的特點，先提出總說的句子：a curious fact, I can think of no satisfactory explanation，然後，如撥開雲霧般，一層層地進行分析和說明，讓讀者心中的疑惑一一解開。翻譯過程中，為了體現漢語句子「意合」的特徵，不僅要有顯性的銜接手段的調整，如去掉原句中的連接詞，將一個長句切分成三個語義銜接的句子等，而且要按照漢語習慣對句子的「隱性」邏輯順序進行調整，體現漢語句子先分析後總結的特點。這樣漢語句子不僅銜接恰當，而且語篇流暢。因此，漢語譯文先分說一些歐洲國家的天氣和尋找美景所需付出的代價，然後語義出現轉折，做進一步的分析和說明，最後高屋建瓴地進行總結：「這是實情，可我怎麼也想不出令人滿意的原因。」漢語句子重心在最後，前面的分析和說明是為最後結論的自然出現做鋪墊，而最後的結論起到了昇華主旨內容的作用。

二、視角的轉換

從社會認知系統上講，東、西方不同的哲學和認識論在社會歷史背景中建構了不同的心理學理論。西方人往往把注意力更多地放在客體和自身目標之上，在觀察事物時，視點更多聚焦於事物而不是觀察者本身；中國人在觀察事物時，更多地是從自己的角度出發。體現在語言結構和邏輯的連貫性上就是英語句子常以物作主語，且一般不能省略，並由此產生謂語形式的被動化。而漢語句子多用人稱主語，當人稱不言而喻時常常對其進行隱藏或省略，從而使漢語中出現大量的省略句和無主句。所以為使語篇連貫，有必要弄清楚兩種語言的思維差異，努力調整自己的思維模式，在翻譯過程中注意視角的轉換，翻譯出地道和連貫的語篇。

例3：This is always a feast about where we are now. Thanksgiving reflects the complexion of the year we're in. Some years it feels buoyant, almost jubilant in nature. Other years it seems marked by a conspicuous humility uncommon in the calendar of American emotions. (November 25th, 2004, *The New York Times*)

譯文：感恩節這一餐總是關乎我們的處境，反應出一年的年景。有些年的感恩節我們心情愉悅，幾乎是喜氣洋洋；但有些年頭我們卻把感恩節過得相當低調，不敢驕傲，這並不是美國人慣有的情緒。（葉子南譯）

解析：英語原文的第三、四句是以 it 作主語的句子，it 指代「感恩節」，有的年份它呈現給我們一派活力萬千、愉悅開心的氣氛，有的年

份它又要求人低調。但在漢語中，感恩節不能和愉悅的心情、喜氣洋洋的氣氛連用，也不能和低調、驕傲等詞搭配，只有感恩節的參與者「我們」才能感受到這份節日的喜悅，體會到那份低調和不敢輕易驕傲的心情。因此為使譯文地道、連貫，譯者有意將原文中的物稱主語變成漢語中的人稱主語，這樣譯文讀起來才順暢、連貫。

例4：Friday started with a morning visit to the modern campus of the 22,000-student University of Michigan in nearby Ann Arbor, where the Chinese table tennis team joined students in the cafeteria line for lunch and later played an exhibition match.

譯文：星期五那天，中國乒乓球隊一早就到安伯亞附近去參觀擁有22,000名學生的密歇根大學的現代化校園。他們和該校學生在校內自助餐廳排隊取午餐，然後進行了一場表演賽。

解析：英語原文是個典型的以物稱 Friday 作主語的句子，表述了那一天所發生的事情。英語中以某個年份、某個日子作主語的句子很多，都表示在某一年或某一天所發生的事情。在漢語譯文中，我們不能照搬原文的結構，不能將原文的物稱作主語，只能從漢語表達習慣和語篇連貫的角度出發，找到動作真正的發出者，調整句子結構，將原文中物稱主語轉換成漢語中的人稱主語。這樣，不僅原語和目標語在語義上是完全對等的，而且譯文在語篇連貫性方面也恰到好處。

Translation Practice

Translate the following sentences into Chinese.

1. Such is human nature in the West that a great many people are often willing to sacrifice higher pay for the privilege of becoming white collar workers.

_____

2. Cosmopolitan Shanghai was born to the world in 1842 when the British man-of-war Nemesis, slipping unnoticed into the mouth of the Yangtze River, reduced the Wusong Fort and took the city without a fight.

_____

3. A study of the letter leaves us in no doubt as to the motives behind it.

_____

4. The happiness—the superior advantages of the young women round a-

bout her, gave Rebecca inexpressible pangs of envy. (W. M. Thackeray: *Vanity Fair*)

5. Poor Joe's panic lasted for two or three days; during which he did not visit the house. (W. M. Thackeray: *Vanity Fair*)

1.4 Focused Writing

Formal Letters

Professional communication is different from personal communication so the style of a formal letter is distinct from that of a personal letter. Formal letters are usually also business letters such as letters sent with a job application, cover letters, letters to institutions such as government ministries or educational establishments and letters to the service industries as well as all the usual day-to-day letters involved in businesses.

Formal letters differ from personal letters in two facets. Firstly, the format of a formal letter is somewhat different from that of a personal letter. Secondly, the language of a formal letter, as the name indicates, is more formal than that of a personal letter. It follows that the intimate and conversational style appropriate for a personal letter is out of place in a formal letter.

The format is, in general, similar in both types of letters in terms of the address of the sender, the date and the main body. However there are some additional points to note as follows.

The addressee's address. In a formal letter, the addressee's address, that is, the address of the recipient which you will also write on the outside of the envelope, is placed on the left, one or two lines below the line of the date (which is still on the right) and above the salutation. In a personal letter, this address is omitted.

The salutation. This usually takes the form 「Dear Mr. ...」 or 「Dear Ms. ...」 if you know the surname of the recipient. Note that only the surname appears after Mr. /Mrs. /Miss. /Ms. It is not correct to address a letter 「Dear Mr. Tom Black」. It should be Dear Tom (informal) or Dear Mr. Black (formal). If you don't know the name of the recipient or you don't know who is supposed to receive the letter, simply write 「Dear Sirs」 or 「Dear Sir or Madam」.

The complimentary close. 「Yours sincerely」 or 「Yours faithfully」 are two most commonly used forms, but their usage should never be confused. 「Yours sincerely」 is used when you know the name of the recipient and have started the letter with their name; whereas, 「Yours faithfully」 should be used if you don't and have therefore started Dear Sir or Dear Madam.

The signature. A formal letter requires your full signature, and usually your full name and title will be printed below your signature. This is because signatures are often unclear.

Headed notepaper. If you are writing on behalf of a business, then it is likely that you will use notepaper that has been preprinted with the name and logo and often the address of the company. If you are writing a business letter on your own behalf, then it is important to ensure that your address is clearly written at the top right of the page so that any reply can be sent.

Two samples of formal letters are given below to help you see how a formal letter should be laid out and the tone of the formal writing.

Sample 1   **A Letter of Enquiry**

> Living Science Weekly
> 45-49 Rush Road
> Nottingham
> NO2, 2ST
> England
>
> June 23rd, 2010
>
> The General Manager
> Ryder Wholesale Medical Supplies Ltd
> 90-100 Rue de la Pompe
> Paris 75004
> France
>
> Dear Sir,
>   The magazine *Living Science Weekly* of which I am Chief Feature Writer will shortly be running a series of articles on scientists who are prominent in different fields of science. We understand that your Senior Research Scientist, Dr J. L. Bonfils, is engaged in research on a new type of anesthetic and we would therefore be very interested in his views for one of our articles.
>   I am writing to you first in case you feel it inappropriate for Dr. Bonfils to talk to us and to assure you that the subject matter of the interview will not in any way breach the confidentiality associated with his current research.
>   I would be most grateful if Dr. Bonfils could spare me a little of his very valuable time, during the next two weeks I can be available at any time to suit Dr. Bonfils except for on the 19th and 24th and would be happy to meet anywhere convenient for him.
>   I look forward to hearing from you.
>
>   Yours faithfully,
>   Edward Sawyer

Note: This is a letter requesting whether a senior member of Ryder Medical Supplies could be available for an interview by a feature writer of a magazine. The writer first briefly introduces himself and then says why he is writing (i.e. asking for an interview). He also indicates why he has not approached Dr. Bonfils directly. Then he mentions that the interview will have to be in the next two weeks (no doubt he has deadlines to meet but it is not necessary for him to go into detail about that) but makes it as easy as possible for Dr. Bonfils to accommodate him since he is asking for a favor.

    The ending 「I look forward to hearing from you」is the best and most commonly used way to indicate that you hope for an early response.

It is important for all business letters to be written as concisely and as clearly as possible so that they are easy to read and understand.

A cover letter is a letter that is included with a document or object to explain why it is being sent to the recipient. For example, a cover letter would be necessary if something was being returned after purchase in order to explain what is wrong and what you expect the seller to do about it. A cover letter should be sent with a CV or resume when applying for a job highlighting the main reason why you think you are suitable for the job and expressing your hope for the opportunity to meet (i.e. to get an interview). In this circumstance the letter should be short, do not be tempted to repeat everything that is in your CV. There are many situations in which a cover letter will be necessary. See the sample below.

Sample 2　　　**A Cover Letter for Manuscript Submission**

>   The Dept of Education
>   University of Birmingham
>   Edgbaston
>   Birmingham
>   B15, 2TT
>
>   June 6th, 2008
>
> The Editorin Chief
> ELT Journal
> Markham Road
> London
> SW18, 9LT
>
> Dear Mr. Drummond,
> 　　I am enclosing a manuscript entitled「Improving Scores on the IELTS Speaking Test」to be considered for publication in the ELT Journal.
> 　　The paper presents three strategies for teaching students who are taking the IELTS speaking test. The first strategy is aimed at improving confidence and uses a variety of self-help materials from the field of popular psychology. The second encourages students to think critically and invokes a range of academic perspectives. The third strategy invites a close inspection and utilization of the marking criteria published in the IELTS handbook. These strategies were applied to a group of students who sat the test in September 2005 and their scores are presented and analyzed. There is evidence that the strategies were effective in raising scores on the speaking component by as much as 12%.
> 　　I confirm that this manuscript has not been published elsewhere and is not under consideration by another journal. The study was supported by a grant from the Wellcome Trust, UK. The author has no conflicts of interest to declare.

> Please address correspondence to:
> Dr. Steve Issitt
> Deputy Director of EAP Summer Courses
> University of Birmingham
> I look forward to hearing from you at your earliest convenience.
>
> Yours sincerely,
> Steve Issitt
> Dr. S. Issitt
> S. Issitt@ bham. ac. ukTel: 0121, 41, 45702

Note: A cover letter for a manuscript submission is your opportunity to directly address the editor of your target journal in order to persuade him or her to consider your paper. The following principals apply in this situation:

• Some journals have different editors for the different areas of research that the journal covers so you should choose the most appropriate editor based on area and occasionally also editor profiles. Always try to address your letter personally to the appropriate editor, e.g.「Dear Dr. Smith」. It is easy to telephone to ask. If one cannot be identified, address your letter to the Editor-in-Chief.

• Begin by providing the title of your manuscript, the section/publication type in which you would like to see it published, and the name of the journal you are submitting it to.

• You then need to provide a very brief background and rationale for your study, explaining why you did what you did. This can be followed by a brief description of the results.

• The following paragraph is very important. You will need to explain the significance of your findings to the research community, and specifically to the readers of your target journal. If you find it difficult to explain why the readers of that journal would be interested in your findings, then you may need to select a more appropriate journal. Editors will only send papers to review that they think will be of interest to their readers. Studying the「aims and scope」of your chosen journal might help with this.

• The last paragraph of the letter should contain any statements or declarations required by the target journal. These usually include declarations of any conflicts of interest, grant support or other sources of funding, a statement that all authors have read and approved the manuscript and a statement that the same manuscript has not been submitted elsewhere. Confirmation of each author's qualification for authorship may also be required.

· Finally, add your contact details and your name printed after your signature.

Writing Assignment

Write a formal letter to a tourist office asking for information about a place you intend to visit. Be sure to be specific about what information you would like to know.

Unit 2 Man and Nature

2.1 Get Started

Ⅰ. This quiz measures your knowledge about humans and nature. Choose the correct answer for each question.

1. Why are volcanoes and landslides considered 「hazardous」 natural earth processes?

  A. These processes are often catastrophic (very fast, and full of destructive energy).

  B. These fairly violent processes can occur where people live.

  C. These processes are fairly slow and relatively nonviolent.

  D. A and B combined.

  E. A and C combined.

  F. B and C combined.

2. The following are ways humans can affect natural geological processes, except _____.

  A. increases in soil erosion due to the clearing of forests

  B. increases in volcanic activity due to the building of cities

  C. increases in fiver flooding due to the clearing of forests

  D. increases in flooding due to the building of cities

3. Who determines which species are endangered?

  A. United Nations (UN).

  B. World Wildlife Fund (WWF).

  C. Conservation International (CI).

  D. International Union for the Conservation of Nature and Natural Resources (IUCN).

4. How many animal species are endangered today worldwide?

  A. About 300.   B. About 1,000.

  C. About 5,000.   D. About 10,000.

5. What is the main reason for plants and animals being endangered?

    A. Climate change.   B. Habitat destruction.

    C. Poaching（偷獵）.   D. Predators（食肉動物）.

6. The following reasons are why animals become extinct, except _____.

    A. changes in climate

    B. increases in human population

    C. fighting and killing between animal species

    D. the hunting and capture of animals by humans

7. The following animal species are already extinct, expect the _____.

    A. Dodo   B. Dinosaur

    C. Steller's Sea Cow   D. White-tailed fish eagle

8. Which description is not true about the blue whale?

    A. It is the largest animal ever known to have lived.

    B. It can live for more than 100 years.

    C. It is listed as one of the endangered species in the world.

    D. It lives only in the cold Waters of the Arctic and Antarctic.

9. When is World Environment Day?

    A. March 12th.   B. June 5th.

    C. October 20th.   D. May 31st.

Ⅱ. Image description: Look at these pictures and describe how a natural ecosystem works.

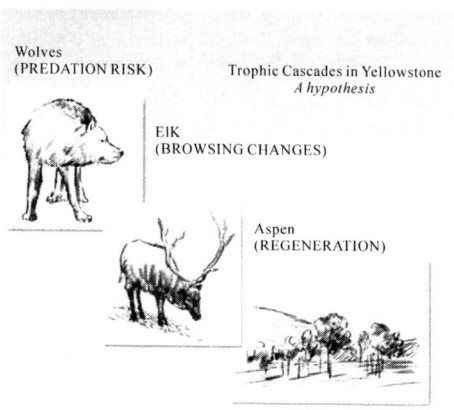

Ⅲ. Discuss in groups the following questions.

1. Many species of wildlife are reported to have become extinct or to be on the verge of extinction. What do you think causes this problem?

2. In your opinion, what measures should be taken to preserve the biodiversity of wildlife?

2.2　Read and Explore

Text A

When the season of winter has overstayed its welcome（因待得太久而不再受歡迎）, nature's promise of spring can be the only thing that keeps one going. Each note of a bird's song, each track on the snow, and every frozen seed is a whisper of spring affirming its arrival.

A Promise of Spring
by *Jeff Rennicke*

Nothing. No tracks but my own are stitched into the dusting of flesh snow, white as birch bark, that fell during the night. No flittering shadows in the trees, not a single sound of bird song in the air.

What sun there is this time of the year shines weakly, halfheartedly through the white clouds, offering not even the slightest pretense of warmth. For nearly a week now the temperatures around my Wisconsin cabin have not risen above zero. The mercury seems painted at the bottom of the thermometer. A shiver runs through me as I stomp my feet for warmth and then listen again for any sign of life. The only sound is from the bare tips of branches chattering like teeth.

At first glance nature doesn't seem to have invested much in this late winter day. The forest can seem like a rough sketch—barren（荒凉的）, lifeless and gray. The sight of flakes（小薄片，雪片）parachuting（空降）onto the front lawn, which swept you up in December, now just means you have to scrape your car windshield. There are subtle beauties—pine branches tipped in white, the pale-blue glow of moonlight off the snow. But deep into winter, you look less for beauty than for signs that spring has not been forgotten.

They are not easy to find. It was once believed that nature simply wiped the slate (板石) clean every winter, which was followed by a miracle rebirth each spring. Mice were thought to regenerate spontaneously from rag piles. Frogs and turtles climbed out of puddles (水窪), spawned (產卵) by magic spring rains. Birds changed into other animals to get through the freezing months.

The real ways nature copes with the cold are almost as amazing as these old tales. Winter gives wildlife two basic choices: leave or tough it out. In some places, the landscape empties like a jug (罐) of water kicked over. Branches bend under the weight of mixed flocks of birds, gathering for mass migrations (遷徙). Two-thirds of the bird species that nest in North America move to warmer climates.

A hundred million butterflies, like wildflowers on wings, travel sometimes 4,000 miles to Mexico, Texas and California. Reindeers (馴鹿) stream out of the high Arctic with the first frosts of winter. Gray whales travel thousands of miles seeking warmth, food and sunlight.

Not all migrations span the globe, however. Many species make short trips, sometimes only a few miles, to take advantage of local conditions known as microclimates. Elk (麋鹿) in Colorado move from high country to nearby valleys. Bald eagles (禿鷹) in Alaska seek open water. White-tailed deer in these Wisconsin woods search out a south-facing slope to catch the morning sun.

Other creatures devise their own way to deal with the harsh realities of winter. Musk oxen (麝牛) stand with their backs to the below-zero wind, slowly breathing through nostrils (鼻孔) that warm the super-cooled arctic air before it is taken into the lungs. Polar bears stay warm by laying on layers of fat up to seven inches thick beneath a coat of fur with nearly 10,000 hairs per square inch. Their rough footpads (足墊) are skid-resistant on the ice.

The survival of some species seems nothing short of miraculous (奇跡的). The chickadee (山雀), for example, weighing just one-third of an ounce, seems a tiny spark of life to throw to the mercy of freezing, 40 m.p.h.

winds.

To keep their internal furnace alive, chickadees eat twice as much food in winter as in summer. They feed almost constantly during daylight to accumulate a layer of fat that will burn slowly through the cold night. They also have 30 percent more feathers in winter and can fluff (抖松) them up, trapping a layer of warm air.

When it gets very cold, chickadees drop their body temperatures as much as 20 degrees below the normal 104, thereby slowing energy consumption. With any hint of warmth, chickadees emerge from their shelters, eating, always eating.

Many cold-blooded species bury themselves in the mud to avoid freezing, slowing themselves to near-death states. Wood flogs actually freeze solid, like lumps of ice, and thaw (融化) out in the coming spring. The frog floods its bloodstream with glucose (葡萄糖), a natural antifreeze that prevents cell damage—a trick also used by some snakes, insects and painted turtles.

I cross a small creek (小溪). Bending down, I shovel (鏟起) the snow off the surface and tap the ice with my hand, imagining a painted turtle somewhere beneath it half-hearing the thud (重擊聲) as it waits patiently for spring.

Somewhere in these woods too are the hibernating (冬眠) black bears. Each fall, triggered (引發) by some ancient memory of winter, black bears go on a feeding frenzy (發狂). They consume up to 20,000 calories (卡路里) a day, adding 30 percent to their body weight. With the first snow, they den (穴居；進洞躲藏) in hollow logs, caves, shallow holes lined with grass. Sometimes they den up to 9 feet high in the broken-off trunk of ancient trees. Their heart rates drop to ten beats a minute and they settle in for four to six months.

The bear's utter faith in the return of spring keeps coming to my mind. Standing here on the thin edge, a few degrees from a climate unsuitable for life, I find it comforting to know that under the snow, bears are sleeping with an innocent belief that the sun will come again and unlock the rivers and make the flowers bloom.

Just as I start to turn back home I hear it: the soft whistle of chickadees.

As I search for them, I see a woodpecker（啄木鳥）spiraling（螺旋形上升）up a birch tree, its blaze（光輝）of red as sharp as a tongue of flame. On the ground, I notice rabbit tracks where moments ago I had seen only unbroken snow.

These slight signs of life make it possible to believe in spring again. They help me appreciate the beauty of what is left of Winter and remind me that the cold won't last forever. Each track, each piece of bird song, each frozen seed, is an affirmation of life, a defiance to the cold, a promise.

Take heart, they seem to say. Spring is coming soon.

Words

1. stitch n. 一針（縫紉或編織中的）；縫法；衣服；縫線（縫合傷口的）vt. 縫；縫補；縫合裂口；縫綴 vi. 縫針，縫紉

2. flitter vi. 飛來飛去，匆忙來往 n. 一掠而過的東西

3. mercury n.［化］汞，水銀；［天］水星；溫度表；精神，元氣

4. stomp n. 跺腳，重踩；頓足爵士舞 v. 踐踏；跺腳，重踩

5. chatter vi. 嘮叨，喋喋不休；鳴，啁啾（鳥等）；振動，打戰（牙齒，機器等）；運動時搖擺或嘎嘎作響 vi. 不假思索地說出 n. 閒聊；咔嗒聲；啁啾聲（動物的）；潺潺流水聲

6. barren adj. 貧瘠的；不結果實的；不孕的；無價值的 n. 荒原，不毛之地

7. flake n. 小薄片，（尤指）碎片；火星，火花；曬魚架，食品擱架；昏過去，不省人事 vi. 脫落，剝落（成小薄片）vt. 把（魚、食物等）切成薄片

8. parachute n. 降落傘；降落傘狀物；［植］風散種子 vt. & vi. 用降落傘投送；用降落傘降落

9. slate n. 石板；板岩，頁岩；行為記錄；石板色，深藍灰色 vt. 用石板瓦蓋，用板岩覆蓋（例如屋頂）；把……加到競選者的名單上；安排或指定 adj. 石板的；石板色的，深藍灰色的

10. puddle n. 水坑；膠土 vt. 使泥濘；把……做成膠土；攪煉 vi. 攪泥漿

11. spawn vt. & vi.（魚、蛙等）大量產（卵）；引起，釀成 n. 子，卵（魚、蛙等的）；絲，菌（裂殖菌類植物的）；產物，結果

12. jug n. 大罐，壺，一大罐（壺）的容量 vt. 用陶罐或壇子煮，炖，煨；把……關進監獄

13. migration n. 遷移，移居

14. reindeer n. 馴鹿

15. elk n. 麋鹿

16. nostril n. 鼻孔

17. footpad n. 足墊

18. miraculous adj. 神奇；奇跡般的；不可思議的

19. chickadee n. 山雀

20. fluff vt. 使鬆軟；搞糟，失去；忘記或說錯了臺詞

21. thaw vi. 解凍，融雪；變緩和；變得不冷淡

22. glucose n. 葡萄糖

23. creek n. 小溪

24. shovel vt. 鏟，鏟出；用鏟子挖；把……胡亂投入；鏟除，挖除

25. thud n. 砰的一聲；重擊聲

26. hibernate vi. 冬眠

27. trigger vt. 引發，觸發；扣……的扳機；發射或使爆炸（武器或爆炸性彈藥）

28. frenzy n. 狂怒；狂亂，狂暴；極度的激動 vt. 使發狂；使狂亂；使狂怒

29. den v. 穴居；藏到洞裡；進窩（冬眠）；把……趕入洞中

30. woodpecker n. 啄木鳥

31. spiral v. 使成螺旋形；螺旋式的上升（或下降）；盤旋上升（或下降）

32. blaze n. 火焰；光輝；爆發；光彩

Proper Names

1. Jeff Rennicke 杰夫·倫尼克（人名）
2. Wisconsin 威斯康星州（美國州名）
3. Mexico 墨西哥（拉丁美洲國家）
4. Texas 德克薩斯州（美國州名）
5. Colorado 科羅拉多州（美國州名）
6. Alaska 阿拉斯加州（美國州名）

Notes

1. Jeff Rennicke (1958 –): an American writer, photographer and teacher. He is the author of over 300 magazine articles for such publications as *National Geographic Traveler*, *Backpacker*, *Reader's Digest* and many others.

2. What sun there is this time of the year shines weakly, halfheartedly through the white clouds, offering not even the slightest pretense of warmth. →The sun seldom appears at this time of the year. And when it does, it shines with no enthusiasm of energy through the white clouds; people do not feel warm at all.

3. The mercury seems painted at the bottom of the thermometer. →It is so cold and the temperature is always below zero that the mercury in the thermometer remains at the bottom and never moves up.

4. At first glance nature doesn't seem to have invested much in this late winter day. →At first glance, it seems that there is nothing attractive in this late winter day.

5. But deep into winter; you look less for beauty than for signs that spring has not been forgotten. →But in late winter, people are more interested in the traces of the coining spring than the beautiful scenery of snow.

6. In some places, the landscape empties like a jug of water kicked over. →Nothing is left on the landscape as no water is left in the jug when it is kicked over and emptied.

7. The survival of some species seems nothing short of miraculous. →It seems that the survival of some species is simply a miracle.

8. seems a tiny spark of life to throw to the mercy of freezing, 40 m.p.h. winds→seems almost too small to survive against bitter winds that can reach a speed of 40 miles per hour.

9. Each fall, triggered by some ancient memory of winter, black bears go on a feeding frenzy. →Each autumn, when they instinctively sense the approach of winter, black bears begin to load their stomachs to the fullest so as to prepare themselves for the coming hibernation.

10. The bear's utter faith in the return of spring keeps coming to my mind. →I was constantly reminded of the bear's strong belief that spring is

certain to be back.

Content Awareness

Ⅰ. Find the right definition in Column B for each italicised word in Column A. Put the corresponding letter in the space provided in Column A. The number of the paragraph in which the target word appears is given in brackets. The first one has been done for you.

Column A

1. __c__ offering not even the slightest *pretense* of warmth (Para. 2):
2. _____ A *shiver* runs through me (Para. 2):
3. _____ to regenerate *spontaneously* from rag piles (Para. 4):
4. _____ a south-facing *slope* (Para. 7):
5. _____ Their rough footpads are skid-*resistant* on the ice (Para. 8):
6. _____ To keep their internal *furnace* alive (Para. 10):
7. _____ make the flowers *bloom* (Para. 15):

Column B

a. a large enclosed fire used for producing hot water or steam
b. a piece of ground going up or down
c. a false appearance intended to deceive people
d. having or showing the act of resisting or the ability to resist
e. without outside force or influence, or without being planned
f. produce flowers
g. a feeling or act of shaking slightly because of cold

Ⅱ. Fill in each blank in the following sentences with a phrase from Text A. Both the meaning and the number of the paragraph in which the target phrase appears are given in brackets.

Example: A whirlwind <u>swept me up</u> and brought me safely to the ground.

(picked me up in one quick powerful movement; Para. 3)

1. Inexperienced as she was, she could _____ the difficulties wonderfully well. (deal successfully with; Para. 5)

2. We're in a difficult situation at the moment, but if we can just _____, things are bound to get better soon. (get through and defeat a difficult situation by having a strong will; Para. 5)

3. He went through drawers and shelves, hoping to _____ the old photo album needed for his autobiography. (find out by searching; Para. 7)

4. It is reported that the Hangzhou citizens consume _____ 3,000 tons of fresh vegetables every day. (to and including; Para. 8)

5. The shut-down of the factory will be _____ a disaster for the people in the area. (nothing less than; Para. 9)

6. The frozen vegetables should _____ first at room temperature before being cooked. (become not frozen, melt; Para. 10)

Ⅲ. Answer the following questions with the information contained in Text A.

1. What are the two primary options the wildlife developed to survive the severe winter?
2. What inspiration does the author draw from the black bears?
3. What do the slight signs of life imply at the end of the author's trip?
4. What does the author think of winter?
5. Why do you think the author is looking forward to signs of spring?

Language Focus

Ⅰ. Complete the following sentences with the words in the boxes below. Change the form where necessary.

| compel   destruction   eternal   output   retreat   threaten   transfer |
| bare   consume   emerge   hollow   mass   miracle   pile   scrape   spark |
| thereby   tip   trigger |

1. If you had had a _____ of consideration for your family, you wouldn't have taken so many stupid risks.

2. Due to the lack of an adequate labor force, even women in this village were _____ to work in the coal mines.

3. We went through lovely countryside with great mountains, some of them beautiful and green and wooded, while others _____ and wild.

4. The cleaner took off his coat and began to _____ the ashes from the furnace with his bare hands.

5. People in that area are already threatened with environmental _____ since 60% of the forest there has been destroyed.

6. The auto company has seen a huge increase in the _____ of private cars this year due to the improved working efficiency.

7. Under severe attack from enemy aircraft, the troops were forced to _____ from the front.

8. When I came up to a giraffe lying on the grasses, I found that it had been killed with a spear _____ with poison.

9. He stayed eight days in an open boat with no food, and he was still alive; his survival was a(n) _____.

10. Survival of the Fittest is a(n) _____ truth of nature.

11. His heart sank when he saw the fresh _____ of mails, memos and telephone messages on his desk.

12. The military government refused to _____ power to a democratically elected civilian government.

13. In that area nearly six million people are affected by the drought and the civil war, and there is a real danger of _____ starvation.

14. Postal service personnel who are severely irresponsible purposely delay sending mail, _____ giving rise to great loss of public trust.

15. With the increase in the number of foreign funded enterprises, various kinds of financial disputes _____.

16. The earthquake may _____ landslides that cause great damage and loss of life.

17. Deforesting and global warming _____ to ruin the current and future state of our environment.

18. It was reported that almost 7 million liters _____ during the 16-day beer festival in Germany that year.

19. On a bitterly cold night, the only shelter he could find was the _____ trunk of a great tree.

II. In the boxes below are some of the expressions you have learned in this unit. Complete the sentences with them. Change the from where necessary.

| as yet   cut down   from head to foot   lire in fear of   show signs of |
| cope with   nothing short of   search out   settle in   take heart   tough it out |

1. Shortly after the government's new policy was put into effect, the economy of our country began to _____ recovery.

2. We knew well what difficulties we had to _____ in bringing our work to a successful conclusion.

3. She _____ getting injured and never participated in any violent sports games.

4. It looks like this snow will stop the food supplies and we shall be hungry for a time, but we've no choice but to _____.

5. Many trees in this area have been _____ to make room for buildings, which has worsened our living environment.

6. In order to avoid possible infection by the unknown viruses, researchers are protected _____ with caps, face masks and white gowns.

7. Despite the warm weather the explorers _____ some snow on the northern slope and boiled it for drinking water.

8. Starting bare-handed, you have built up so many steel plants. This is _____ miraculous!

9. _____ we haven't felt the need for any extra hands, but it's only a matter of time.

10. While one cannot choose one's birthplace, one can certainly decide, based on what one has experienced, the best place to _____.

11. Parents who spend time and money teaching their children music, can _____ from a new Canadian study, which shows young children who take music lessons have better memories than their nonmusical peers.

III. Study the following sentences from Text A and point out the grammatical function of each of the present participles used as an adverbial.

1. What sun there is this time of the year shines weakly, halfheartedly

through the white clouds, *offering* not even the slightest pretense of warmth. (Para. 2)

___

2. Musk oxen stand with their backs to the below-zero wind, slowly *breathing* through nostrils... (Para. 8)

___

3. They also have 30 percent more feathers in winter and can fluff them up, *trapping* a layer of warm air. (Para. 10)

___

4. ... chickadees drop their body temperatures as much as 20 degrees below the normal 104, thereby *slowing* energy consumption. (Para. 11)

___

5. *Being* down, I shovel the snow off the surface and tap the ice with my hand, *imaging* a painted turtle somewhere beneath it half-hearing the thud as it waits patiently for spring. (Para. 13)

___

6. They consume up to 20,000 calories a day, *adding* 30 percent to their body weight. (Para. 14)

___

7. *Standing* here on the thin edge, a few degrees from a climate unsuitable for life, I find it comforting to know that under the snow, bears are sleeping with an innocent belief... (Para. 15).

___

Ⅳ. Complete the following sentences by translating the Chinese in brackets into English, using a present participle as an adverbial.

1. The war went on for years, _____ (奪去了成千上萬人的生命).

2. The farmers used a new insecticide (殺蟲劑), thus _____ _____ (將平均產量提高了 15%).

3. Einstein watched the toy in delight, _____ (想推導出它的運轉原理).

4. _____ (看到大家都在聚精會神地看書), we stopped talking and began to study.

5. _____ (好久沒有收到父母的來信了), he was worried about them.

6. The old scientist died all of a sudden, _____ (留下了未完成的項目).

7. _____ (向右轉彎), you will find a path leading to his cottage.

8. _____ (不想使病人緊張), the doctor did not explain the seriousness of his illness.

V. Complete the following passage with words chosen from this unit. The initial letter of each is given.

Man has a blood tie with nature and nobody can live outside nature. Nature provides us with everything we need: the air we breathe, the water we drink, and the food we eat.

For quite a long time after man began to live in the r_____ of nature, he lived in fear of its destructive forces. He used to regard nature with its e_____ forces as something hostile to him. And even the forest was something wild and frightening to him. Very often, he was unable to o_____ the merest daily necessities though he worked together with others s_____ and collectively with his imperfect tools. Through his interaction with nature, man changed it gradually. He cut down forest, cultivated land, t_____ various species of plants and animals to different climatic conditions, changed the shape and climate of his environment and t_____ plants and animals. He s_____ and disciplined electricity and compelled it to serve the interests of society.

Nonetheless, with the constant e_____ of agriculture and industry, man has robbed nature of too much of its i_____ resources, polluted his own living environment and caused about 95% of the species that have existed over the past 600 million years to become e_____ and still many others to be endangered. The previous d_____ balance between man and nature is on the v_____ of breaking down. Man is now faced with the problem of how to stop, or at least to m_____ the destructive effect of technology on nature.

The crisis of the e_____ situation has become a global problem.

The solution to the problem depends on r_____ and wise organization both of production itself and care for Mother Nature. This can only be done by all humanity, rather than by individuals, enterprises or separate countries.

VI. Translate the following sentences into English, using the words or expressions given in brackets.

1. 這個村子離邊境很近，村民們一直擔心會受到敵人的攻擊。(live in fear of)
_____

2. 這個國家僅用了 20 年的時間就發展成了一個先進的工業強國。(transform)
_____

3. 看到項目順利完成，那些為此投入了大量時間和精力的人們都感到非常自豪。(invest... in)
_____

4. 鑒於目前的金融形勢，美元進一步貶值（devalue）是不可避免的。(inevitable)
_____

5. 現在的汽車太多了，這個地區的道路幾乎無法應對當前的交通狀況。(cope with)
_____

6. 天氣沒有出現好轉的跡象，所以政府號召我們做好防洪的準備。(show signs of; call upon)
_____

7. 那場車禍以後愛麗絲十幾年臥床不起，所以她的康復真是一個奇跡。(nothing short of)
_____

8. 這些同學對世界盃十分關注，每天至少花兩個小時看比賽的現場直播。(be concerned about; at least)
_____

9. 托馬斯說他家半個多世紀前就在佛羅里達定居了。(settle in)
_____

10. 尋求他人的幫助，別自己一個人扛著。我很早就吸取了這個教訓。(tough it out)

Text B

As we know, nature is the most important to human life. People depend on nature to live, and humans need fresh air, water and vegetables, which all come from nature. Industry needs fuel and other raw materials, which also come from nature. What is more, humans also belong to nature, and are regarded as the highest natural form of life. As a consequence, if we destroy nature, to some extent, we diminish ourselves.

Thinking Like a Mountain
by *Aldo Leopold*

A deep chesty bawl echoes from rimrock to rimrock, rolls down the mountain, and fades into the far blackness of the night. It is an outburst of wild defiant sorrow, and of contempt for all the adversities of the world.

Every living thing (and perhaps many a dead one as well) pays heed to that call. To the deer it is a reminder of the way of all flesh, to the pine a forecast of midnight scuffles and of blood upon the snow, to the coyote a promise of gleanings to come, to the cowman a threat of red ink at the bank, to the hunter a challenge of fang against bullet. Yet behind these obvious and immediate hopes and fears there lies a deeper meaning, known only to the mountain itself. Only the mountain has lived long enough to listen objectively to the howl of a wolf.

Those unable to decipher the hidden meaning know nevertheless that it is there, for it is felt in all wolf country, and distinguishes that country from all other land. It tingles in the spine of all who hear wolves by night, or who scan their tracks by day. Even without sight or sound of wolf, it is implicit in a hundred small events: the midnight whinny of a pack horse, the rattle of rolling rocks, the bound of a fleeing deer, the way shadows lie under the spruces. Only the ineducable tyro can fail to sense the presence or absence of wolves, or the fact that mountains have a secret opinion about them.

My own conviction on this score dates from the day I saw a wolf die. We were eating lunch on a high rimrock, at the foot of which a turbulent river elbowed its say. We saw what we thought was a doe fording the torrent, her breast awash in white water. When she climbed the bank toward us and shook out her tail, we realized our error: It was a wolf. A half dozen others, evidently grown pups, sprang from the willows and all joined in a welcoming mêlée of wagging tails and playful maulings. What was literally a pile of wolves writhed and tumbled in the center of an open flat at the foot of our rimrock.

In those days we had never heard of passing up a chance to kill a wolf. In a second we were pumping lead into the pack, but with more excitement than accuracy: how to aim a steep downhill shot is always confusing. When our rifles were empty, the old wolf was down, and a pup was dragging a leg into impassable slide-rocks.

We reached the old wolf in time to watch a fierce green fire dying in her eyes. I realized then, and have known ever since, that there was something new to me in those eyes—something known only to her and to the mountain. I was young then, and full of trigger-itch; I thought that because fewer wolves meant more deer, that no wolves would mean a hunters' paradise. But after seeing the green fire die, I sensed that neither the wolf nor the mountain agreed with such a view.

Since then I have lived to see state after state extirpate its wolves. I have watched the face of many a newly wolfless mountain, and seen the south-facing slopes wrinkle with a maze of new deer trails. I have seen every edible bush and seedling browsed. First to anemic desuetude, and then to death. I have seen every edible tree defoliated to the height of a saddle horn. Such a mountain looks as if someone had given God a new pruning shears, and forbidden Him all other exercise. In the end the starved bones of the hoped, for deer herd, dead of its own too-much, bleach with the bones of the dead sage, or molder under the high-lined junipers.

I now suspect that just asa deer herd lives in mortal fear of its wolves, so does a mountain live in mortal fear of its deer. And perhaps with better cause, for while a buck pulled down by wolves can be replaced in two or three years, a range pulled down by too many deer may fail of replacement in as many decades.

So also withcows. The cowman who cleans his range of wolves does not realize that he is taking over the wolf's job of trimming the herd to fit the range. He has not learned to think like a mountain. Hence we have dust bowls, and rivers washing the future into the sea.

We all strive for safety, prosperity, comfort, long life, and dullness. The deer strives with his supple legs, the cowman with trap and poison, the statesman with pen, the most of us with machines, votes, and dollars, but it all comes to the same thing: peace in our time. A measure of success in this is all well enough, and perhaps is a requisite to objective thinking, but too much safety seems to yield only danger in the long run. Perhaps this is behind Thoreau's dictum: In wildness is the salvation of the world. Perhaps this is the hidden meaning in the howl of the wolf, long known among mountains, but seldom perceived among men.

Words and Expressions

1. anemic adj. 沒有活力的，無精打采的

2. awash adj. 被水或其他液體漫過的

e.g. The river overflowed until the streets were awash.

3. bawl v. 叫嚷，大喊 n. 叫嚷，大喊

4. bleach v. 使（顏色）變淡，使變白；漂白；曬白

e.g. The sun had bleached her hair.

5. coyote n. （北美西部和墨西哥的）叢林狼

6. decipher v. 辨認；解釋

e.g. I always wonder how people manage to decipher my doctor's handwriting.

7. defiant adj. 違抗的；挑釁的；蔑視的

e.g. With a final defiant gesture, they sang a revolutionary song as they were led away to prison.

8. defoliate v. （用脫葉劑）使……脫落

9. desuetude n. 廢棄；不用

10. dictum n. （由受人尊敬的或有權威的人士正式發表的）斷言，意見，宣言

e.g. It is a sad fact that one of feminism's most important dictums, that 「women have a right to choose,」 has been so jeopardized （危及，損害）by women's insecurities.

11. doe n. 雌兔；雌鹿

12. dust bowl n. 干旱而多塵暴的地帶

13. extirpate v. 消滅；根除

e.g. It is far more common for a bird to be extirpated from a particular region, while surviving elsewhere.

14. fang n.（蛇，野狗等的）尖牙

15. ford v. 涉水而過（河）

e.g. They were guarding the bridge, so we forded the river.

16. gleanings n. 費力搜集到的零星信息

17. juniper n. 檜，刺柏

18. maul v. 撕……的肉，抓裂

e.g. A man was mauled after climbing into the lion's enclosure at the London Zoo.

19. maze n. 迷宮似的街道、小路、電線等

20. mêlée n.（人們四處亂竄的）混亂局面

21. molder v. 腐爛，腐朽；漸漸崩塌

e.g. Your scripts have been moldering under your bed for ages.

22. rattle n.（碰撞而發出的）格格聲，嘎嘎聲

e.g. There was a rattle of rifle fire.

23. requisite n. 必需品

24. sage n. 鼠尾草，洋蘇菜（其灰綠色葉子可用於烹調）

25. scuffle n. 扭打（不太猛烈的短時打鬥）

e.g. A few isolated scuffles broke out when police tried to move the demonstrators.

26. seedling n. 籽苗，種苗，幼苗

27. shears n. 大剪刀

28. spruce v.（使）（自己或某物）顯得更加整齊乾淨

e.g. The cottage had been spruced up a bit since her last visit.

29. supple adj.（身體）柔軟的；靈活的

30. tingle v.（尤指皮膚）感到刺痛

e.g. My cheeks tingled with the cold.

31. torrent n. a large amount of water moving very rapidly and strongly in

a particular direction（水的）湍流，急流

e.g. A torrent of water swept down the valley.

32. tyro n. 新手，生手，初學者

33. wag v. (狗) 搖 (尾巴)

e.g. The dog wagged its tail with pleasure.

34. whinny v. (馬) 輕聲嘶叫 n. (馬) 嘶叫

35. willow n. 柳樹；柳木

36. writhe v. (尤指因痛苦而) 劇烈地扭動身體

e.g. He was writhing on the ground in agony.

37. pay heed to sth. 注意某事；慎重考慮某事

e.g. You should pay heed to her advice as she has had a similar experience.

Proper Names

1. Aldo Leopold 奧爾多·利奧波德
2. Thoreau 梭羅 (1817—1864，美國作家，哲學家)

Notes

1. Aldo Leopold (1887—1948) is widely acknowledged as the initiator of modern wildlife conservation in the United States. He was best known for his collections *A Sandy County Almanac*, from which this text is extracted. The essays are stories of Leopold's observations of nature around him, the passing of seasons, and of wildlife, based on the belief that every living thing has a niche in the ecosystem.

2. The phrase「the way of all flesh」means「living and dying as other people (beings); suffering the same change or danger, as other people (beings) do」.

3. The phrase「red ink" is used figuratively here. In US English, it refers to (financial) deficit, a situation in which one owes more money than one has.

e.g. Fallout from investments in the risky subprime mortgage market has forced Wall Street banks to write down more than $150 billion—and more red ink is expected.

4. Here,「a pack horse」refers to a horse used for carrying heavy loads,

also there are 「pack donkeys or camels」, etc.

5. The writer uses 「elbow」 to show how the river flowed and turned round so fast, as if it were a person struggling for a way forward.

6. The first letter of 「Him」 is capitalized in the middle of a sentence to refer to 「God」 specifically.

7. The subjunctive mood is used in this sentence to refer to the serious destruction of the mountains by a large number of deer and other herbivore (食草動物).

8. Henry David Thoreau (1817-1862, born David Henry Thoreau) is a US author, naturalist, transcendentalist, development critic, philosopher and abolitionist, best known for *Walden*, a reflection upon simple living in natural surroundings, and his essay *Civil Disobedience*, an argument for individual resistance to civil government in moral opposition to an unjust state. Thoreau's books, articles, essays, journals and poetry total over 20 volumes. Among his lasting contributions are his writings on natural history and philosophy, where he anticipated the methods and findings of ecology and environmental history, two sources of modern day environmentalism.

Content Awareness

Ⅰ. The text can be divided into four parts. Deduce the main idea of each part with your partner, and provide arguments and supporting evidence.

Part I Every living thing pays heed to the wolf's bawl	A. Different interpretations of the meaning of the wolf callSupporting evidence: a. ___ b. ___ c. ___ d. ___ e. ___ f. ___ B. Traces of wolves' existence. Supporting evidence: a. ___ b. ___ c. ___ d. ___ e. ___ f. ___

表(續)

Part II The author's experience of killing a wolf	When did the author see the wolves? How did the author kill the wolves? Why did the author kill the wolves?
Part III The chain consequence of killing wolves and cows	Arguments: a. _____ b. _____ c. _____
Part IV The long-term relationship between nature and humans	Conclusion: _____

Ⅱ. Reading the following statements and decide whether they are true or false according to the text. Put 「T」 before a true statement and 「F」 before a false one.

_____ 1. The wolf bawl reminds the deer that they could be eaten by wolves.

_____ 2. Nothing except the mountain knows what the wolf howl really means.

_____ 3. The deer in the water is fleeing because it is being chased by a wolf.

_____ 4. The wolves the author saw one day were fighting with each other for food.

_____ 5. The author killed the wolf in order to relieve the hunters' burden.

_____ 6. Wolfless mountains are paradise for deer to live happily forever.

_____ 7. A large number of deer will do harm to a mountain.

_____ 8. The cowman voluntarily trims the herd to suit the range.

_____ 9. The constant decrease of wolves will eventually lead to dust bowls and drained rivers.

_____ 10. According to Thoreau, we will know how to achieve permanent peace from the laws of the nature.

Language Focus

Ⅰ. Choose the answer closet in meaning to the underlined word or phrase in the sentence.

1. The howl of a coyote echoed across the valley.
    A. spread   B. sounded repeatedly
    C. rang   D. reflected
2. He has contempt for those beyond his immediate family circle.
    A. attempt   B. disobedience
    C. hatred   D. scorn
3. I'm still no closer to deciphering the code.
    A. decoding   B. finding out
    C. checking   D. understanding
4. My own conviction on this score dates from the day I saw a wolf die.
    A. persuasion   B. belief
    C. experience   D. opinion
5. The police couldn't control the turbulent demonstrations, so troops came to give them a hand.
    A. disorderly   B. crowded
    C. prevalent   D. impatient
6. Stock market prices tumbled after rumors of a rise in interest rates.
    A. stumbled   B. mumbled
    C. rambled   D. fell
7. In those days we had never heard of passingup a chance to kill a wolf.
    A. diminishing   B. exceeding
    C. eliminating   D. missing
8. I now suspect that, just as a deer herd lives in mortal fear of its wolves, so does a mountain live in mortal fear of its deer.
    A. deadly   B. Moral
    C. constant   D. everlasting

9. Stress is widely <u>perceived</u> as contributing to coronary heart disease (冠心病).

  A. viewed   B. believed

  C. spotted   D. received

10. An understanding of accounting techniques is a major <u>requisite</u> for the work of the analysts.

  A. component   B. feature

  C. necessity   D. benefit

Ⅱ. Fill in each of the blanks with an appropriate word from each group. Change the form if necessary. Some words may be used more than once.

1. outburst burst outbreak

 A. There has been another angry _____ against the new local tax introduced today.

 B. Terri keeps _____ into tears for no reason.

 C. A (n) _____ of food poisoning led to the deaths of five people.

2. adversity adverse advise

 A. Despite the _____ conditions, the road was finished in just eight months.

 B. They continue to fight in the face of _____.

 C. It was his doctor who _____ that he change his job.

3. distinguish distinguished distinct

 A. There is something about music that _____ it from all other art forms.

 B. Now that Tony was no longer present, there was a _____ change in her attitude.

 C. His grandfather had been a _____ professor at the University.

4. sight view outlook vision

 A. I use my sense of sound much more than my sense of _____.

 B. Do you have a (n) _____ about what we should do now?

 C. The _____ of the economy is still uncertain.

D. Maybe you had _____ of being surrounded by happy, smiling children.
5. implicit   underlying   implied
   A. He has a (n) _____ belief in the goodness of people.
   B. I feel there is some _____ criticism about the gift you have chosen.
   C. To prevent a problem you have to understand its _____ causes.
6. awash   wash   washing
   A. You are going to have your dinner, get _____, and go to bed.
   B. The roads were _____ with mud and rainwater.
   C. My mother always did the _____ on Mondays.
7. spring   jump   leap
   A. He _____ to his feet, and grabbed his keys off the coffee table.
   B. To the north are the hot _____ of Banyas de Sant Loan.
   C. Think twice before you _____.
   D. The number of crimes _____ by 10% last year.
8. track   trail   trace (n. & v.)
   A. He left a _____ of muddy footprints.
   B. He was following a broad _____ through the trees.
   C. I can't _____ the file you want on disk C.
   D. After graduation we find it difficult to keep _____ of our old friends.
   E. The intruders were careful not to leave any _____ behind them.
9. sense (n. & v.)   sensible   sensational   sensitive
   A. She probably _____ that I wasn't telling her the whole story.
   B. This seems to be a _____ way of dealing with the problem.
   C. Winning an award would give me a great _____ of achievement.
   D. Carol takes his work seriously and is _____ to criticism.

E. Experts agreed that it was a truly _____ performance.

10. prosperity   prospect   prosperous   prophecy

   A. With economic expansion comes the promise of a more _____ future.

   B. We hope that the 21st century brings peace, happiness and _____, with us learning to respect our differences rather than fight about them.

   C. The _____ for employment in the technology sector are especially good right now.

   D. His _____ that she would one day be a star came true.

Ⅲ. Complete the following extract with information from the text.

A wolf gives out a deep chesty howl in the valley one night. It _____ from rimrock to rimrock. Every living thing _____ the call. Although it has different _____ meanings to different animals, it is only the mountains that can listen _____ to the call, because it has lived long enough. Those who can't _____ the hidden meaning of the howl can still sense the wolves' _____ through their tracks, sights or sounds. Whatever the fact is, I believe that the mountains have a secret opinion about the wolves.

This _____ on this score dates from the day when I witnessed a wolf die. We thought we saw a doe when we were eating lunch on a high rimrock. When we realized that it was a wolf and there were still a half dozen others, we _____ at them out of excitement and trigger-itch. At that time, I thought I helped the hunters, _____, when I saw the green fire die in the wolf's eyes, I found I might be wrong.

Sine then, I have seen the _____ of wolves state after state, which eventually lead to nearly _____ mountains. The same is true to cowmen who have to _____ the herd to fit the range. All creatures in the valley _____ each other, and they should be kept in balance. If one link breaks down, it might cause dramatic change to others. We all _____ for safety, prosperity, comfort, long life, and dullness, but too much safety seems to _____ only danger in the long run.

Ⅳ. Translate the following passage into English.

人類生活在大自然的王國裡。他們不僅是大自然的居民，也是大自然的改造者。隨著社會的進步和經濟的發展，人們對大自然的直接依賴越來越少，而對其間接的依賴卻越來越多。

人類與大自然血肉相連，誰都無法生存於大自然之外。然而，人與自然之間原來存在的動態平衡已經出現崩潰的跡象。人口爆炸、生態失衡、資源匱乏等問題已成為阻礙人類社會進一步發展的主要因素。

斯伯金教授認為，要解決這一問題，人類唯一的選擇就是明智地協調好生產和對大自然的關愛之間的關係。

2.3　Practical Translation

語境與語篇的翻譯

語境（context）是指語言交際所涉及的不同環境，離開語境孤立地看語言，是無法準確地理解其真正含義的。語境大致可分為言內語境（linguistic context）和言外語境（non-linguistic context）兩大類。

所謂言內語境，就是指文章的上下文以及和語言本身相聯繫的各種因素。例如，volume 這個詞在 The volume of traffic on the roads has increased dramatically in recent years. 中，是指「總量」，而在 The volume of the container measures 10,000 cubic meters. 中，表示「體積、容積」。

言外語境是指語言本身之外的各種主、客觀環境，可分為情景語境

和社會文化語境。情景語境指語言交際活動發生時的具體情景。例如，When did you call me last time? 這個句子根據說話人的身分不同，使用的場景不同有不同的解釋，可以表示簡單的詢問或者是抱怨太長時間沒有打電話了。而社會文化語境指交際者各自不同的經驗、經歷、知識、文化背景等。在翻譯中，應該考慮到社會文化差異，並做適當的調整。

例1：The meeting was not hold due to the airline strike. It was held to discuss the impact an aging society would have on our environment.

譯文：不是因為航空公司罷工才舉行會議的。召開這個會議是為了討論老齡化社會對環境造成的影響。

解析：原文中，如果孤立地看第一句話，就會存在歧義。它可以理解成：（1）不是因為航空公司罷工才舉行會議的。或者（2）因為航空公司罷工，會議被取消了。聯繫下文，根據言內語境，不難看出第一種理解才是正確的。

例2：There was nothing to do in London the evening except to go to the saloon, an old board building with swinging doors and a wooden side walk awning. Neither prohibition nor repeal had changed its business, its clientele, or the quality of its whisky. In the course of an evening every male inhabitant of London over fifteen years old came at least once to the Buffalo Bar, had a drink, talked a while and went home.

There would be a game of the mildest kind of poker going on. Timothy Ratz, the husband of my landlady, would be playing solitaire, cheating pretty badly because he took a drink only when he got it out. I've seen him get out five minutes in a row. When he won he piled the cards neatly, stood up and walked with great dignity to the bar. Fat Carl, the owner and bartender, with a glass half filled before he arrived, asked,「What'll it be?」

「Whisky,」said Timothy gravely.

譯文：在洛曼小鎮，晚飯後除了去鎮上唯一的那家酒館便無事可做。酒館是一座老式的木制建築，有一扇轉門，門前人行道上方有一塊木制雨篷。無論是政府的禁酒令還是後來廢除禁酒令的法令都未曾改變過它生意的興隆、顧客的數量，也未曾改變過它威士忌的質量。每天晚飯後，鎮上十五歲以上的男子至少要光顧布法羅酒館一次，喝杯酒，聊聊天，然後回家。

酒館裡常有人玩撲克牌，不過其輸贏聊勝於無。我那位房東太太的

丈夫蒂莫西·羅茲就經常在那裡玩單人紙牌游戲。他玩牌老愛作弊，因為他只在贏牌時才買上一杯酒喝。我曾見過他一口氣連贏五盤。贏牌後他便把紙牌整整齊齊地疊好，然後直起身，神氣十足地走向吧臺。酒館老闆兼伙計胖子卡爾不等他走近吧臺便會端起已斟了半杯酒的酒杯問：「來杯什麼酒？」「威士忌。」蒂莫西總是莊重地回答。(《中國翻譯》，2002 年第 2 期)

解析：原文選自於 1938 年發表的美國著名作家約翰·斯坦貝克的小說《約翰尼·伯爾》。原文第一段的第二句中，prohibition 雖然沒有首字母大寫，但是從作品反應的年代以及小說的上下文來看，prohibition 應該指 1920 年至 1933 年間的美國禁酒令。而 repeal 指 repeal of the prohibition，即廢除禁酒令的法令。

第二段的最後一句話 what'll it be，根據情景的不同，可以有很多不同的理解。不過，原文中該句出現的情景是：在酒館中，酒館老闆兼伙計向贏錢後打算買一杯酒喝的客人詢問；並且下文中客人的回答是「威士忌」。據此，這句話的翻譯應該是：來杯什麼酒。

Translation Practice

Translate the following paragraph into Chinese.

I am a journalist, not a historian, and while this book is an effort to describe a moment in the past, it is less a work of history than of personal reminiscence and reflection. Essentially, it is an account of my own observations and experiences in wartime Washington, supplemented by material drawn from interviews and other sources. I have tried to create out of it all a portrait of the pain and struggle of a city and a government suddenly called upon to fight, and to lead other nations in fighting, the greatest war in history, but pathetically and sometimes hilariously unprepared to do so.

This is bound to be somewhere close to the last reporting from that period based on firsthand sources. One after another, with unsettling rapidity, those in positions of power and responsibility during World War II are passing from the scene. Several who agreed to recall and describe their experiences in the war years died before I could get to them.

I have not dealt here in any detail with the grand strategy of the war in Europe and the Pacific. Instead, I have tried to report mainly on what I saw and heard and learned in Washington during years now fading into a misty past, the wartime experience of a country two-thirds of whose people are now too young to remember any of it. The result is a sort of Our Town at war, the story of a city astonished and often confused to find itself at the center of a worldwide conflict without ever hearing a shot fired. A strange city, set up in the first place to be the center of government and, like government itself at that time, a city moving slowly and doing little.

2.4 Focused Writing

Letters of Application

The role of a letter of application

A letter of application will almost certainly be required when applying for any position, be it a job, an internship or a place on a graduate/professional program. The role of the application letter is to draw a clear link between the position you are seeking and your qualifications as listed in your resume. It must not merely repeat the contents of your resume but should highlight the most relevant information emphasizing why you are right for the position.

The format of a letter of application

An application letteris customarily laid out as follows:
The sender's address;
The date;
The addressee's address;
The salutation;
The body of the letter, which is usually comprised of:
　—an introductory paragraph, stating the purpose of the letter. When applying for a job, people usually indicate the source of their information about the job, say, a newspaper advertisement or a personal contact. If applying for a graduate program, people usually mention by name their sponsor, mentor or a senior tutor who has recommended that they apply;
　—main body paragraphs, highlighting the main qualifications and pres-

enting evidence closely tied to the job or the graduate program;

—a closing paragraph, indicating your hope to be able to meet to explore further how you may be of help to the company;

The complimentary close;

The signature.

Differences between academic and business letters of application

Though academic and business letters of application are very similar in terms of function and layout, the content differs significantly in quantity and kind. When you are applying for a graduate program or a faculty position with a college or university, the application letter needs to leave a strong impression as a promising researcher or teacher. Thus, an academic application letter should be long enough to highlight in some detail your accomplishments during your academic years. However, the application letter for other job vacancies is relatively brief and concise because it is usually accompanied by a copy of your CV.

Sample 1 **An Academic Application Letter**

Tel: 008810, 4509, 876	The School of Management
Email: limin@hotmail.com	Shanghai Jiaotong University
	535, Fahuazhen Road
	Shanghai,
	P. R. China, 200052

July 5th, 2009

The American Graduate School
of International Management
15429 N. 59th Ave.
Glendale Arizona 85306-6003

Dear Sir or Madam,

    With the enclosed application and supporting documentation, I am expressing my sincere interest in being accepted into the Master of International Management Graduate Program at The American Graduate School of International Management. | The introductory paragraph: Li Min states his interest in being admitted.

    I feel confident that I am well equipped for graduate studies in international business, and I feel certain I could one day become a distinguished alumnus of your fine institution. As you will see from my resume, I already hold a B. Sc. degree in Business and Marketing and I read, write, and speak English fluently. My English language skills were refined and improved while working as an interpreter at the 2008/2009 Canton Fair (China) and as a tour guide for foreign delegations. | Main body paragraphs: supporting evidence of his eligibility for the graduate program①.

    In addition to my experience as an interpreter and tour guide, I have extensive work experience which I believe will help to make me a valuable member of the MIM program. While working in summer and part-time jobs to finance my college education, I gained experience in a wide range of positions working in retail: sales and marketing and in the construction, hospitality, and transportation industries. | Supporting evidence of his eligibility for the graduate program②.

    As you will see when you read my essay, my goal is to become the chief executive officer of a company doing business in Asia, and I feel my background thus far, combined with the program of graduate studies offered by the American Graduate School of International Business, will help me achieve that aim. I feel I would be a credit to the business community because of my strong conviction of the economic necessity that making a profit must be balanced by regard for customers and respect for employees. | Supporting evidence of his eligibility for the graduate program③.

    I can assure you in advance that I would be an asset to the next entering class and as a graduate. If I can provide any further information please do not hesitate to contact me. Thank you for your consideration of my application.

    I look forward to hearing from you. | The closing paragraph, re-emphasizing his confidence and offering more information if required.

Yours sincerely,
Li Min
Enclosures: Application Form, Essay, Resume, Letter of Reference

Sample 2 **A Business Application Letter**

        34 Second Street
        Troy
        New York 12180

        May 4th, 2009

MS. Gail Roberts
Recruiting Coordinator
Department DRR 1201
Data base Corporation
Princeton, New Jersey 05876

Dear MS. Roberts,
  Your advertisement for software engineers in the January issue of the IEEE Spectrum caught my attention. I was drawn to the ad by my strong interest in both software design and Database.   *Introduction: the source of information about the job vacancy.*

  I have worked with a CALMA systemin developing VLSI circuits, and I also have substantial experience in the design of interactive CAD software. Because of this experience, I can make a direct and immediate contribution to your department I have enclosed a copy of my resume, which details my qualifications and suggests how I might be of service to Database.   *Main body: supporting evidence of his qualifications for position.*

  Iwould like very much to meet with you to discuss your open positions for software engineers. If you would like to arrange an interview, please contact me at the above address or by telephone at (518) 271-9999 or email: jsmith@yahoo.com   *Closing: requesting an interview and facilitating that request.*

  Thank you for your time and consideration.
  Yours sincerely,
  Joseph Smith Encl: Resume

Writing Assignment

1. Write a letter of application for an internship at an international company.

2. Write a letter of application for a position on a doctoral program at Cornell University in America.

Unit 3 Man and Technology

3.1 Get Started

I. Work in pairs or groups and discuss the following questions.

1. What changes have taken place in our life with the advancement of technology?

2. Do you think technology makes your life easier? Could you give some examples?

3. Is the advancement of technology always a good thing?

II. Study the following quotes about man and technology and discuss in pairs what you can learn from them.

1. The saddest aspect of life right now is that science gathers knowledge faster than society gathers wisdom.

——Isaac Asimov

2. Education makes machines which act like men and produces men who act like machines.

——Erich Fromm

3. The production of too many useful things results in too many useless people.

——Karl Marx

4. It is difficult to say what is impossible, for the dreams of yesterday are the hopes of today, and the realities of tomorrow.

——Robert H. Goddard

3.2　Read and Explore

Text A

In the present era, all of us are enthusiastically pursuing technological advancement and take it for granted that the development of technology will make us happier. However, little evidence can be found to prove the correlation between technology and happiness once material and technological advances reach a certain level. The text below may provide you with some insights into this issue.

Technology and Happiness
by James Surowiecki

In the 20th century, Americans, Europeans, and East Asians enjoyed material and technological advances that were unimaginable in previous eras. In the United States, for instance, gross domestic product per capita tripled from 1950 to 2000. Life expectancy soared. The boom in productivity after World War II made goods better and cheaper at the same time. Things that were once luxuries, such as jet travel and long-distance phone calls, became necessities. And even though Americans seemed to work extraordinarily hard, their pursuit of entertainment turned media and leisure into multibillion-dollar industries.

By most standards, then, you would have to say that Americans are better off now than they were in the middle of the last century. Oddly, though, if you ask Americans how happy they are, you find that they are no happier than they were in 1946 (which is when formal surveys of happiness started). In fact, the percentage of people who say they are 「very happy」 has fallen slightly since the early 1970s—even though the income of people born in 1940 has, on average, increased by 116 percent over the course of their working lives. You can find similar data for most developed countries.

The relationship between happiness and technology has been an eternal subject for social critics and philosophers since the advent of the Industrial Revolution. But it's been left largely unexamined by economists and social scientists. The truly groundbreaking work on the relationship between prosperity and well-being was done by the economist Richard Easterlin, who in 1974 wrote a famous paper entitled 「Does Economic Growth Improve the Human Lot?」 Easterlin showed that when it came to developed countries, there was no real correlation between a nation's income level and its citizens' happiness. Money, Easterlin argued, could not buy happiness—at least not after a certain point. Easterlin showed that though poverty was strongly correlated with misery, once a country was solidly middle-class, getting wealthier did not seem to make its citizens any happier.

This seems to be close to a universal phenomenon. In fact, one of happiness scholars' most important insights is that people adapt very quickly to good news. Take lottery winners for example. One famous study showed that although winners were very, very happy when they won, their extreme excitement quickly evaporated, and after a while their moods and sense of well-being were indistinguishable from what they had been before the victory.

So, too, with technology: no matter how dramatic a new innovation is, no matter how much easier it makes our lives, it is very easy to take it for granted. You can see this principle at work in the world of technology every day, as things that once seemed miraculous soon become common and, worse, frustrating when they don't work perfectly. It's hard, it turns out, to keep in mind what things were like before the new technology came along.

Does our fast assimilation of technological progress mean, then, that technology makes no difference? No. It just makes the question of technology's impact, for good or ill, more complicated. Let's start with the downside. There are certain ways in which technology makes life obviously worse. Telemarketing, traffic jams, and identity theft all come to mind. These are all phenomena that make people consciously unhappy. But for the most part, modern critiques of technology have focused not so much on specific, bad technologies as the impact of technology on our human relationships.

Privacy has become increasingly fragile in a world of linked databases. In many workplaces, technologies like keystroke monitoring and full recordings of phone calls make it easier to watch workers. The notion that technology disrupts relationships and fractures community gained mainstream prominence as an attack on television. Some even say that TV is chiefly responsible for the gradual isolation of Americans from each other. Similarly, the harmful effects of the Internet supposedly further isolate people from what is often called 「the real world」.

This broad criticism of technology's impact on relationships is an interesting one and is especially relevant to the question of happiness, because one of the few things we can say for certain is that the more friends and the closer relationships people have, the happier they tend to be.

Today, technological change is so rapid that when you buy something, you do so knowing that in a few months there's going to be a better, faster version of the product, and that you're going to be stuck with the old one. Someone else, in other words, has it better. It's as if disappointment were built into acquisition from the very beginning.

Daily stress, an annoying sense of disappointment, fear that the government knows a lot more about you than you would like it to—these are obviously some of the ways in which technology reduces people's sense of well-being. But the most important impact of technology on people's sense of well-being is in the field of health care. Before the Industrial Revolution, two out of every three Europeans died before the age of 30. Today, life expectancy for women in Western Europe is almost 80 years, and it continues to increase. The point is obvious: the vast majority of people are happy to be alive, and the more time they get on earth, the better off they feel they'll be. But until very recently, life for the vast majority of people was nasty, rough, and short. Technology has changed that, at least for people in the rich world. As much as we should worry about the rising cost of health care and the problem of the uninsured, it's also worth remembering how valuable for our spirits as well as our bodies are the benefits that medical technology has brought us.

On a deeper level, what the technological improvement of our health and our longevity emphasizes is a paradox of discussion of happiness on a national or a global level: even though people may not be happier, even though they are wealthier and possess more technology, they're still as hungry as ever for more time. It's like that old joke: the food may not be so great, but we want the portions to be as big as possible.

Words and Expressions

1. gross adj.（無比較級）總共的，全部的

2. gross domestic product 國內生產總值（指國民生產總值中減去國外投資的淨收益，略作 GDP）

3. per capita 按人口計算的（地）；人均

4. triple vi. 增至三倍

5. life expectancy 預期壽命，平均（期望）壽命

6. boom n. 繁榮（時期），迅速增長（期），景氣

7. productivity n.［U］生產力；生產率，生產效率

8. at the same time：together 一齊；同時

9. jet n. 噴氣式飛機

10. be better off：be in a more satisfactory or desirable situation 較自在；較幸運；較幸福

11. formal adj.［尤指術語］規範的；書面語要求的；正規的，正式的；公文的

12. survey n. 調查

13. on average：in most cases；usually 大多情況下；通常；平均

14. critic n.（尤指文學、藝術）評論家，批評家

15. advent n.（事件、時期、發明等的）出現，來臨

16. groundbreaking adj. 有創造力的，以創造力和創新為特徵的

17. prosperity n.［U］發達，興隆，昌盛，繁榮

18. when it comes to：when it concerns 當提到……

19. correlation n.［C］（常與 between 連用）相互關係；關聯

20. solidly adv. 可信賴地；實實在在地

21. close to：almost；nearly 接近於；差不多

22. universal adj. 普遍的，一般的

23. phenomenon n. /pl.（尤指不尋常或具科學性的）現象

24. indistinguishable adj.（常與 from 連用）難以分辨（區別）的

25. dramatic adj. 戲劇性的；激動人心的；不尋常的

26. frustrating adj. 令人沮喪的

27. assimilation n.［U］充分理解，掌握

28. make no difference：not matter at all 沒有影響；都一樣

29. for good or ill：whether the results are good or bad 不論好歹

30. downside n. 不利方面

31. telemarketing n.［U］電話推銷（術）

32. theft n.［C；U］偷竊，盜竊；竊案

33. come to mind：make (one) suddenly think of 使想到

34. critique n. 評論文章；評論

35. fragile adj. 脆的，易碎的，易損壞的

36. database n.（電腦系統的）數據庫，資料庫（同 data bank）

37. keystroke n. 按鍵，（在打字機等鍵盤上的）一次按擊

38. disrupt vt. 使混亂，擾亂

39. fracture vt.［術語，尤指醫用術語或正式術語］（使）折斷，（使）斷裂，破裂

40. mainstream n.（思想或行為的）主流

41. prominence n.［U］突出，顯著；重要

42. gradual adj. 逐漸的，逐步的

43. isolation n.［U］隔絕孤立，隔離

44. similarly adv. 同樣地，相同地

45. supposedly adv. 據認為，據推測，據稱；一般相信，一般看來

46. for certain：without doubt 肯定地

47. be stuck with：have or deal with sth. unwanted unwillingly 被……纏住無法擺脫

48. build... into：make (sth.) a part of a system, agreement, etc. 使……成為組成部分

49. acquisition n.［U］（常與 of 連用）獲得，取得，習得

50. annoying adj. 惱人的，討厭的

51. health care 醫療保健

52. nasty adj. 醜惡的；令人不愉快的；令人作嘔的

53. rough adj.（食物）粗制的；（生活環境、條件）簡陋的，不舒服的

54. uninsured adj. 未保過險的

55. longevity n.［U］［正式］長壽；［術語］壽命

56. paradox n. 似非而是的雋語；似矛盾而正確的說法

Notes

1. The text is taken from *Technology Review*, January 2005.

2. James Surowiecki (1967-): an American journalist. He is a staff writer at *The New Yorker*, where he writes a regular column on business and finance. Surowiecki's writing has appeared in a wide range of publications, including *The New York Times*, *The Wall Street Journal*, etc.

3. gross domestic product: In economics, gross domestic product (GDP) is defined as the total value of all goods and services produced within that territory during a specified period (or, if not specified, annually). It is often seen as an indicator of the standard of living in a country.

4. The Industrial Revolution: the major social, economic and technological change in the late 18th and early 19th century. It began with the introduction of steam power and powered machinery in Great Britain. The technological and economic progress of the Industrial Revolution spread throughout Western Europe and North America, eventually affecting the rest of the world.

5. Richard Easterlin (1926-): a professor of economics at the University of Southern California. He is a member of the National Academy of Sciences and the American Academy of Arts and Sciences. He is well known for his researches in social trends, the Baby Boom generation, the economic status of the young and the old, and materialism.

6. By most standards, then, you would have to say that Americans are better off now than they were in the middle of the last century. →Judged by most standards, one has to admit that Americans today are wealthier than they were in the middle of the last century.

7. it's been left largely unexamined by economists and social scientists. →economists and social scientists have hardly studied this issue at all.

8. people adapt very quickly to good news→people tend to feel happy and excited on hearing good news but they soon take it for granted.

9. their extreme excitement quickly evaporated→their intense excitement lasted only a short period of time.

10. Does our fast assimilation of technological progress mean, then, that

technology makes no difference? →Does it mean that technological advancements and their timely application have not brought about any changes in our lives?

11. Telemarketing, traffic jams, and identity theft all come to mind. → You may think of such unpleasant situations as salespeople trying to sell products to you on the phone, your car being stuck in heavy traffic and your personal information being stolen.

12. But for the most part, modern critiques of technology have focused not so much on specific, bad technologies as the impact of technology on our human relationships. →However, current comments on technology have mostly centered on the bad effects of technology on our human relationships rather than particular, harmful technologies.

13. The notion that technology disrupts relationships and fractures community gained mainstream prominence as an attack on television. →People's criticism of television mainly focuses on the claim that television interferes with the smooth development of relationships between people and breaks up community unity.

14. you're going to be stuck with the old one→you will have to keep the old one even if you don't like it anymore.

15. It's as if disappointment were built into acquisition from the very beginning. →It seems as if people were doomed to disappointment the moment they bought the product.

16. the more time they get on earth, the better off they feel they'll be→ the longer life people live in the world, the happier they feel they'll be.

17. it's also worth remembering how valuable for our spirits as well as our bodies are the benefits that medical technology has brought us. →also, we should not forget that medical technology has benefited us both mentally and physically.

18. what the technological improvement of our health and our longevity emphasizes is a paradox of discussion of happiness on a national or a global level→the fact that technology has greatly improved people's health and life expectancy is just contradictory to the general claim at any level that technology cannot bring happiness to people.

Content Awareness

Ⅰ. Answer the following questions with the information contained in Text A.

1. Did material and technological advances make Americans happier according to the survey?

2. What is the relationship between money and happiness according to Easterlin?

3. How does technology affect human relationships according to the author?

4. In which field does technology have the most important impact on people's sense of well-being according to the author?

5. What does the author think of the relationship between technology and happiness?

Ⅱ. Text A can be divided into five parts with the paragraph number (s) of each part provided as follows. Write down the main idea of each part.

| Part | Paragraph (s) | Main Idea |
| One | 1~2 | |

Two	3~5	_____
Three	6~9	_____
Four	10	_____
Five	11	_____

Ⅲ. Read the following sentences carefully and discuss in pairs what the author intends to say by the italicised parts.

1. And even though Americans seemed to work extraordinarily hard, *their pursuit of entertainment turned media and leisure into multibillion-dollar industries.* (Para. 1)

_____

_____

2. Money, Easterlin argued, could not buy happiness—*at least not after a certain point.* (Para. 3)

_____

_____

3. *The notion that technology disrupts relationships and fractures community* gained mainstream prominence as an attack on television · (Para. 7)

_____

_____

4. It's like that old joke: *the food may not be so great, but we want the portions to be as big as possible.* (Para. 11)

_____

_____

Language Focus

Ⅰ. You will read six pairs of words which are similar in meaning but are different in usage. Reflect on the differences in usage between the words in each group and fill in each blank with a proper one. Change the form if necessary.

exterior   external

1. The picture shows the _____ view of Cairo International Conference Center.

2. All countries in the region have the right to protect themselves against

_____ threat.

delightful   pleasant

3. The _____ tourist guide speaks very good Chinese.

4. We were enjoying a (n) _____ conversation until she sailed in with her unpleasant remarks.

isolate   separate

5. You are confusing two different concepts—you should try to _____ them out in your mind.

6. The president's decision could _____ his country from the other permanent members of the United Nations Security Council.

companion   company

7. We visited the museum in _____ with some foreign tourists yesterday afternoon.

8. Both my travelling _____ and I wanted to go to Waterloo—that historic battlefield.

acquire   ripe

9. If you want to _____ profound knowledge, you must start from the ABC.

10. The children _____ singing, dancing, drawing, and the like in the kindergarten.

mature   ripe

11. The Minister of Foreign Affairs told reporters that he thought the time was _____ for the normalization of relations between the two countries.

12. Tom is only ten years old, but he is very _____ for his age.

Ⅱ. Fill in each blank with one of the words listed below in the appropriate form, paying special attention to the meaning and spelling.

expect *conj.*   expect *vt.*   accept *vt.*   excerpt *n.*

loose *vt.* & *adj.*   lose *vt.*   loss *n.*

depress *vt.*   suppress *vt.*   oppress *vt.*

1. The letter from the bank asks him to _____ their sincere apologies for the error in his bank statement.

2. The black people suffered from domestic political discrimination and _____.

3. Dr. Bethune served the wounded soldiers wholeheartedly, regardless of his personal gain or _____.

4. What follows are some _____ of the famous speech Martin Luther King Jr. delivered in Washington, D. C.

5. It is said that during the economic _____ half of the machines in the factory lay idle.

6. Would you please help Mike _____ the nail? It is rusty and won't come out of the wood.

7. She remembered nothing about her grandpa _____ that his hair was thin and grey.

8. Her weakness after the illness is only to be _____ and you must accept the fact.

9. Only a short-sighted man would _____ sight of the importance of education.

10. The reactionary government attempted to _____ dissatisfaction among the masses, but failed completely.

Ⅲ. Translate the following sentences into English, using the words and expressions given in brackets.

1. 他的確懂得很多理論，但是一碰到實際工作就顯得非常無知。(when it comes to)

_____

2. 最新調查表明，大多數市民支持政府再建一個新圖書館的計劃。(survey)

_____

3. 這兩個國家之所以能夠成功地達成科學技術合作協定是因為有利於他們進行合作的好幾種因素一直在發揮作用。(at work)

_____

4. 我在上小學時就看過那部電影，可就是一時想不起它的名字來。(come to mind)

_____

5. 儘管每天平均工作約12小時，他仍然陷於重重債務之中。(on overage; be stuck with)

6. 有必要知道他的身高嗎？在我看來，這與他能否成為一個好的律師沒有關係。(not relevant to)

7. 櫥櫃被安裝到牆裡，既節約空間，又使用方便。(build... into...)

8. 這些工人掙的錢比我們多，可話又說回來，他們的工作也危險得多。(the other side of the coin)

9. 海倫在大學裡學的是經濟學，與此同時，她把哲學作為第二專業來學習。(at the same time)

10. 重要的是你們要自己發現問題和解決問題，我是否到現場去無關緊要。(make no difference)

Ⅳ. Translate the following passage into English.

目前，許多人都享受著過去歷代人想像不到的物質和技術進步帶來的好處。隨著科學技術的發展，人們的生活水準越來越高，壽命也大幅度提高。

然而，奇怪的是，許多人並不感到比以前幸福。可見，人們的收入和幸福並非密切相關，畢竟幸福是金錢買不到的。

儘管大多數人對生活並不十分滿意，可還是樂意活著。他們在地球上生活的時間越長，感覺越好。重要的是，僅在物質上富有是不夠的，

人們還需要精神上的幸福。

___

Text B

I Have His Genes But Not His Genius

It's Christmas Eve 2040, and I'm the only bartender still working that afternoon, and the house is practically empty. I see this guy down at the end of the bar, sitting by himself. I bring him a fresh drink and wish him greetings of the season. He looks at me, sort of funny, and says:「Do you know who I am?」

I admit I don't.

「Here, maybe this will help?」he says, and he pulls a little picture out of his wallet. An old portrait, really old, like centuries old. It's a young man in profile: sharp nose, weak chin, definite resemblance to my friend here. At the bottom, there's a caption:「W. A. Mozart.」

Now it's my turn to look at him funny. Then it hits me like a brick. 「You're that clone guy,」I say,「The guy in the papers back in the 20s.」

「In the flesh. Wolfgang Amadeus Mozart. I have his brain, his heart, his DNA. He's my father and my mother and my brother. He's my identical twin, except I was born 247 years later.」

So he starts talking. It takes him a long time to explain, and I don't get it all, but I get a lot.

In 2001, Congress passed a ban on cloning humans, but of course mad scientists went ahead with secret cloning.

And then, there was this software billionaire who was nuts about Mozart, and was especially nuts about Mozart's 20 *Requiem*. He set up a secret institute in Switzerland and hired some top biologists and told them they'd get ＄1 million each for every baby they cloned from Mozart's DNA.

In 2003, the institute managed to bring four babies to term. Two died shortly after birth. Two survived. But then this software billionaire died, and his company collapsed, and so did his cloning institute. One baby Mozart was put up for adoption anonymously. No one knows what happened to that one. The other baby was adopted by one of the scientists, who was a big Mozart fan herself.

「And that's me,」he says.

His mother, of course, didn't tell him or anyone else who he was, but she told the boy how special he was, how he was a genius, what a great composer he could be, trying to push her little Mozart toward music.

But the 2010s weren't the 1760s. The boy may have had talent, but he also had his own priorities, and they didn't include violin sonatas. He liked rock music and he liked it loud, and then as he got older he liked beer and girls. The harder his mother pushed him to be a great composer, the less he wanted to be one. After a while his mother gave up. By the time he was 20, he had a decent job working in a frame shop. And that's when the roof fell in.

Some reporter got wind of the institute and the cloning experiment and tracked him down. But no one could prove he was a clone of Mozart without digging up the original, so the media treated him as a joke. It just crushed him. He tried running away. He joined a Buddhist monastery in Japan. One day, while he was there, he heard the *Requiem*. Not for the first time, but this time it was different.

「My God, it was beautiful!」he says,「I felt a realization explode inside my head. I just felt it somehow: It rang inside of me. I'd finish it, or die trying.」He knew that if he could finish the *Requiem*, he'd be famous for real, a genius instead of a fool. He immersed himself in Mozart's music. Nights, weekends, all the time, he drove himself, working on the *Requiem*.

「And? What happened?」

「I turned 37 four months ago. I've been working on the *Requiem* for 15 years. Mozart died when he was 35. I should have finished the Requiem two years ago.」

「And you haven't.」

He looks at me for a while and shakes his head,「You don't understand. I have his genes but not his genius.」

And with that he drops a tip on the bar and is gone. I never saw him again. If the Requiem was ever finished, I never heard about it.

Words and Expressions

1. bartender n. 酒吧間銷售酒精飲料的人，酒吧間男招待
2. portrait n. 肖像，肖像畫
3. resemblance n. 相似，形似；外表，外觀；相似物，相似點；肖像
4. caption n. 字幕；標題，說明文字，字幕
5. identical adj. 同一的；完全同樣的，相同的
6. go ahead with 繼續進行（去做某事）
7. collapse vi. 崩潰；倒塌；折疊；坐下（尤指工作勞累後）
8. anonymously adv. 不具名地，化名地
9. priority n. 優先，優先權；優先考慮的事；［數］優先次序
10. decent adj. 正派的；得體的；相稱的，合宜的（服裝等）；相當好的
11. dig up 掘出；發現
12. immerse vt. 沉迷……中，使陷入

Notes

1. Mozart's *Requiem*: Mozart labored on the *Requiem*, while suffering from delusions that he had been poisoned. He died with the Requiem unfinished. The cause of his death is uncertain and has been the subject of much speculation.

Content Awareness

Ⅰ. Fill in the blanks with the information from the passage. Don't refer back to it until you have finished.

　　W. A. Mozart was a great _____ who lived in the 18th century. He died young, leaving his masterpiece *Requiem* unfinished. At the _____ of the 21st century, a billionaire who was crazy about the *Requiem* set up a _____ institute and hired some top biologists to _____ babies from Mozart's DNA. The institute succeeded in producing four babies but only two survived. One was _____ by a woman, who was also among the research group. She had been trying to push the little Mozart toward _____. However, the boy had his own priorities, and all the mother's efforts turned out fruitless. The boy grew up into an _____ person. Then something happened, and totally changed his life. A reporter heard about the institute and the experiment, and found the young man. As he couldn't _____ that he was the copy of Mozart, the media treated him as a _____. It was a great blow to him. He swore to finish the *Requiem* to show to the whole world. He immersed himself in the Requiem day and night. Fifteen years passed, and he achieved nothing. Eventually he realized that he only had Mozart's genes but not his _____.

Language Focus

Ⅰ. Find two more collocates (words that are frequently used together) for each of the following samples from the passage and then make a sentence with each collocation.

flesh	adj.→	drink	I bring him a fresh drink, and wish him greeting of the season.
	e.g.	look	We really need to take a fresh look at our test-driven education.
		____	_____
identical	adj.→	twin	He's my identical twin, expect I was born 247 years later.
		____	_____
		____	_____
decent	adj. →	job	By the time he was 20, he had a decent job working in a frame shop.
		____	_____
		____	_____
pass	v. →	a ban	In 2001, Congress passed a ban on cloning humans...
		____	_____
		____	_____

adopt	v.	→	a baby	The other baby was adopted by one of the scientists...
			___	_____
			___	_____
drop	v.	→	a tip	And with that he drops a tip on the bar and is gone.
			___	_____
			___	_____

II. Match the idioms in the left column with their definitions in the right, and then rewrite the sentences below with the idioms listed.

1. hit sb. like a brick   a. to find sb./sth. after a difficult or long search
2. in the flesh   b. to go to great effort to find sb. or sth.
3. be nuts about   c. to hear about, find out about
4. the roof falls in   d. to like a lot, be crazy about
5. get wind of   e. sth very bad that suddenly happens
6. track sb./sth. down   f. suddenly the meaning becomes clear to sb.
7. dig sb./sth. up   g. in person (instead of a photo of the person)

1. As I walked out of the room I realized that she was a teacher instead of a student.

(hit sb. like a brick) _____

2. For the first six years of my life I was happy. Then my father died and everything changed.

(the roof falls in) _____

3. I browsed in all those secondhand stores, trying to find out something valuable.

(dig sb./sth. up) _____

4. Not believing that her father had died in the war, she spent years trying to find him.

(track sb./sth. down) _____

5. If they know about what we are doing, we'll then be in a very passive position.

(get wind of) _____

6. If you like ice-creams very much, this is the very place to enjoy yourself.

(be nuts about) _____

7. When I turned back, suddenly I saw Julia in person, standing right in front of me!

(in the flesh) _____

Ⅲ. Translate the following paragraphs into English.

1. 那時，我過度沉溺於電腦游戲的虛擬世界，幾乎每分鐘都是在電腦前度過的。後來我父母禁止我用電腦，敦促我做功課。「做個好學生，想想你的當務之急。」他們的話給了我當頭一棒，在我腦中回響。我開始看書學習，終於考上了大學。

_____
_____

2. 他的描述和事實幾乎完全不符。事實上就在公司倒閉之後不久，一位匿名億萬富翁設法建立了這家工廠，聘請了幾位頂級科學家，開始了一模一樣的項目。他們這個項目至今已經進行了兩年，兩個月前就該結束，但實際上卻沒有取得任何成果。如果沒有實質性的進展，這家工廠很快就會被出售。

_____
_____
_____

3.3　Practical Translation

語篇層次的翻譯——銜接

語篇（discourse）是在交際功能上相對完整和獨立的一個語言片斷。為了進行有效的交際活動，語篇應銜接（cohesion）得當，連貫性（coherence）好。銜接手段（cohesive device）是一種謀篇手段，是生成語篇的重要條件之一，也是譯者在翻譯過程中首先要考慮的問題，因為它直接關係到譯文的質量。銜接自然的譯文讀起來通順、流暢、連貫；缺乏銜接或銜接不當的譯文晦澀難懂，影響閱讀，也影響交際功能的實現。

英語和漢語分屬不同的體系：英語屬於印歐語系（Indo-European Family），漢語屬於漢藏語系（Sino-Tibetan Family）。它們在許多方面

都有各自的規律和特點。從語篇層面上說，需要強調英、漢兩種語言在形合（hypotaxis）和意合（parataxis）方面的差異。英、漢兩種語言邏輯思維的不同。英語重形合，句子內部的連接或句子間的連接採用顯性的語言手段來實現，主要是通過各種語法手段和詞彙手段，來表示其結構和邏輯關係。因此，英語中長句多。漢語重意合，句中各成分之間或句子之間的結合少用甚至不用形式銜接手段，主要靠句子內部的隱性邏輯聯繫，注重邏輯事理的順序以及意義和主旨上的銜接和連貫。因此，漢語中短句多，短句間的邏輯關係靠意義來表達，語法處於次要地位。在翻譯過程中，要牢記英、漢兩種語言在形合和意合上的差別，注意形合和意合之間的轉換和調整。

例1：I had so worked upon my imagination as really to believe that about the whole mansion and domain there hung an atmosphere peculiar to themselves and their immediate vicinity—an atmosphere which had no affinity with the air of heaven, but which had reeked up from the decayed trees, and the grey wall, and the silent tam—a pestilent and mystic vapor, dull, sluggish, faintly discernible, and leaden-hued. (Edgar Allan Poe: *The Fall of the House of Usher*)

譯文：我如此沉湎於自己的想像，以至於我實實在在地認為那宅院及其周圍懸浮著一種它們所特有的空氣。那種空氣並非生發於天地自然，而是生發於那些枯樹殘枝、灰牆暗壁，生發於那一汪死氣沉沉的湖水。那是一種神祕而致命的霧靄，陰晦、凝滯、朦朧、沉濁如鉛。（曹明倫譯）

解析：這個例句選自美國作家愛倫・坡的小說名篇《厄舍府之倒塌》。整段話其實只有一個完整的句子，共70個字，它不僅通過多個消極、晦澀、陰暗的形容詞，如：decayed, grey, silent, pestilent, mystic, dull, sluggish, leaden-hued 來營造一種淒涼、蕭瑟的自然氛圍和壓抑、沉悶的心理氣氛，而且通過一個典型形合的長句來烘托這種乏味、陰晦的自然氛圍和心理氣氛。這個形合長句主要採用各種語法手段（如並列句、狀語從句、同位語從句、定語從句）以及詞彙手段（如詞彙 atmosphere 的重複）等來表示其結構關係，並進行有機的銜接。在翻譯過程中，原語中「顯性的語法和詞彙手段」不能完全照搬到目標語中。也就是說，不能用帶有各種成分的長句來處理這個句子，否則整個漢語句子就會顯得拖沓、冗長。因此在正確理解原文內容、弄清原文內在結

構的基礎上，譯文用三個分句來處理這個長句。分句之間雖然也運用了一定的詞彙和語法手段，如重複「空氣」一詞和運用並列結構「生發於……」「生發於……」。分句之間的銜接主要還是靠意義和邏輯關係的連接，先是講「我」想像的內容，然後講想像內容──「空氣」和周圍環境的關係，最後講這種空氣的實質。三個分句環環相扣、層層展開，如果缺少了分句中意義和邏輯關係的銜接，整個句子就無法成為一個有機而連貫的漢語句子。

例2：She had a very thin face like the dial of a small clock seen faintly in a dark room in the middle of a night when you waken to see the time and see the clock telling you the hour and the minute and the second, with a white silence and a glowing, all certainty and knowing what it has to tell of the night passing swiftly on toward further darkness but moving also toward a new sun. (Ray Douglas Bradbury：*Fahrenheit 451*)

譯文：（她的）容貌那麼清秀，就像半夜裡醒來時在黑暗中隱約可見的小小的鐘面，報告時刻的鐘面。它皎潔而安靜，深知時間在飛馳，深信黑暗雖然越來越深沉，卻也越來越接近新生的太陽。（苗懷新譯）

解析：這個例句選自美國作家布拉德伯利的著名的反烏托邦小說《華氏451度》。整段話共80個字，是一個完整而典型的形合句，主要是採用各種語法手段（如被動句、定語從句、賓語從句、並列句）以及運用修辭手法來進行有機的銜接，使原文一氣呵成。在翻譯過程中，要正確理解原文內容、理清原文內在結構，原語中「顯性的語法和詞彙手段」，除了兩組重複的詞（「鐘面」「深知」和「深信」）以及前後指代（「鐘面」和「它」）外，大部分都被隱去，取而代之的是漢語中意義和邏輯上的銜接和連貫。譯文充分利用漢語的短句形式，按照原文的邏輯順序，把整個句子切分成兩個單句、七個部分。每個部分間層層相連、環環相扣，讀起來有讀原文那種一氣呵成的感覺。如果脫離了漢語句子間意義和邏輯的銜接，整個句子將支離破碎，讀起來拗口、別扭。

Translation Practice

1. I've been spared a lot, one of the blessed of the earth, at least one of its lucky, that privileged handful of the dramatically prospering, the sort whose secrets are asked, like the hundred-year-old man.

2. And so Franklin Roosevelt found that he had, in effect, to recruit an

entirely new and temporary government to be piled on top of the old one, the new government to get the tanks and airplanes built, the uniforms made, the men and women assembled and trained and shipped abroad, and the battles fought and won.

3.4 Focused Writing

Personal Letters

Apersonal letter is a letter which provides communication between a small number of people, usually two. There are many types of personal letters and they are written for a wide variety of reasons, for example:

obtaining information from an individual or a business;

telling somebody about themselves, for example, pen pals;

sending an individual or a business a social note, such as a thank-you or congratulations;

contacting an acquaintance, a friend or family member, for example, to exchange information.

The format of a Letter

In general, a letter, be it personal or formal, is comprised of the same parts. Let's take a look at the following specimen format of a personal letter. (See Unit 1 for formal letters)

	Sender's address (not punctuated in current practice) ←Date
Salutation →	
	← Body of the letter
Complimentary close → Name or → Signature	

The address of the sender. The sender's address is written on the top right-hand corner of the page. Remember that the address of the receiver, which is often referred to as the receiver's or addressee's address, is not appropriate in a personal letter.

The date. The date is written below the sender's address with a blank line in between. In the month-day-year system, popular in the United States, a comma is used between the day and the year, as in「September 10, 2009」whereas British people tend to adopt the day-month-year mode, as in「10th September 2009」or「10-9-2009」.

The salutation. The salutation always appears at the left-hand side of the page. The customary「Dear」is used along with the recipient's first name, if appropriate.

The body of the letter. It is the most important part, conveying information to the recipient of the letter. Personal letters are usually「newsy」(信息丰富的) and are written in a chatty or conversational style in most cases. Thus, such contractions like「I'll」or「doesn't」, incomplete sentences like「Wonderful news」and colloquial expressions are acceptable.

The complimentary close. It can be placed either on the right-hand or left-hand side below the body of the letter. The most common forms of closing a personal letter are 「Yours sincerely」or 「Kind regards」. Some other closing phrases, such as 「Yours affectionately」and 「Love」can also be used where appropriate as a mark of intimacy.

The name or signature. It is placed directly below the complimentary close. The first name only is usual in personal letters e.g. 「Kind regards, Jane」. However, the full name or signature may be used in formal letters or when writing to businesses. e.g. 「Yours sincerely, Jane White or J. M. White」.

Sample

Suite 975
495 West Village Way
New York
10023

October 15th, 2009

Dear Mavis,

    Please accept my heartiest congratulations on your recent selection for inclusion on the short-list for the NY City Writers Prize.

    I just heard the news today from Francis Goodspeed when she dropped into my office with the marked-up proofs for her latest collection of stories. As you can imagine, Fran was very excited too! I am so proud of you. As you know, I have been a long-time promoter of your work, and in my mind it's about time they finally recognized your talent. In fact, I believe that your selection for the NYCWP short-list is long overdue.

    I have already read two of the other books that are short-listed and in my opinion they don't hold a candle to your *No Turning Bock*. I will read the other three books nominated and let you know what I think although I could hardly be considered an objective reviewer on this one.

    Once again Mavis, my sincere congratulations on your nomination. Just being nominated for the NYCWP is an honor in itself. I will be keeping my fingers crossed for you until they announce the Winner on March 1st.

Best wishes,

Brad

Writing Assignment

Write a letter to your cousin in UCLA (University of California, Los Angeles) asking him to extend all possible help to your teacher and his or her family who plan to visit Los Angeles.

Unit 4 Education

4.1 Get Started

Ⅰ. Before reading Passage A, try to tell what you feel is the best part of you college life, and what is not so good as you used to expect.

1. Lecture
2. Class
3. Cafeteria
4. Library
5. Degree
6. Reading

4.2 Read and Explore

Text A

Bachelor's Degress:
Has It Lost Its Edge and Its Value?
by *Lee Lawrence*

Once the hallmark of an educated and readily employable adult, the bachelor's degree is losing its edge. Quicker, cheaper programs offer attractive career route alternatives while the more prestigious master's is trumping it, making it a mere steppingstone.

Studies show that people with four-year college degrees earn more money than those without over their lifetime, that they are more likely to find jobs and, once employed, are almost twice as likely to be selected for on-the-job training.

This has prompted a stampede through college and university gates.

But studies are like photographs: They record the past. They say nothing about the clear and present danger that the bachelor's degree is losing value.

⌈As more and more people get a bachelor's degree, it becomes more commonplace,⌋ says Linda Serra Hagedorn, immediate past president of the Association for the Study of Higher Education and associate dean and professor at Iowa State University in Ames, Iowa.

And, she adds, ⌈not all bachelor's degrees are equal.⌋ In many communities around the country, the bachelor's degree is not enough to make you stand out. ⌈ ⌈A bachelor's in what?⌋ That's the question,⌋ Professor Hagedorn says.

⌈A bachelor's is what a high school diploma used to be,⌋ suggests Caryn McTighe Musil of the American Association of colleges and Universities.

After World War II and through decades of postwar economicgrowth, college attendance morphed from an exception into the desired norm. In 1950, some 34 percent of adults had completed high school; today, more than 30 percent have completed a bachelor's. In 2009, colleges and universities handed out more than 1.6 million bachelor's degrees, a number the National Center for Education Statistics (NCES) expects will grow to almost 2 million by 2020.

Spiraling degree inflation is what Richard Vedder, professor of economics at Ohio University and adjunct scholar at the American Enterprise Institute, calls it. The danger he sees is that growing numbers of Americans will be unnecessarily saddled with hefty student loans.

⌈The fact is that it is not a sure shot you're going to get the high-paying job,⌋ Professor Vedder says, and the notion that the earnings differential ⌈is continuing to grow and expand is somewhat suspect.⌋

Bachelor's degree-holders may well earn 66 percent more than high school graduates and 35 percent more than people with two-year degrees, he says. But for every bachelor's degree-holder earning more than $54,000 a year, he notes, there is a mail carrier, taxi driver, bartender, parking attendant or other worker with a bachelor's earning less. Indeed, almost 16 percent of the country's bartenders and almost 14 percent of its parking lot attendants have a bachelor's or higher.

Vedder predicts more and more college-educated people will be in jobs that do not require a four-year degree.

Michael Hughes and Amanda Kusler met in just such a job, working as servers in a restaurant in Ann Arbor, Mich. It was 2007, and both had graduated from high school three years earlier.

Soon after they started dating, Kusler encouraged Hughes to re-enroll and pursue a degree. 「Especially nowadays,」 she believes, 「it's a norm to get your BA—doesn't matter what it's in.」

「That was certainly the case for decades,」 says Anthony Carnevale, director of the Georgetown University Center on Education and the Workforce, 「but not anymore.」

「It used to be that just getting the bachelor's made you employable,」 Mr. Carnevale says. But the research increasingly shows 「that the BA in and of itself is not what's valuable. Now, it more and more depends on what the degree is in.」

Kusler's aim was to work with children as a physical therapist, and there was no way to do that without a graduate degree.

But even in occupations that do not formally require postgraduate education, some employers have begun using graduate degrees as a filter.

「There's been some slight shifting to hiring more advanced degrees, particularly the master's,」 says Edwin Koc, director of strategic and foundation research at the National Association of Colleges and Employers. He notes that a number of his organization's members are now hiring people with a master's in engineering for jobs he'd assumed require only a bachelor's.

There is, however, also the undeniable fact that the supply of Americans with master's degrees is exploding. There are 50 percent more people in the job market today with a master's than there were in 2000. And the rate of growth is accelerating: When the economy is in turmoil and jobs are scarce, graduate enrollments typically rise.

This, in turn, fuels the feeling that Green, the accelerated master's student at Emory University, has: 「The master's seems like what you have to get where you want to go.」

With few good jobs immediately available and cuts in such postgrad havens as the Peace Corps, many are postponing these experiences to get their masters sooner rather than later.

Ironically, the push for master's degrees underscores the increasing need for the bachelor's while highlighting its weaknesses.

In theory, four years of undergraduate study nurtures critical thinking and the ability to adapt to a rapidly changing workplace.

But US college education has come under heavy criticism of late, and a bachelor's degree no longer guarantees that someone has actually acquired these crucial skills.

「There is this credential race going on,」 says Richard Arum, coauthor of 「Academically Adrift」. 「where there is less attention to the substance of the education and more to the credentials that are useful as signals in the labor market.」

Even though more than half of this year's college graduates have received no job offers, and even though the class of 2010 faced record unemployment, college graduates are still faring much better than those without a bachelor's.

「If nothing else,」 says Mr. McKendry, the California recruiter, 「a bachelor's shows that somebody has the mental capability and the initiative to complete something that less than 30 percent of the US population has achieved.」 But McKendry and his counterpart in a Snellings Staffing Services in New Jersey, Koleen Singerline, have independently lost their faith in the bachelor's as a predictor, in and of itself, of workplace success.

They point primarily to what they judge as a lack of work ethic and an attitude of entitlement in the new generation. Still, they are forced by employers to use college degrees as a benchmark.

「There are really good people with a wonderful track record,」 says Ms. Singerline. 「but I often cannot get a client to Consider them because the company policy is that to become a manager you must have a degree.」

This is where cultural factors come to bear. 「People would feel that it's unfair to report to somebody who has a lesser degree of education than they have.」 Hagedorn explains, 「That usually leads to an uncomfortable situation in the company.」

The crux is that 「education is still respected」, as Hagedorn points out, and there will probably always exist an economic and social divide between those who have it and those who don't.

But workplace and educational institutions are evolving, and attitudestoward the bachelor's are also showing signs of change. Some employers are more interested in experience, skills, and attitude than they are in degrees; others require higher levels of education from the start.

Then, as Jack Hollister, president of the Employers' Association serving Northwest Ohio and Southeast Michigan, reports, there are employers who only 「look at bachelor's from certain schools and certain areas of study and require a minimum GPA」.

In other words, they no longer take a bachelor's at face value.

Words and Expressions

1. bachelor n. 學士
2. hallmark n. 檢驗印記；特點，標志；質量證明
3. prestigious adj. 受尊敬的，有聲望的
4. stampede n. 驚逃；人群的蜂擁
5. commonplace adj. 平凡的，陳腐的；平庸的，普通的
6. morph vt. 改變
7. norm n. 規範；標準；準則；定額（勞動）
8. hang out 掛出，晾曬
9. inflation n. 通貨膨脹；膨脹；誇張；自命不凡
10. adjunct adj. 附屬的
11. exception n. 例外，除外；反對，批評；［法律］異議，反對
12. pursue vt. 追求
13. therapist n. 治療專家，特定療法技師
14. filter n. 濾波器；濾光器；濾色鏡
15. undeniable adj. 無可爭辯的；不可否認的；無法抵賴的；確實優秀的；無爭議的
16. accelerate vi. 加快，加速
17. turmoil n. 混亂；焦慮
18. postgrad n. 研究所人數；官方網站

19. nurture vt. 培育；養育
20. credential n. 文憑；憑證
21. recruiter n. 招聘人員
22. initiative n. 主動性；主動權；首創精神
23. counterpart n. 合作者
24. independently adv. 獨立地，自立地，無關地
25. entitlement n. 授權；應得權益；命名、被定名
26. benchmark n. 基準，參照
27. crux n. 癥結；關鍵；中心

Content Awareness

Ⅰ. Skim the text and then answer the following questions.

1. What is the title of the article?

_____

2. What are the challenges for a bachelor's degree?
    A. Cheaper programs.　　　B. Master's degrees.
    C. Both A and B

3. Which of the following is not created by the 「spiraling degree inflation」?
    A. More and more Americans will be burdened with heavy student loans.
    B. The earnings differential will continue to grow and expand.
    C. More and more college-educated people will be in jobs that do not require a bachelor's degree.

4. College graduates tend to do better in the job market than those without a bachelor's degree because _____.
    A. they have mastered critical thinking skills
    B. they have the mental capability and the initiative to complete something
    C. they have the potential to obtain a master's degree

5. People's attitudes toward a bachelor's degree _____.
    A. are ambiguous　　　B. are changing
    C. are not clear

6. The main idea of this article is that _____.

    A. a bachelor's degree has lost its value

    B. a bachelor's degree will regain its value

    C. a bachelor's degree is no longer taken at face value

II. According to the text, decide whether each of the following statements is True (T) or False (F).

1. People with bachelor's degrees always earn more than those without.

2. Not all bachelor's degrees are equal.

3. More and more college-educated people may be employed in jobs that do not require a four-year degree.

4. A master's degree highlights the weaknesses of a bachelor's degree and decreases the need for it.

5. Employers are more interested in a master's degree than in anything else.

6. People's attitude toward a bachelor's degree indicates that education is no longer respected.

Language Focus

I. Fill in the blanks with the correct forms of the given words.

Employ   economy   attend   graduate   pursue

Engineer   enrollment   criticize   academically   evolution

1. He enrolled with an _____ agency for a teaching position.

2. In recent years our country has placed great importance on _____ development.

3. _____ at Professor Smith's lecture fell off sharply that evening.

4. This university aims to more than double their _____ student population in five years.

5. Life, liberty, and the _____ of happiness have been called the inalienable rights of man.

6. Their inventions have contributed to the development of electrical _____.

7. I must _____ the children for piano lessons before next week.

8. All of our cultural heritage which is useful should be inherited, but in

a _____ way.

9. Many scholars were annoyed by his injection of politics into _____ discussion.

10. He argued that organisms _____ gradually by accumulating small hereditary changes.

II. Fill in the blanks with words that are often confused.

attitude   aptitude

1. Does she show any _____ for music?

2. He shows a very positive _____ to his work.

require   acquire

3. To remove any ambiguity we have to _____ more accurate information.

4. If you _____ further information, you should consult the registrar.

search   research

5. The new law empowered the police to _____ private houses.

6. Recent _____ has cast new light on the causes of the disease.

III. Fill in each blank with one suitable word.

Education is not an end, but a means to an end. In _____ words, we do not educate children _____ for the purpose of educating them; our purpose is to fit them for life.

In many modern countries it _____ for some time been fashionable to think that, by free education for all, one can solve all the problems of society and build a perfect nation. But we can already see that free education for all is not enough: we find in _____ countries a far larger number of people with university degrees _____ there are jobs for them to fill. Because of their degrees, they _____ to do what they think 「low」 work; and, in fact, work with the hands is thought to be dirty and shameful in such countries.

But we have only to think a moment to that the _____ that the work of a completely uneducated farmer is far more important than _____ of a professor: we can live _____ education, but we die if we have no food. _____ no one cleaned our streets and took the rubbish away from our houses, we should get terrible diseases in our towns.

In fact, when we say that all of us must be educated to fit us for life, it means that we must be _____ to do whatever job is suited to our brain and ability, and to realize that all jobs are necessary to society, that it is very _____ to be ashamed of one's work, or to scorn someone else's. Only such a type of education can be called valuable to society.

Text B

Home Schooling
by *Rebecca Axe, Amy Syvertsen*

When it comes to the education of today's youth, the idea of home schooling is a highly debated topic. Many people are for home schooling; similarly, many people are against it. The basis of this debate is one of great importance: our children need an education that prepares them for the world. It is the parents' fight to decide how best to obtain this goal.

Advantages unique to home schooling include its convenience, less strict attendance policies, and individualized attention. Of special importance to the community is that with more home schooled children, the cost of running public schools is reduced. With fewer enrollments, there is less demand for facilities and supplies, thus reducing overall costs.

Home schooling is much more convenient for parents and children because there is no formal schedule. With home schooling, parents do not need to wake up early in order to get their children dressed and fed before the bus arrives. Similarly, they do not need to double-check that their child has his or her homework and lunch money packed.

Another aspect relating to the convenience of home schooling is the issue of an attendance policy. In most public schools, students are required to attend school for 180 days. With home schooling however, there is no set number of days that the student must be in attendance. This seeks to remove problems that might cause a child to miss public school. And, for families that do long-distance traveling, go on prolonged family vacations, or for a child who has a serious illness, this is a blessing.

For parents who wish to have their children home schooled, it is fairly simple to accomplish, if one parent is willing to stay at home and be the teacher. In the state of New Jersey, U.S., no certification is needed for a parent to begin home schooling. Parents teach their children to the best of their ability with the knowledge and skills they themselves already possess. In cases where a parent has previously earned a college degree and is currently out of work or is working at home, it can be beneficial to both the parent and the child.

Parents who home school their children argue that their children receive a better education because of the individualized attention. Today's public schools are becoming too overcrowded and the quality of education is decreasing. Home schooling requires no set curriculum. With this, parents can be more focused on teaching their child subjects that truly interest them. In some cases, the child also receives a greater depth of knowledge because there is more time to complete research. With public schooling comes test pressure and anxiety. Testing is not required for children who are home schooled. This is a beneficial aspect of home schooling because children need to enjoy what they are learning in order to keep knowledge; testing just increases the stress.

On the other hand, by spending his or her day in the home, a child misses many opportunities to interact with peers. Critics charge that home schooled children are isolated from the outside world and are socially disabled. By being kept from the real world, children are seldom presented with me opportunities to learn truly needed social interaction skills. It is easy to understand why this is a concern. When attending a public school, a child is able to experience a wide variety of teachers and classmates. This fosters the child's interpersonal skills and teaches them how to work with others.

When one is home schooled, however, one is limited to only one teacher and, at best, brothers and sisters as one's classmates. Certainly this limits the amount of unique ideas being shared and explored. Home schooled ⌈children are seldom exposed to the various beliefs and backgrounds mat they would face in most public, school classrooms. Furthermore, if the child joins outside groups to try to reduce this limitation, the participants usually are a very limited group who for the most part share similar values, background, and social class. Such groups are unlike what the child will experience in college, on the job, and in the real world.

Public school teachers have been trained in specific content areas. They also have been trained in how to motivate and manage a classroom. Malay parents lack this training. Consequently their ability to teach in a home schooling environment may be doubtful. Compared to public school teachers, parents will have some problem in giving feedback because they are teaching their own child. The result is that the child may be graded too easily or too hard.

Parents may only teach areas in which they are skilled, thus leading to more obvious strengths and weaknesses in their child's abilities. This is true even for parents who have college training. Even parents holding doctoral degrees in mathematics and science are often poorly educated in literature, history, and the foundations of our civilization. As a child moves from elementary school to secondary school, the level of knowledge needed to teach them appropriately increases. In public schools, as the child moves on to the secondary level, there are teachers for each content area; in the home there is only the parent.

In addition to limited knowledge, it may be hard for the parent to balance the duty of teaching and other day-to-day tasks. Teaching requires dedication and self-discipline. Procrastination has to be a major problem in a home setting. It is easy to start a little later or delay learning so the parent can do something claimed to be very urgent. Some parents give in too easily to the complaints of their children and change things to meet the desires of the child. It also may be hard to separate the home and school when it comes to things such as discipline. It is pointed out that not every parent or guardian has the ability to teach or the resolve to stay with it. Knowing materials and having resources to use still does not provide everyone with the skills to teach young minds. As kids get older, they also show a natural rebellion to parents, which makes them harder to teach.

Another concern regarding home-schooling is that children will be limited in what resources are present to help facilitate their learning. Everything has a price and the limited amount of family income can create serious barriers for the child's education. As Romanowski points out: Limited resources affect their ability to provide adequate educational opportunities and equipment, such as computers; field trips and other experiences that cost money such as entrance fees to museums; science materials such as microscopes and other laboratory facilities; access to tutors to teach courses such as Spanish or to other needed specialized professional assistance; and simple everyday school materials.

This lack of resources can prevent the child from learning moreabout subjects that interest him or her. It also places a barrier on how much can be taught within the home.

It is also possible that children who are home schooled will be limited in their extra-curricular activities. A home school simply cannot provide all kinds of activities such as band, orchestra, choral activities, and many sports without some cooperation from some educational institution. And while some home schooling parents feel as though they are able to provide theses activities for their children, they may not be as good as those of other educational institutions.

As with all other forms of education, there are several advantages and disadvantages to home schooling. While it is the parent's right to choose how their children are educated, it is important that one make an informed decision. Our children are our future and they should have the best preparation possible.

Words and Expressions

1. adequate adj. 適當的，充分的
2. appropriately adv. 恰如其分地，適當地
3. beneficial adj. 有益的，有助的
4. certification n. 證明；證明書
5. choral adj. 合唱隊的
6. critic n. 批評家，評論家
7. currently adv. 當前
8. curriculum n. 課程
9. debate vt. 爭論，辯論
10. enrollment n. 註冊人數；入學人數；登記，註冊

11. extra-curricular adj. 課外的，業餘的

12. facilitate vt. 使容易，促進

13. feedback n. 反饋

14. foster vt. 鼓勵；養育

15. guardian n. ［律］監護人

16. institution n. （慈善、宗教等性質的）公共機構；協會；學校

17. interact vi. 相互作用，相互影響

18. microscope n. 顯微鏡

19. orchestra n. 管弦樂隊

20. procrastination n. 拖延，耽擱

21. rebellion n. 叛亂；反抗

22. self-discipline n. 自律；自我約束

23. a variety of 種種；各種各樣

24. at best 至多，充其量

25. for the most part 就大部分而言；在很大程度上

26. give in 屈服，讓步

27. to the best of one's ability 盡全力

Content Awareness

Ⅰ. Read the passage and decide on the best choice according to the passage.

1. According to this passage, how to educate children is decided by _____.

    A. children themselves　　B. parents
    C. the local government　　D. the national government

2. Which of the following is NOT included in the advantages of home schooling?

    A. Individualized attention.
    B. Less strict attendance policies.
    C. More interaction with different people.
    D. Convenience.

3. Which of the following statements is NOT true?

    A. No certification is required of a parent to begin home schooling.

    B. Home schooling does not require to set curriculum.

    C. Testing is not required for home schooled children.

    D. Special training is required before parents start home schooling.

4. Which of the following is NOT the advantage of public school?

    A. Exposure to more beliefs and backgrounds.

    B. Well trained teachers in different content areas.

    C. More flexible curriculum.

    D. Easier access to various resources.

5. Critics argue that home schooled children _____.

    A. have better interpersonal skills

    B. are less sociable

    C. have more unique ideas

    D. show less respect for teachers

6. The author supposes that many home schooling parents _____.

    A. lack training in specific content areas

    B. are better at controlling their children

    C. care more about their children's grades

    D. are more able to give feedback

7. Home schooled children are likely to be limited in _____.

    A. access to public library

    B. time for study

    C. time for play

    D. extra-curricular activities

8. In the author's opinion, it is advisable for parents to _____.

    A. think carefully before starting home schooling

    B. ask teachers for help while home schooling their child

    C. be further educated to get certificates for home schooling

    D. send their children to public schools

Language Focus

Ⅰ. Use the context to decide on the best meaning or synonym for each underlined word or phrase. Do not use a dictionary before making a guess.

    1. When it comes to the education of today's youth, the idea of home

schooling is a highly debated topic.

  A. heated   B. mentioned

  C. argued   D. introduced

2. Home schooling is much more convenient for parents and children because there is no formal schedule.

  A. meetings   B. subject

  C. term paper   D. program of classes

3. And, for families that do long-distance traveling, go on prolonged family vacations, or for a child who has a serious illness, this is a blessing.

If you prolong a vacation, you _____ it.

  A. shorten   B. lengthen

  C. delay   D. cancel

4. For parents who wish to have their children home schooled, it is fairly simple to accomplish, if one's parent is willing to stay at home and be the teacher.

  A. take in   B. bring about

  C. carry out   D. take over

5. When attending a public school, a child is able to experience a wide variety of teachers and classmates.

  A. a few   B. many kinds of

  C. a small group of   D. a couple of

6. Public school teachers have been trained in specific content areas. They also have been trained in how to motivate and manage a classroom.

  A. stimulate   B. control

  C. change   D. support

7. In addition to limited knowledge, it may be hard for the parent to balance the duty of teaching and other day-to-day tasks.

  A. Except   B. Besides

  C. Despite   D. Without

8. It is pointed out that not every parent or guardian has the ability to teach or the resolve to stay with it.

  A. determination   B. interest.

  C. confidence   D. possibility

9. Another concern regarding home schooling is that children wilt be limited in what resources are present to help facilitate their learning.

  A. continue   B. start

  C. make… easier   D. make… harder

10. Limited resources affect their ability to provide adequate educational opportunities and equipment, such as computers.

  A. superior   B. expensive

  C. advanced   D. enough

Ⅱ. Translate the following sentences or parts of sentences into English.

1. 當談論小汽車時，湯姆顯示出很大的興趣。

_____

2. 目前，很多父母樂於把孩子們送到國外去讀書。

_____

3. 必須指出，在家教育存在一些弊端。

_____

4. Many people find it hard to _____ （在工作和家庭生活之間取得平衡）.

5. He lives in a small house near the sea, _____ （與外界完全隔絕）.

6. You can engage in whichever job, _____ （重要的是你自己喜歡）.

4.3　Practical Translation

縮譯法

  翻譯過程中根據原文的邏輯關係和譯文的表達習慣，把原文中的一個句子緊縮成譯文中另一個句子的組成部分的翻譯方法叫「縮譯法」（condensation）。相比較而言，英譯漢時，拆譯法比縮譯法更為常見，畢竟英語是一種「形合」的語言，主要靠形式上的銜接來實現語意的連貫。英語句子較長，有許多修飾成分，呈現出環環相連、盤根錯節的樹幹結構；而漢語是一種「意合」的語言，主要採用脈絡分明、語意

連貫的竹式結構。但有時為了處理那些只是出於行文需要、為了表達某種語氣或烘托某種氣氛而本身並無多大意義的英語短語，英譯漢過程中也會使用縮譯法。這樣處理比較符合漢語語言洗練簡潔的特點，從而避免譯文囉唆及拖泥帶水。

一、縮譯短語

例1：Darkness came down on the field and the city: And Amelia was praying for George, who was lying on his face, dead, with a bullet through his heart. (Thackeray: *Vanity Fair*)

譯文：夜色四罩，城中之妻方祈天保夫無恙，戰場上其夫僕臥，一彈穿心，死矣。（錢鐘書譯）

例2：He seated himself close to her; he gazed at her in silence, or told her stories of the days gone by, of her childhood and of the convent.

譯文：他坐在她身旁，靜靜地望著她，或者和她談談往事，她的童年和她在修道院的情景。

解析：例1中的短語 the field and the city 和例2中的短語 stories of the days gone by 都是為了烘托某種氣氛，出於英語行文的需要。我們可以用縮譯法處理這兩個短語，前一短語縮譯成「四罩」，融合了 the field and the city 的含義；後一短語被縮譯成了只有兩個字的漢語名詞短語「往事」，體現了漢語洗練簡潔的特點。

二、縮譯複合句

例3：The liquid water is heated so that it becomes steam.

譯文：液態水受熱而變成蒸汽。

例4：No one has told them about the British custom of lining up for a bus so that the first person who arrives at a bus stop is the first person to get on the bus.

譯文：誰也沒有跟他們說過，英國人有排隊候車、先到先上的習慣。

解析：例3是一個含有結果狀語從句的複合句，例4是一個含有目的狀語從句和定語從句的複合句。由於從句的使用，兩個英文原句的結構略顯複雜，如果我們照此結構把從句都翻譯出來，漢語句子就會顯得冗長、拖沓。因此根據原文的意思，對例3的狀語批句進行了縮譯和省略的處理，整個複合句被融合成一個簡單句。漢語句子意思清楚、邏輯清晰。例4的目的狀語從句和定語從句都被融合在一起，縮譯成了漢語

中的「四字格」：「排隊候車、先到先上。」譯文地道、簡潔，易被漢語讀者接受和喜歡。

三、縮譯兩個簡單句

例5：Two men occupied the same hospital room. They were both seriously ill.

譯文：兩位重病患者住在同一間病房裡。

例6：Her experiment got nowhere. There is no sign of progress since.

譯文：她的實驗已陷入僵局，並且至今也沒取得任何進展。

解析：例5和例6中都含有兩個簡單句，兩個簡單句的主語相同，意思都非常清楚。例5的主語是「兩人」，例6的主語是「她的實驗」，兩個簡單句都用來描述或說明主語的情況。在這種情況下，我們可以將兩個簡單句縮譯成一個簡單句，將它們共同的主語作為句子的主語。例5原文中後一個簡單句處理成了漢語譯文中的前置定語，句子簡潔明晰。例6原文中後一個簡單句處理成了漢語譯文中的一個並列結構，邏輯清楚，語義連貫。

Translation Practice

Translate the following sentences into Chinese, using the technique of condensation.

1. In the course of the same war, a serious epidemic broke out.

2. A receptor is shaped in such a way that it can receive only a certain messenger.

3. The structure of the steel and resulting properties will depend on how hot the steel gets and how quickly or slowly it is cooled.

4. Take care of the pence, and the pounds will take care of themselves.

4.4　Focused Writing

Letters of Recommendation

What is a letter of recommendation?

A good letter of recommendation can be an asset to any application. For example, during admissions to post graduate courses, most universities expect to see at least one, preferably two or three, letters of recommendation for each applicant.

A letter of recommendation is a written document from your referee to an employer or graduate school that discusses your skills, abilities and worthiness for the position or program into which you are seeking enhance.

What is included in a letter of recommendation?

All letters of recommendation differ; however, most good letters of recommendation need at least three paragraphs containing the following types of information. The letter should spill over onto a second page, if possible.

· Identify yourself and the student. Explain your affiliation, the capacity in which you have come to know the student, and for how long you have known him or her. Include course names. State what grades the student earned in your course and mention how you would rank the student in relation to other students that you have known.

· Make detailed references to specific projects or activities in which the student participated, or work that was produced. You should be detailed and fulsome (豐富的; 大量的) where appropriate and highlight any relevant aspects from the following:

—Intellectual ability (overall intelligence, analytical skills, creativity, academic record, retention of information)

—Knowledge of area of specialty

—Communication skills (writing skills, oral articulateness)

—Personal qualities (industry, self-discipline, motivation, maturity, initiative, flexibility, leadership, team work spirits, perseverance, energy, competitiveness)

· Referees should be willing to receive follow-up calls from employers or schools, so you should include your business or home phone number and email in the letter.

What should be noted?

Bear in mind the following particular 「dos」 when producing a letter of recommendation.

1. Do be specific. Give examples of the student's work, completed pro-

jects, participation in extra-curricular activities and any relevant information that shows the student's abilities and character.

2. Do be objective. Although you are giving a personal recommendation, you must be fair and reasonable. Report specific examples to back up your comments. If you want to attest to a student's interpersonal skills, mention how you observed the student's interactions with others, rather than merely stating what a 「nice person」 she or he is.

3. Do be both honest and positive. If your experience with the student is negative in any way, ask the student to find another letter writer. Obviously, making negative comments about a student's performance will have serious consequences on the student's chances at the job, scholarship, or acceptance being sought. Remember that your experience with the student may not be typical, so the student should find someone who can make positive comments. In addition, writing negative comments can potentially affect you as well, if there is ever any doubt about the reliability of your judgment with respect to the student.

Sample 1

School of Sciences
Zhejiang University
Hangzhou, China, 310058

December 22nd, 2009

To Whom It May Concern:

    It is my great pleasure to recommend Ms. Ma for the Master's Finance and Economics program at the London School of Economics. As her former calculus professor, I have known Ma Xiaoming since autumn 2005 and have met with her regularly over the past four years. I knew that she had made up her mind to pursue a degree in finance at LSE some years ago and I am delighted she has asked me to write a letter of recommendation for her.

    Ms. Ma is a gifted, diligent and intensely rigorous student with strong academic performance At the very beginning of my calculus course at the Chu Kochen Honors College, affiliated to Zhejiang University, she appeared to be no more than a diligent student who always sat at the right corner of the front row. Yet soon, she stood out as one of the few very outstanding and talented students who come along from time to time. She easily understood my lectures and often raised thought-provoking questions. Through questions and discussions, I found her intensely meticulous and persistent, for she would never stop scrutinizing (詳審) a problem until all uncertainty was unraveled. As you know, these qualities a re most useful in research and I strongly believe that she will go on to make an excellent PhD candidate one day. Her scores at Zhejiang were exceptional, achieving 99%, the highest grade, in both Calculus I and Calculus II final papers. I understand from her other professors that she has performed equally well in all her other mathematics courses such as Linear Algebra, Probability Theory, Mathematical Statistics, and Ordinary Differentiation. I believe Ms. Ma's undergraduate training in mathematics and exceptional learning ability will undoubtedly prove useful to her graduate study in finance and economics.

    Another point that I would like to mention is her enrollment in the Mathematical Modeling Competition. During the competition, she combined her knowledge of mathematics and finance so well that her team won Second Prize. In addition, as the leader of her team, she skillfully managed the available resources and drew out the potential of each team member. Such experience and the leadership she showed indicated a level of maturity somewhat beyond her years.

    Ms. Ma is warm-hearted and straightforward. My recollection is of her frequent and patient explanations to confused classmates before and after my calculus classes. During my 4-year contact with her and her classmates, she was always willing to offer her help and was a great comfort to a classmate who lost her Father in tragic circumstances. She shows excellent time management skills, her assignments were always handed in on time and she has been able to combine a healthy social life in the Debating Society and on the tennis courts with her studies.

    I know she isvery keen to study for a degree in your program, and your positive consideration will be greatly appreciated. Please do not hesitate to contact me at 086-571-88206033 if I can be of any further assistance in her application.

Yours faithfully,
YY
Dean of Department of Mathematics, Zhejiang University

The salutation can also be 「Dear Admissions Committee Members」.
Opening: stating how you knew the applicant and your pleasure to recommend her.
Main body: supporting evidence ①of the applicant's academic abilities.

Supporting evidence ②of the applicant's extracurricular achievements.

Supporting evidence ③ of the applicant's good character and personality.

Closing: indicating willingness to be contacted and offer of further help.

Sample 2

> 55 Baima Lu
> Changsha
> Hunan
>
> November 19th, 2009
>
> To Whom It May Concern:
>
>   I have great pleasure in writing to recommend Yang Hailin. I have known him in my capacity as a friend of the family and Neighborhood Watch Officer since he was a child and watched him grow into an intelligent and hard working young man. His school years were marred by difficulty as his Father died when he was only six and his Mother struggled to support the family. Despite this Hailin has completed his high school diploma showing especial aptitude in art and Chinese literature. He would seem to be ideally suited for a job in advertising where his artistic ability would provide interesting and unusual images.
>
>   At school he was a diligent student who worked hard at his studies and entered into the school life with a quiet commitment. His attendance was excellent and he was well liked by all the teachers. He helped to organize optional artistic outings for students so that they could expand the types of subjects they could draw and showed such enthusiasm for making the event fun yet productive that they became very well attended. He made a number of good friend.
>
>   Hailin was a quiet yet thoughtful child and has grown into a caring and considerate adult. He has shown great kindness to an elderly neighbor who he has spent many hours reading to and showing her how to paint. Hailin was also a willing and conscientious member of the team that cleaned and replanted out local pond and has helped each year to plant trees in our neighborhood. He is honest, careful and sensible in all he does and will be a loyal asset to any company that employs him. I have no hesitation in recommending this excellent young man.
>
> Yours faithfully,
> Yang Fanmei
> Deputy Neighborhood Watch Officer

Writing Assignment

  1. Suppose you are a professor at Peking University. Write a letter of recommendation for Li Ming, one of your students, who aims to pursue a course of study at Harvard University.

  2. Suppose you are a high school teacher. Write a letter of recommendation to a potential employer about one of your students.

Unit 5 Work and Career

5.1 Get Started

Ⅰ. Work in pairs or groups and discuss the following questions.

1. What do you think work can provide?

2. What factors do you think one should take into account when choosing a career?

3. What kind of job do you think will be suitable for you?

Ⅱ. Study the following quotes about work and career and discuss in pairs what you can learn from them.

1. Work is something you can count on, a trusted, lifelong friend who never deserts you.

—Margaret Bourke-White

2. You've achieved success in your field when you don't know whether what you're doing is work or play.

—Warren Beatty

3. Genius is one percent respiration and ninety-nine percent perspiration.

—Thomas Edison

4. Far and away the best prize that life has to offer is the chance to work hard at work worth doing.

—Theodore Roosevelt

5.2 Read and Explore

Text A

Work
by *Bertrand Russell*

Whether work should be placed among the causes of happiness or among the causes of unhappiness may perhaps be regarded as a doubtful question. There is certainly much work which is exceedingly irksome, and an excess of work is always very painful. I think, however, that, provided work is not excessive in amount, even the dullest work is to most people less painful than idleness. There are in work all grades, from mere relief of tedium up to the profoundest delights, according to the nature of the work and the abilities of the worker. Most of the work that most people have to do is not in itself interesting, but even such work has certain great advantages. To begin with, it fills a good many hours of the day without the need to think of anything sufficiently pleasant to be worth doing. And whatever they decide on, they are troubled by the feeling that something else would have been pleasanter. To be able to fill leisure intelligently is the last product of civilization, and at present very few people have reached this level. Moreover the exercise of choice is in itself tiresome. Except to people with unusual initiative it is positively agreeable to be told what to do at each hour of the day, provided the orders are not too unpleasant. Most of the idle rich suffer unspeakable boredom as the price of their freedom from drudgery. At times, they may find relief by hunting big game in Africa, or by flying round the world, but the number of such sensations is limited, especially after youth is past. Accordingly the more intelligent rich men work nearly as hard as if they were poor, while rich women for the most part keep themselves busy with innumerable trifles of whose earth-shaking importance they are firmly persuaded.

Work therefore is desirable, first and foremost, as a preventive of boredom, for the boredom that a man feels when he is doing necessary though uninteresting work is as nothing in comparison with the boredom that he feels when he has nothing to do with his days. With this advantage of work another is associated, namely that it makes holidays much more delicious when they come. Provided a man does not have to work so hard as to impair his vigor, he is likely to find far more zest in his free time than an idle man could possibly find.

The second advantage of most paid work and of some unpaid work is that it gives chances of success and opportunities for ambition. In most work success is measured by income, and while our capitalist society continues, this is inevitable. It is only where the best work is concerned that this measure ceases to be the natural one to apply. The desire that men feel to increase their income is quite as much a desire for success as for the extra comforts that a higher income can procure. However dull work may be, it becomes bearable if it is a means of building up a reputation, whether in the world at large or only in one's own circle. Continuity of purpose is one of the most essential ingredients of happiness in the long run, and for most men this comes chiefly through their work. In this respect those women whose lives are occupied with housework are much less fortunate than men, or than women who work outside the home. The domesticated wife does not receive wages, has no means of bettering herself, is taken for granted by her husband (who sees practically nothing of what she does), and is valued by him not for her housework but for quite other qualities. Of course this does not apply to those women who are sufficiently well-to-do and make beautiful houses and beautiful gardens and become the envy of their neighbors; but such women are comparatively few, and for the great majority housework cannot bring as much satisfaction as work of other kinds brings to men and to professional women.

The satisfaction of killing time and of affording some outlet, however modest, for ambition, belongs to most work, and is sufficient to make even a man whose work is dull happier on the average than a man who has no work at all. But when work is interesting, it is capable of giving satisfaction of a far higher order than mere relief from tedium. The kinds of work in which there is some interest may be arranged in a hierarchy. I shall begin with those which are only mildly interesting and end with those that are worthy to absorb the whole energies of a great man.

Two chief elements make work interesting; first, the exercise of skill, and second, construction.

Every man who has acquired some unusual skill enjoys exercising it until it has become a matter of course, or until he can no longer improve himself. This motive to activity begins in early childhood: a boy who can stand on his head becomes reluctant to stand on his feet. A great deal of work gives the same pleasure that is to be derived from games of skill. The work of a lawyer or a politician must contain in a more delectable form a great deal of the same pleasure that is to be derived from playing bridge. Here of course there is not only the exercise of skill but the outwitting of a skilled opponent. Even where this competitive element is absent, however, the performance of difficult feats is agreeable. A man who can do stunts in an aero plane finds the pleasure so great that for the sake of it he is willing to risk his life. I imagine that an able surgeon, in spite of the painful circumstances in which his work is done, derives satisfaction from the exquisite precision of his operations. The same kind of pleasure, though in a less intense form, is to be derived from a great deal of work of a humbler kind. All skilled work can be pleasurable, provided the skill required is either variable or capable of indefinite improvement. If these conditions are absent, it will cease to be interesting, when a man has acquired his maximum skill. A man who runs three-mile races will cease to find pleasure in this occupation when he passes the age at which he can beat his own previous record. Fortunately there is a very considerable amount of work in which new circumstances call for new skill and a man can go on improving, at any rate until he has reached middle age. In some kinds of skilled work, such as politics, for example, it seems that men are at their best between sixty and seventy, the reason being that in such occupations a wide experience of other men is essential. For this reason successful politicians are apt to be happier at the age of seventy than any other men of equal age. Their only competitors in this respect are the men who are the heads of big businesses.

Words and Expressions

1. exceedingly adv. 非常，極其，特別，十分
2. irksome adj. 令人厭煩的
3. tedium n. 單調乏味，令人生厭，冗長
4. drudgery n. 苦工，賤役，單調沉悶的工作
5. innumerable adj. 不可勝數；無數的，數不清的
6. impair vt. 損害，削弱
7. zest n. 興趣，熱情；風味，滋味
8. procure vi. 取得，獲得
9. continuity n. 連續性，繼續
10. hierarchy n. 分層，層次
11. feat n. 功績，偉業；卓絕的手藝，技術，本領
12. be apt to 傾向於

Notes

1. Bertrand Russell (1872−1970) was educated at Trinity College, Cambridge. He published his first book, *The Study of German Social Democracy*, in 1896; subsequent books on mathematics and on philosophy quickly established his international reputation. His pacifist opposition to World War I cost him his appointment at Trinity College, and won him a prison sentence of six months. While serving this sentence he wrote his *Introduction to Mathematical Philosophy*. In 1940 an appointment to teach at the College of the City of New York was withdrawn because of Russell's unorthodox moral views. But he was not always treated shabbily; he won numerous awards, including a Nobel Prize in 1950. After World War II he devoted most of his energy to warning the world about the dangers of nuclear war. This essay comes from a book called *The Conquest of Happiness*.

2. a doubtful question→a question the nature of which people are uncertain.

3. There is certainly much work which is exceedingly irksome, and an excess of work is always very painful. →Of course, a large amount of work is extremely irritating, and too much work is always very painful.

exceedingly→extremely.

e.g. Though they lost the game in the end, the national basketball team played exceedingly well.

irksome→irritating, annoying.

e.g. The neighbors were tired of the couple's irksome complaints.

4. There are in work all grades, from mere relief of tedium up to the profoundest delights→What work can bring workers varies from just setting them free from boredom to the greatest happiness.

tedium→boredom, the state of being tedious, too long, slow, or dull.

e.g. Since they were tired of the tedium of car journeys, this time they decided to go by air.

5. To be able to fill leisure intelligently is the last product of civilization…→Only people who live in a highly civilized society are able to well utilize leisure.

6. initiative→ energy and resourcefulness enabling one to act without prompting from others (主觀能動性; 主動).

e.g. Always remember to use your initiative, imagination, and common sense.

7. Most of the idle rich suffer unspeakable boredom as the price of their freedom from drudgery. →Those rich people who don't go to work do not have to suffer like most people: to do dull and uninteresting work. But the price for not having to do dull work is to suffer extreme boredom.

drudgery→hard, dull, uninteresting work.

e.g. Few people enjoy the everyday domestic drudgery.

8. hunting big game→hunting big wild animals.

game→ (mass noun), wild mammals or birds hunted for sport or food.

9. … while rich women for the most part keep themselves busy with innumerable trifles of whose earth-shaking importance they are firmly persuaded. →… rich women busy themselves with countless small, insignificant things, but they make themselves believe that the things they do are important.

10. … it makes holidays much more delicious when they come. →Work makes holidays much more enjoyable and people appreciate their holidays

more.

11. Provided a man does not have to work so hard as to impair his vigor... →As long as a person does not have to work until he has no physical strength left.

　　impair→weaken or damage (especially a human faculty or function).
　　e.g. A noisy job could permanently impair the workers' hearing.

12. Continuity of purpose is one of the most essential ingredients of happiness in the long run→Eventually one of the indispensable components of happiness is always having a goal ahead and working persistently towards it.

13. The domesticated wife does not receive wages, has no means of bettering herself, is taken for granted by her husband→The housewife does not receive wages, nor can she achieve a higher status. Her husband thinks that everything she does is what she should do, so he does not appreciate her work.

14. affording some outlet, however modest, for ambition→Work makes it possible for the worker to realize his desire for success and achievement. Even if it is only a small opportunity, it is still an opportunity.

15. may be arranged in a hierarchy→may be classified into distinctive levels.

　　hierarchy→a system or organization in which people or groups are ranked one above the other according to status or authority (等級制度).

16. those that are worthy to absorb the whole energies of a great man→Those kinds of work that are so interesting and challenging that a great man is willing to devote the whole of his life and talents to them.

17. do stunts in an aero plane→特技飛行，航空表演.

18. ... the skill required is either variable or capable of indefinite improvement→The author is of the opinion that if a certain type of work requires skill, then this work brings pleasure to the worker. However, this is not enough. If there is no variation in the skill required, once you have mastered it and become proficient, you will feel under-challenged and bored. Therefore, only when work requires ever-improving skill or a worker is able to improve his skill continuously in work will he derive tremendous pleasure from work.

19. ... in such occupations a wide experience of other men is essential→

In politics and some other kinds of skilled work, it is very important to get to know and learn from a lot of people.

Content Awareness

I. Answer the following questions with the information contained in Text A.

1. What's the author's opinion to the work that most people have to do is not in itself interesting? Why?

_____

_____

2. What's the advantage of most paid work according to the text?

_____

3. What's the chief elements to make work interesting?

_____

_____

4. Some people think that idleness is more comfortable than work, but we all might have experienced the sense of boredom amid an unusually long vacation. What does work mean to you?

_____

_____

Language Focus

I. For each blank in the following passage, choose the most suitable word from the following list of words. Each word can be used only once.

could   human   had   humane   set
would   routine   grow   should   warning
forbidding   substitute

It is foolish to dream of reversing history. We cannot pass laws _____ science and technology. The computing machines are here, and they will not merely stay, they will grow bigger, faster, and more useful every year. They will _____ because engineers want to build them, scientists want to use them, industrialists want to employ them, soldiers want to enlist

Unit 5 Work and Career

111

them in new weapons system, politicians want their help in the processes of government. In short, they will flourish because they enable us to finish tasks that _____ never before have been undertaken, no matter how many unskilled laborers we might have _____ to work. Computers will continue to amplify our intelligence for just the same reason that engines continue to amplify our muscles. The question we must ask is not whether we shall have computers or not have computers, but rather, since we are going to have them, how can we make the most _____ and intelligent use of them?

Obviously, there _____ be no point in investing in a computer if you had to check all its answers, but people _____ also rely on their own internal computers and check the machine when they have the feeling that something has gone wrong.

Questioning and _____ double-checks must continue to be as much a part of good business as they were in pre-computer days. Maybe each computer should come with the _____: for all the help this computer may provide, it should not be seen as a _____ for fundamental thinking and reasoning skills.

II. Sentence Recasting: For each of the sentences below, write a new sentence as similar as possible in meaning to the original sentence. You are required to use the word given in capital letters without any alteration.

Example: He didn't turn up for the meeting yesterday. (FAILED)
Answer: He failed to turn up for the meeting yesterday.

1. You cannot go into that restaurant without a tie. (UNLESS)

2. I paid the plumber $5 for mending the cold tap. (CHARGED)

3. Charles regretted his foolish behavior. (WISHED)

4. We took more books than we needed on holiday. (NEEDN'T)

5. We listened to records the whole evening. (SPENT)

Ⅲ. Paraphrasing: Paraphrase the following sentences in your own words.

1. There are in work all grades, from mere relief of tedium up to the profoundest delights.

2. To be able to fill leisure intelligently is the last product of civilization.

3. Continuity of purpose is one of the most essential ingredients of happiness in the long run.

4. The domesticated wife does not receive wages, has no means of bettering herself, is taken for granted by her husband.

5. Here of course there is not only the exercise of skill but the outwitting of a skilled opponent.

Ⅳ. Translate the following passage into English.

有些人認為只要自己準時上下班就算完成任務了，從不思索什麼是工作和為什麼要工作。其實，「工作」涉及智慧、熱情、想像力和創造力等各方面的素質。

要做好工作，工作者必須有奉獻精神，能夠吃苦耐勞，此外他還應該具有主動性和創造性。所謂主動性，就意味著工作者要隨時把握住機會，展現自己非凡的工作才能。

其次，工作者要弄清楚自己所從事的工作的性質和意義，對自己的所作所為負起責任，以旺盛的熱情投入到工作中去。如果能做到這一點，他就會發現，工作不再是一種負擔，而是他生活中不可或缺的一個重要組成部分。不管從事什麼工作，他總能從工作中找到價值和樂趣，在平凡的崗位上取得不平凡的成績。

Text B

Choosing an occupation is an important decision. When making a decision such as this, it is essential to look critically at yourself, and examine your values, interests, abilities, etc. The following text provides you with some insightful advice on the factors worth considering when choosing an occupation or career.

Choosing anOccupation or Career
by *Gerald Corey*

What do you expect from work? What factors do you give the most attention to in selecting a career or an occupation? In my work at a university counseling center I've discovered that many students haven't really thought seriously about why they are choosing a given vocation. For some, parental pressure or encouragement is the major reason for their choice. Others have idealized views of what it will be like to be a lawyer, engineer, or doctor. Many people I've counseled regarding career decisions haven't looked at what they value the most and whether these values can be attained in their chosen vocation. In choosing your vocation or evaluating the choices you've made previously, you may want to consider which factors really mean the most to you.

Making vocational choices is a process that spans a considerable period of time, rather than an isolated event. Researchers in career development have found that most people go through a series of stages in choosing the occupation or, more typically, occupations that they will follow. The following factors have been shown to be important in determining a person's occupational decision-making process: self-concept, interests, abilities, values, occupational attitudes, socio-economic level, parental influence, ethnic identity, gender, and physical, mental, emotional, and social handicaps. Let's consider some of these factors related to career decision making, keeping in mind that vocational choice is a process, not an event. We'll look at the role of self-concept, occupational attitudes, abilities, interests, and values in choosing a career.

Self-Concept

Some writers in career development believe that a vocational choice is an attempt to fulfill one's self-concept. People with a poor self-concept, for example, are not likely to picture themselves in a meaningful or important job. They are likely to keep their ambitions low, and thus their achievements will probably be low also. They may select and remain in a job that they do not enjoy or derive satisfaction from, based on their conviction that such a job is all they are worthy of. In this regard, choosing a vocation can be thought of as a public declaration of the kind of person we see ourselves as being.

Occupational Attitudes

Research indicates that, among the factors that influence our attitudes toward occupational status, education is important. The higher the educational requirements for an occupation, the higher its status.

We develop our attitudes toward the status of occupations by learning from the people in our environment. Typical first-graders are not aware of the different status of occupations. Yet in a few years these children begin to rank occupations in a manner similar to that of adults. Other research has shown that positive attitudes toward most occupations are common among first-graders but that these preferences narrow steadily with each year of school. As students advance to higher grades, they reject more and more occupations as unacceptable. Unfortunately, they rule out some of the very jobs from which they may have to choose if they are to find employment as adults. It is difficult for people to feel positively about themselves or their occupation if they have to accept an occupation they perceive as low in status.

Abilities

Ability, or aptitude, has received as much attention as any of the factors considered significant in the career decision-making process, and it is probably used more often than any other factor. There are both general and specific abilities. Scholastic aptitude, often called general intelligence or IQ, is a general ability typically considered to consist of both verbal and numerical aptitudes. Included among the specific abilities are mechanical, clerical, and spatial aptitudes, abstract reasoning ability, and eye/hand/foot coordination. Scholastic aptitude is particularly significant because it largely determines who will be able to obtain the levels of education required for entrance into the higher-status occupations.

Interestingly, most studies show little direct relationship between measured aptitudes and occupational performance and satisfaction. This does not mean that ability is unimportant, but it does indicate that we must consider other factors in career planning.

Interests

Interest measurement has become popular and is used extensively in career planning. Interests, unlike abilities, have been found to be moderately effective as predictors of vocational success, satisfaction, and persistence. Therefore, primary consideration should be given to interests in vocational planning. It is important to first determine your areas of vocational interest, then to identify occupations for which these interests are appropriate, and then to determine those occupations for which you have the abilities required for satisfactory job performance. Research evidence indicates only a slight relationship between interests and abilities.

Values

It is extremely important for you to identify, clarify, and assess your values so that you will be able to match them with your career.

In counseling college students on vocational decision making I typically recommend that they follow their interests and values as reliable guides for a general occupational area. If your central values are economic, for example, your career decisions are likely to be based on a desire for some type of financial or psychological security. The security a job affords is a legitimate consideration for most people, but you may find that security alone is not enough to lead to vocational satisfaction. Your central values may be social, including working with people and helping people. There are many careers that would be appropriate for those with a social orientation.

Of course, the factors I've mentioned are only a few of the many considerations involved in selecting a vocation. Since so much time and energy are devoted to work, it's extremely important to decide for ourselves what weight each factor will have in our thinking.

In short, you stand a greater chance of being satisfied with your work if you put time and thought into your choice and if you actively take steps toward finding a career or an occupation that will bring more enrichment to your life than it will disruption. Ultimately, you are the person who can best decide what you want in your work.

Words

1. occupation n. 職業，工作
2. counseling n.（對個人，社會以及心理等問題的）諮詢服務
3. idealize vt. 使理想化；幻想化
4. evaluate vt. 評價；求……的值（或數）；對……評價
5. previously adv. 以前；事先；倉促地
6. vocational adj. 職業的
7. derive vt. 得到；源於，來自
8. conviction n. 定罪；信念；確信；說服
9. declaration n. 宣言，布告，公告，聲明
10. aptitude n. 傾向；才能，資質，天資
11. scholastic adj. 學校的，教育上的
12. verbal adj. 言辭的；口頭的
13. numerical adj. 數字的
14. spatial adj. 空間的；立體的
15. coordination n. 協調，和諧
16. moderately adv. 適度地；普通地；不過度地
17. appropriate adj. 適當的；合適的；恰當的
18. orientation n. 取向
19. enrichment n. 豐富
20. disruption n. 擾亂
21. ultimately adv. 根本；最後，最終；基本上

Proper Names

1. Gerald Corey　杰拉爾德·科里（人名）

Notes

1. This text is taken and adapted from *I Never Knew I Had a Choice*: *Explorations in Personal Growth* (Seventh Edition) by Gerald Corey and Marianne Schneider Corey. Wadsworth Publishing Co., 2005.

2. Gerald Corey: a professor emeritus (榮譽退休的) of Human Services and Counseling at California State University at Fullerton and a licensed psychologist. With his colleagues he has conducted workshops in various countries with a special focus on training in group counseling.

3. IQ: IQ (intelligence quotient) is a number that shows a person's level of intelligence, measured by a special test called an IQ test. An IQ of 100 is the average. The test consists of problems related to letters, numbers, and shapes. Some people criticize this test because it only measures one specific type of intelligence, and it may not be fair to people from certain races or social backgrounds.

4. Others have idealized views of what it will be like to be a lawyer, engineer, or doctor. →Other students have unrealistically high hopes of what it means to be a lawyer, engineer or doctor.

5. If your central values are economic, for example, your career decisions are likely to be based on a desire for some type of financial or psychological security. →If what you want most out of life is money, for example, you will probably choose a job that is likely to be a good and steady source of income.

6. you stand a greater chance of being satisfied with your work if you put time and thought into your choice and if you actively take steps toward finding a career or an occupation that will bring more enrichment to your life than it will disruption. →if you take the matter of career decision seriously and if you can find out what kind of occupation may enrich your life and bring about a sense of true fulfillment, then you are more likely to end up with a career that is going to make you happy.

Content Awareness

Ⅰ. Find the right definition in Column B for each italicised word in Column A, Put the corresponding letter in the space provided in Column A. The number of the paragraph in which the target word appears is given in brackets. The first one has been done for you.

Column A

1. ____e____ *idealized* views (Para. 1)
2. _____ the choices you've made *previously* (Para. 1)
3. _____ *ethnic* identity (Para. 2)
4. _____ *Scholastic* aptitude (Para. 6)
5. _____ *mechanical*, clerical, and spatial aptitudes (Para. 6)
6. _____ *predictors* of vocational success (Para. 8)

Column B

a. before now of before a particular time
b. of a racial, national, or tribal group
c. of schools and/or teaching
d. those who can describe a future happening in advance
e. imagined or represented as perfect or as better than reality
f. of machinery

Ⅱ. Fill in each blank in the following sentences with a phrase from Text B. Both the meaning and the number of the paragraph in which the target phrase appears are given in brackets.

Example: That area's future weather pattern might <u>consist of</u> long, dry periods. (be made up of: Para. 6)

1. It often helps to talk to someone when you're _____ a crisis. (suffering of experiencing; enduring: Para. 2)

2. The union is the largest in the country and _____ is best placed to serve its members. (in this respect: Para. 3)

3. The police haven't _____ yet murder after days of investigation into the case. (stopped considering the possibility of: Para. 5)

4. You'll _____ of getting a better job if you hold a Master's degree. (have the possibility of succeeding or achieving sth.: Para. 12)

Ⅲ. Paraphrase the following sentences, paying special attention to the italicised parts.

1. Many people I've counseled regarding career decisions haven't looked

at *what they value the most and whether these values can be attained in their chosen vocation.* (Para. 1)

_____

2. In this regard, choosing a vocation can be thought of *as a public declaration of the kind of person we see ourselves as being* . (Para. 3)

_____

3. *It is difficult for people to feel positively about themselves or their occupation* they have to accept an occupation they perceive as low in status. (Para. 5)

_____

4. Interestingly, most studies show *little direct relationship between measures optitudes and occupational performance and satisfaction.* (Para. 7)

_____

5. Interests, unlike abilities, have been found to be *moderately effective as predictors of vocational success, satisfaction, and persistence.* (Para. 8)

_____

Language Focus

Ⅰ. Complete the following sentences with an appropriate word form the box.

job   career   post   position   profession   trade   vocation   work

1. Teaching children ought to be regarded as a _____, not just as a means of earning a living.

2. The company advertised some _____ for university graduates in yesterday's newspapers.

3. Some professional people used to look down upon people who are engaged in _____.

4. The factory closed down last month and she lost her _____ a-

gain.

5. It is difficult to find _____ in the present economic climate.

6. Dr. Green showed great ability in pleading for the accused. After all, he is a lawyer by _____.

7. As a diplomat, he spent most of his _____ in the United States of America.

8. She retired from her _____ as marketing director due to health reasons.

II. Turn the following complex sentences into simple sentences.

Example: We couldn't agree as to whom we should select.

We couldn't agree as to whom to select.

1. I don't remember I have ever borrowed anything from you.

_____

2. She'll stay here for a couple of weeks before she goes on to New York.

_____

3. The prospect that Professor Smith was to come to visit us cheered us all.

_____

4. Jim, who was a man of strong character, naturally didn't give in.

_____

5. When he arrived at the school gate, he found his classmates had already assembled.

_____

III. Complete the following passage with words chosen from this unit. The initial letter of each is given.

Most people have work to do. With work, they can e_____ their lives. However, people who did p_____ labor were looked clown upon in the past. Many people were c_____ to take manual labor because it was an absolute n_____ for them to earn a living and to s_____ their families. By contrast, people who did m_____ work were highly respected. Under the influence of this idea, even today some people still i_____ their future when making choices for their career. What they care most about is whether the job can give them enough social s_____

121

rather than whether they can realize their v_____ in it. In their eyes, those who do manual labor should still be c_____ as inferior in social status.

In fact, there is no e_____ difference between those who work with their hands and those who work with their m_____. Whether a job is labor of work does not depend on the job itself but on people's a_____ towards it. As long as you like your job, you will think you are f_____ enough to take it and you will do it enthusiastically.

Ⅳ. Translate the following sentences into English, using the words or expressions given in brackets.

1. 隨著她個人生活的細節越來越多地被媒體披露出來，她不得不辭去公司總經理的職務。(compel)

2. 她對自己的新工作很滿意，因為這份工作正好與她的興趣相符。(coincide with)

3. 我買了這件襯衣，因為它的價格從300元降到了80元。(reduce)

4. 為了把孩子們撫養成人，這位母親真是歷經了各種磨難。(go through)

5. 警方在老太太的死亡案中已經排除了謀殺的可能性。(rule out)

6. 市政府承諾將盡快採取有效措施，解決空氣污染的問題。(take steps)

7. 因為腿部受傷，我沒有參加上個月學校舉行的網球錦標賽。(go in for)

8. 要是能得到大多數女生支持的話，你贏得選舉成為學生會主席的機會是很大的。(stand a chance)

9. 他寫的書並非都像這一本這麼成功，所以我建議你從圖書館把它借來讀一下。(recommend)

10. 在2004年雅典奧運會上，劉翔打破男子110米欄（110-meter hurdles）世界紀錄，獲得冠軍，這個記錄以前是由一個美國運動員保持的。(previously)

5.3 Practical Translation

拆譯法

相比漢語而言，許多英語文本，尤其是英語議論文和科技文獻，句子一般較長，且包含許多信息。這些信息通過「形合」法連接成句，進而形成語篇。英譯漢時，如果應用語法分析和邏輯判斷的手段，對英語語篇加以分析拆解，就能使譯文更加體現漢語「意合」的特點。我們稱這種化整為零的處理方法為「拆譯法」（division）。拆譯法需要按照意群，將英語句子中某些成分，比如詞、短語、複合句從句子的主幹中拆分出來，或變成短句，或變成獨立句等。這些成分可根據邏輯順序和英漢兩種語言的差異，改變它們在原句中的位置，以利於譯文句子的總體安排，使譯文自然、流暢。

一、拆譯單詞

例1：He shall be glad of your company on the journey.

譯文：如果你能陪他一塊兒去，他會很高興的。

例2：She had a sound fleeing that idiom was the backbone of a language and she was all for the racy phrases.

譯文：她感到習語是語言的支柱，因此特別主張用生動的短語，她的想法是完全正確的。

解析：這兩個句子雖然不長，但都包含多層意思。例1包含兩層意思：「他高興」和「你陪他一塊兒去」，因此原句中的 glad 在譯文中被拆分出來，譯成了一個短句「他會很高興的」。例2包含三層意思：「她的想法完全正確」「習語是語言的支柱」和「她主張用生動的語言」，因此原文中的 sound 在譯文中被拆分出來，譯成了短句「她的想法是完全正確的」。在翻譯這類句子時，我們要先對句子進行有效的拆分，譯出句子的層層意思，然後按照漢語「先分析後結論」的句式特點，得出地道、連貫的譯文。

二、拆譯短語

例3：「But we have a lot of small, very disruptive day-in-and-day-out problems on the factory floor.」one industrialist said.

譯文：一位實業家說：「在工廠辦公樓裡，我們面臨許多很小但破壞性卻很大的問題，它們日復一日，無休無止地發生。」

例4：Thunderstorms in spring and summer often come with intensity great enough to cause flash-flooding.

譯文：春夏兩季，雷雨交加，猛烈異常，往往會導致暴雨成災。

解析：這兩個句子都是完整的長句。例3中的 problems 前面有四個修飾語：a lot of, small, very disruptive, day-in-and-day-out，如果不做任何拆譯，讓所有的修飾語全部作定語修飾 problems，那定語部分就會顯得過長，句子會出現「頭重腳輕」的問題。因此有必要對句子進行拆譯，讓直接修飾 problems 的定語前置，而把說明問題發生頻率的短語 day-in-and-day-out 置於句尾，譯成一個獨立句。這樣句子的意思和結構就變得清晰明了。例句4的原文是一個完整而有氣勢的句子，但如果我們不做任何拆譯，句子的結構就會顯得拖沓，意思表達不清，讀者會不知所雲，因此有必要拆譯句子，並用漢語中常用的「四字格」來處理，使句意清晰，氣勢依舊。

三、拆譯複合句

例5：In the course of decay of the vegetable and the animal matter in the soil, various acids and gases are formed which help to decompose the rock particles and other compounds needed for the plan foods.

譯文：動植物在泥土裡腐爛的過程中，形成各種酸和氣體。這些酸和氣體有助於分解岩石粒和其他化合物，以供植物作養料。

例6：Considerable attention has been focused on the dilemma presented by the patient with chest pain who, on angiographic study, has normal coronary arteries and no other objective evidence of heart disease.

譯文：有一種胸痛病人，其冠狀動脈造影檢查正常，又無心臟病的其他客觀特徵，其診斷上的困難引起了人們的極大重視。

解析：這兩個句子都是含有定語從句的複合句，對於這類句子，我們往往可以按照句子的意群，使用拆譯法將從句和主句分開譯。例5的關係代詞 which 前面是一個完整的句子，我們可先譯出前面的句子，而 which 所指代的 acids 和 gases 又是後面句子的主語，因此我們可以重複這兩個先行詞，再譯後面的句子。而後面句子中的 needed 其實是另一個定語從句 which are needed 省略 which are 而來，因此按照意群，我們可以在這裡進行第二次拆譯，將後半句譯成兩個語義連貫的短句。例6的情況也是一樣，我們可以按照句子的意群，將關係代詞 who 作為拆譯的一個標誌詞，在它的前面進行拆分，將句子一分為二。而這個定語從句本身是一個並列句，我們有必要將並列的兩個成分進行拆分。從思維方式來說，原句是典型的「先結論後分析」的英語句子結構，譯成漢語時，要使句子符合漢語的邏輯思維，就需採用「先分析後結論」的句子結構，對整個句子的結構和順序進行較大的調整。

四、拆譯整個句子

例7：This development is in part a result of experimental studies indicating that favorable alterations in the determinants of myocardial oxygen consumption may reduce ischemic injury and that reduction after load may be associated with improved cardiac performance.

譯文：從某種程度上講，這方面的進展是實驗研究的結果。實驗結果表明，有效改善心肌耗氧量的決定因素可減輕局部損害，並且負荷的減輕也能改善心肌功能。

例8：Could any spectacle, for instance, be more grimly whimsical than that of gunners using science to shatter men's bodies while, close at hand, surgeons use it to restore them?

譯文：例如：炮兵利用科學毀壞人體，而就在附近，外科醫生用科學搶救被炮兵毀壞的人體，還有什麼情景比這更怪誕可怕的嗎？

解析：這兩句如果按照英文結構直接翻譯成漢語，勢必造成邏輯關係混亂、表意不清，使人難以理解。因此我們要根據漢語多用短句的句法特點，按照英語原文的意群，將較長的英語句子拆譯為兩個或兩個以上的單位，以求在充分「達意」的基礎上，符合漢語的表達習慣。因此例 7 的譯文將原句拆譯成兩個完整的句子，含五個分句。例 8 的譯文將原句拆譯成五個分句，這樣處理後，句子層次分明、表意明確、邏輯性強。

但是，拆譯是有一定限度的，拆譯的目的並不是要把句子弄得七零八落，支離破碎。拆譯應該按照英文原句的意群，使拆譯後的漢語主謂結構完整、層次分明、邏輯清晰，否則拆譯的意義也就不復存在了。

Translation Practice

Translate the following sentences into Chinese, using the technique of division.

1. They vainly tried to find out the stranger's name.

2. The infinitesimal amount of nuclear fuel required makes it possible to build power reactors in that mountainous area.

3. It all began in the mid-1850s, when Lowe's experiments with balloons led him to believe in the existence of an upper stream of air that moved in an easterly direction, no matter what direction the lower currents flowed.

4. More puzzling is the remarkable increase in occurrence of this disease which has happened since World War II in a number of western countries where standards of hygiene were continuously improving.

5.4　Focused Writing

Resumes and CVs

What is a resume or CV?

A resume or a curriculum vitae (CV) is a document that honestly outlines and summarizes your qualifications, training, work experience, and interests. Prospective employers or admissions committee members will need to know your educational attainments, any work experience you already have and your skills, achievements and interests.

How is resume or CV organized?

A resume (US) or a CV (UK) should be limited to one page if possible so that a potential employer can see at a glance who you are and what he or she can expect you to be able to do. Therefore, take time to lay out the page so that it looks tidy and is easy to read. You should tailor your resume or CV to fit the needs and expectations of each company and job position by ensuring the information you include is relevant. There is no point in making a lot of your ability to teach children how to play the flute if you are applying for a position as an accountant—though you should of course mention any abilities that you do have.

What is included ina resume or CV?

Generally speaking, a resume or CV should include any of the following information that is relevant.

Personal details at the top, such as name in bold type, address, contact numbers and, if the subject has one, an e-mail address.

Career objective (This is optional and is not always included in a CV.)

Education: Listing of academic degrees beginning with the degree in progress or most recently earned. Include: name of institution, city and state, degree type (B. A., B. S., M. A., etc.) and area of concentration, month and year degree was (will be) received. If you are an undergraduate and your GPA is 3.5 or higher, it is appropriate to include it.

Work Experience: Listing of jobs (part-time, full-time, volunteer, temporary or permanent). Include: company name, department, agency, or organization; city and state; job/position title; dates; a brief description of your duties and responsibilities, using strong action verbs. List these in reverse chronological order, i. e. latest first.

Honors and Awards (if appropriate): List any competitive scholarships, fellowships or scholastic honors, teaching or research awards, if relevant. Do not include minor awards but these could be referred to in your cover letter, e. g.「I also received awards for swimming while at university.」

Qualifications or skills: A summary of particular or relevant strengths or skills which you want to highlight.

Publications (if appropriate): Give bibliographic citations fusing the format appropriate to your particular academic discipline) for articles, pamphlets, chapters in books, research reports, or any other publications that you have authored or co-authored. (This section may be omitted but can be referred to in your cover letter, or if comprehensive, listed separately.)

Hobbies and Interests (Optional but you can provide a short list)

References: (Optional) end a resume or CV with the statement「Available upon Request」.

Five Cs in writing a resume or CV

Clear—well-organized and logical

Concise—relevant and to the point

Complete—including everything relevant

Consistent—don't mix styles or fonts

Current—up-to-date

A Sample CV

Wang Xiaoming	
PERSONAL INFORMATION	
Address:	Tel: (86-21) 5163-0222
School of Economics and Finance	Mobile: (86) 136-8888-2222
Fudan University, Shanghai,	E-mail: wxm123@163.com
China, 200043	

EDUCATION
Sep. 2005–July 2009
—Bachelor of Economics, Majored in Finance of Fudan University, Shanghai, China (GPA: 3.98/4, ranked Top 1st in 160 students)

WORK EXPERIENCE
July 2008–Aug. 2008
—Research Assistant at Hengdian Capital, Hangzhou, China. Collected and processed data, developed PowerPoint slides, translated subprime crisis articles in magazines such as Economists and Business Week and wrote an industry analysis report

Summers 2008 and 2007
—Research Assistant at State Street Technology Instit., Shanghai. Produced a review of the evolution of the New Basel Accord, gathered data and helped analysis of sub-prime crisis

PROJECTS AND RESEARCH EXPERIENCE
Sep. 2007–Present
—Student Research Training Program
—Focused on the growing environment and macro-policy influence for small and medium sized enterprises (SMEs) in Shanghai: collated literature, designed questionnaires, and currently conducting field work in Shanghai.

June–Aug. 2008「Mid-Term Evaluation of the 11th Five-Year Plan of Shanghai Municipality」Project, Shanghai
—Took charge of the social insurance and social service section, collected local information, and wrote the social insurance and social service part of the report

May 2008「The Present Situation of Shanghai Real Estate Market and Potential Financial Risk」Project, Local Commercial Bank
—Collected and processed data on the real estate market of Shanghai, gathered local real estate market information, and wrote the report

Dec. 2007–Jan. 2008「Developmental Finance Supporting Shanghai」Project, National Development Bank
—Collected data, wrote part of the report, and developed PowerPoint slides

RESEARCH INTERESTS
Econometrics, Financial Economics, and Chinese Economic Reform

LANGUAGESKILLS
Native Language: Chinese
English Language: TOEFL 113/120 GRE V 620/800 Q 800/800 AW 4/6
COMPUTERSKILLS

COMPUTER EXPERIENCE
Microsoft Office, Visual Basic, C, Matlab

STATISTICAL PACKAGES
SPSS, Eviews, Excel

ACTIVITIES AND INTERESTS
Activities: Volunteer for the 2008 International Workshop on Chinese Productivity Member of IAESTE
Interests: Swimming, Calligraphy, and Chinese Cooking

REFERENCES
Available upon request.

A Sample Resume

JIM SMITH
jsmith@ dd. email. him

Present Address	Permanent Address
123 Riverwood Dr.	222 Hometown Dr.
Collegetown, USA 12345	Parentville, USA 45678
(xxx) 555-7756	(xxx) 444-1111 (after May 15th, 2009)

CAREER OBJECTIVE

   To obtain a position working with environmental issues where I can utilize my analytical skills to assist a company with research goals.

EDUCATION

   University of Nebraska, Lincoln, Nebraska
   Bachelor of Science, May 2009
   Major: Geology Minor: History
   GRA: 3. 75/4. 00
   Significant Coursework: Research Methods, Peer Leadership, Global Environmental Issues, Technical Writing.
   Computerskills: Lotus, 1-2-3, COBOL, SPSS

PROFESSIONAL EXPERIENCE

   Intern, Carson Geological Consultants
   Denver, Colorado, May 2009-August 2009
   * Assisted Senior Geologist with collection of field samples
   * Performed laboratory chemical composition tests
   * Input data for statistical software packages
   * Met with clients to discuss project status
   Student Assistant, University of Nebraska Department of Geology
   Lincoln, Nebraska, September 2008-May 2009
   * Compiled and indexed statistical information from soil sample tests
   * Inspected and cataloged incoming soil sample tests
   * Streamlined procedures for testing and grading core samples
   * Wrote reports summarizing results of soil sample tests
   President, Lambda Lambda Lambda Fraternity
   University of Nebraska, Lincoln, NE, September 2006-August 2008
   * Organized meetings for a group of 25 house members
   * Coordinated activities and intramural participation during Greek Week
   * Proposed new and successful fund raising activities for the house

ACTIVITIES AND HONORS

   Kappa Delta Psi, Geology Honorary, 2006-2008
   Tutwiler Scholarship Award, 2007
   Dean's list, last six semesters
   History Club, 2006-2008

REFERENCES
Available upon request.

Writing Assignment

Suppose you are applying for an internship at all international manufacturing company. Write your resume for the company so that the Human Resources Department gains a fundamental understanding about you. Remember that special attention should be paid to the layout or format of a resume.

Unit 6   Attitudes to Life

6.1   Get Started

Ⅰ. Work in pairs or groups and discuss the following questions.

1. Have you ever experienced any difficult time in your life? Please say something about it.

2. What do you think is the right attitude towards problems in one's life?

3. What qualities do you think one should possess to survive tough times?

Ⅱ. Study the following quotes about attitudes towards life and discuss in pairs what you can learn from them.

1. Attitude is a little thing that makes a big difference.

—Winston Churchill

2. Life is ten percent what happens to you and ninety percent how you respond to it.

—Lou Holtz

3. Human beings, by changing the inner attitudes of their minds, can change the outer aspects of their lives.

—William James

4. When one door of happiness closes another opens, but often we look so long at the closed door that we do not see the one which has been opened for us.

—Helen Keller

6.2　Read and Explore

Text A

Many people dream of living a full, joyous and worthy life. However, to live our life to the fullest, we need to have a deep sense of responsibility, inspire and believe in others, exercise diligence and endurance, look beyond life's rewards, and devote ourselves to a selfless cause.

Let Yourself Go!

by *Barbara Hatcher*

Several years ago I received a post card from a friend in Jackson Hole, Wyo., who wrote, 「I am skiing with abandon!」 I wondered what he meant, for when I ski it is always with anxiety and fear. I believe he meant he was skiing skillfully, joyfully, peacefully and confidently. Although I have no hopes of ever skiing that way. I do dream of living with abandon. I believe that men and women through the ages who have led successful lives have captured these five secrets of living life to the fullest.

1. Have a self you respect. This means having a deep sense of responsibility for your thoughts and actions. It means keeping your word, and being faithful to yourself, family and work. It means believing in what you do and working hard. It means setting your own internal standards, and not comparing yourself to others. It's not a question of being better than someone else; respect and integrity demand that you be better than you thought you could be.

Winston Churchill exemplified integrity and respect in the face of opposition. During his last year in office, he attended an official ceremony. Several rows behind him two gentlemen began whispering: 「That's Winston Churchill.」「They say he is getting old.」「They say he should step aside and leave the running of the nation to more dynamic and capable men.」 When the ceremony was over, Churchill turned to the men and said, 「Gentlemen, they also say he is deaf!」

Churchill knew that one secret to a self you can respect is to choose a course of action based on what is right, and not waver from it when criticized.

2. Commit yourself to others. Believe in others, and take time to nurture their dreams. A wise man said, 「If you want one year's prosperity, grow grain. But if you want ten years' prosperity, grow men and women.」

You can build into the lives of your family. Friends and colleagues by providing nutrients of gratitude and encouragement, and by investing your time and energy in their aspirations. If a tree is given minimal nourishment, it will live, but it will not grow. But if nourishment is given over and beyond what is needed for life, the tree will live and grow upward, producing fruit.

3. Turn disappointments into strengths. Individuals who live with abandon have discovered that personal trials make them more sensitive and loving, while building endurance and character. They have learned that achievements worth remembering are accompanied with the blood of diligence and the scars of disappointment.

The pages of history are filled with the heroic stories of brave men and women who triumphed over disabilities and adversities to demonstrate victorious spirits. Raise him in poverty, and you have an Abraham Lincoln. Make her blind and deaf, and you have a Helen Keller.

4. Enjoy life's process, not just life's rewards. We live in a goal-oriented society that wants problems resolved now. We want three-minute fast food, one-hour dry cleaning, and instant success. But to live with abandon, we must live one day at a time, savoring the little victories, realizing that life is an endless journey in self-discovery and personal fulfillment. It means taking time to hug your kids, kiss your spouse and let the other fellow ahead of you on the freeway.

「I was one of those people who never go anywhere without a thermometer, hot water bottle, raincoat and parachute,」wrote author Don Herold. 「If I had my life to live over, I would go barefoot earlier in the spring. I would ride more merry-go-rounds. I would take more chances, and I would eat more ice cream.」

5. Become involved in something bigger than yourself. I do not believe you will live happily if you set out to live life for yourself alone. Choose a

cause bigger than you are and work at it in a spirit of excellence. It will become a part of you as you see your goals through to the end. Measure success not by what you've done, but what you could do.

Words and Expressions

1. ski vi. 滑雪，滑冰
2. exemplify vt. 是……的典型；例示，舉例證明
3. grain n. 穀物，糧食
4. heroic adj. 有英雄氣概的，英雄的，英勇的
5. fulfillment n. 實現；完成；滿足（感）
6. abandon n. 放任，放縱；完全屈從於壓制
7. dynamic adj. 充滿活力的，精力充沛的
8. gratitude n. 謝意；感激，感謝；感激的樣子
9. triumph vi. 戰勝；獲勝；克服；打敗
10. barefoot adj. & adv. 赤腳的；光著腳的；赤著腳地
11. faithful adj. 忠實的；忠誠的；正確的
12. commit vt. 犯罪，做錯事；把……托付給；保證（做某事、遵守協議或遵從安排等）；承諾，使……承擔義務
13. aspiration n. 強烈的願望
14. victorious adj. 勝利的；得勝的
15. integrity n. 完整；正直，誠實
16. prosperity n. 繁榮；成功；興旺，昌盛
17. nourishment n. 食物；滋養品，營養品
18. waver vi. 猶豫
19. nutrient n. 營養品
20. minimal adj. 極少的；最低的
21. diligence n. 勤奮
22. parachute n. 降落傘
23. keep one's word 遵守諾言，守信用；說話算數；信守諾言
24. set out to do 著手做某事；開始去做；開始著手做某事
25. dry cleaning 干洗
26. step aside 走到一邊；從權威地位退下；讓開
27. live over 重溫；重新過（某種日子）

28. work at 在……工作；從事於……，致力於……

Proper Names

1. Barbara Hatcher 芭芭拉・哈徹（人名）
2. Jackson Hole 杰克遜谷地（美國懷俄明州地名）
3. Wyoming 懷俄明州（美國州名）
4. Winston Churchill 溫斯頓・丘吉爾（人名）
5. Abraham Lincoln 亞伯拉罕・林肯（人名）
6. Helen Keller 海倫・凱勒（人名）
7. Don Herold 唐・赫羅爾德（人名）

Notes

1. The text is taken from *Reader's Digest*. Vol. 131 No. 787, 1987.

2. Barbara Hatcher: a professor of Southwest Texas State University. This text is the speech she made at the graduation ceremony of the university in December, 1986.

3. Jackson Hole: a valley in the US state of Wyoming. It is located in west-central Wyoming, and gets the name「hole」from early trappers（狩獵者）who primarily entered the valley from the north and east and had to descend down into the valley along relatively steep slopes, giving the feeling of entering a hole. The Jackson Hole Mountain Resort and the nearby Yellowstone national parks are major tourism attractions.

4. Wyoming: a state in the Rocky Mountains in the northwestern US. Although it covers a large area, it is the least populous state in the US. It produces minerals, beef, and wool. The capital and largest city of Wyoming is Cheyenne.

5. Abraham Lincoln (1809-1865): the 16th President of the US (1861-1865). He led the Union during the Civil War and emancipated slaves in the South. He was assassinated shortly after the end of the war by John Wilkes Booth. He is considered to be one of the most important US presidents.

6. Don Herold (1889-1966): an American humorist, writer, illustrator, and cartoonist who wrote and illustrated many books and was a contributor to many national magazines.

7. It means setting your own internal standards, and not comparing yourself to others. →It means establishing your own standards, rather than comparing your own achievements with those of others.

8. They say he should step aside and leave the running of the nation to more dynamic and capable men. →They say that Churchill should resign and leave the opportunity of leading the nation to those who are younger, more energetic and more capable.

9. You can build into the lives of your family. Friends and colleagues by providing nutrients of gratitude and encouragement, and by investing your time and energy in their aspirations. →You will become inseparable in the lives of your family, friends and colleagues if you show your gratitude and encouragement to them and devote your time and energy to helping them fulfill their aspirations.

10. achievements worth remembering are accompanied with the blood of diligence and the scars of disappointment→success worth remembering comes with hard work and the pains of disappointment.

11. who triumphed over disabilities and adversities to demonstrate victorious spirits→who succeeded after overcoming handicaps and unfavorable conditions to show their victorious spirits.

Content Awareness

Ⅰ. Find the right definition in Column B for each italicised word in Column A. Put the corresponding letter in the space provided in Column A. The number of the paragraph in which the target word appears is given in brackets. The first one has been done for you.

Column A

1. ___d___ *exemplified* integrity and respect (Para. 3)
2. _____ nutrients of *gratitude* and encouragement (Para. 6)
3. _____ investing your time and energy in their *aspirations* (Para. 6)
4. _____ a tree is given minimal *nourishment* (Para. 6)
5. _____ the blood of *diligence* (Para. 7)
6. _____ brave men and women who *triumphed* over disabilities

(Para. 8)

7. _____ an endless journey in self-discovery and personal *fulfillment* (Para. 9)

8. _____ go *barefoot* earlier in the spring (Para. 10)

Column B

a. strong desires; ambitions

b. the quality of being hardworking or showing steady effort

c. satisfaction after successful effort

d. gave an example of

e. gratefulness; appreciation

f. without shoes on the feet

g. something that people and other living things need to grow and keep healthy

h. gained victory or success, esp. in dealing with a very difficult situation

Ⅱ. Fill in each blank in the following sentences with a phrase from Text A. Both the meaning and the number of the paragraph in which the target phrase appears are given in brackets.

Example: It is amazing that Daniel has won the election <u>in face of</u> such strong opposition from his opponents. (in spite of; against: Para. 3)

1. Branson had fully _____ on not seeing or communicating with Joan for three months. (done what one had promised: Para. 2)

2. Morris should _____ as a chairperson until the investigation is completed. (leave one's official position: Para. 3)

3. Knowing she has missed something important in her life, she wishes that she would have her life to _____. (live again, experience again Para. 10)

4. The new administration _____ to develop a better immigration policy for the country. (started doing or making plans to do: Para. 11)

5. Most couples would agree that for a marriage to succeed, both parties should _____ it. (try hard to improve: Para. 11)

Ⅲ. Answer the following questions with the information contained in Text A.

1. Why did Churchill say 「Gentleman, they also say he is deaf!」?

2. What is the wise way to give people long-term prosperity according to the author?

3. What should people do when faced with disappointments according to the author?

4. What does the author intend to tell us by quoting Don Herold's lines?

5. How can we live happily according to the author?

Language Focus

Ⅰ. Complete each of the following sentences with an appropriate word from the box. Change the form if necessary.

alter   change   convert   modify   revise   transcribe   transform   vary

1. In his speech, he urged people to _____ their attitudes to the environment in the 21st century.

2. The photochemical reactions _____ the light into electrical impulses (電脈衝).

3. In doing translation, one should not _____ the meaning of the original to suit one's own taste.

4. The old barn we bought to _____ into flats was practically tumbling down.

5. In view of the present situation, we'll have to _____ our original plan.

6. The committee did not reach an agreement about how to _____

the policy.

7. Children _____ considerably in the rate at which they learn these lessons.

8. He gave up trying to write for the guitar and decided to _____ the work for the piano.

II. You will read three groups of words which are similar in meaning but different in usage. Reflect on the differences in usage between the words in each group and fill in each blank with a proper one. Change the form if necessary.

journey   tout   travel   trip

1. I have the honor of introducing to you Mr. Smith, who will address you on his recent _____ abroad.

2. It took the young couple a long time to save enough money for a _____ to Europe.

3. After he graduated from college, he spent a year _____, mostly in Africa and Asia.

4. It is a two-hour train _____ from my hometown to Beijing.

choose   elect   pick   select

5. Which place in the world would you _____ as your perfect home?

6. The presidential nominee was advised to _____ a woman as a running mate.

7. We had to find a flat in a hurry—there was no time to _____ and choose.

8. Farmers could _____ legislators or congressmen from rural districts, who would represent their interests.

normal   average   ordinary   regular

9. From the moment I met her, I knew she was no _____ kind of girl.

10. In this shop discount (折扣) is given only to our _____ customers.

11. James Joyce would probably not be familiar to the _____ French person.

12. As a handicapped child, she wished she could run around and play like _____ children.

Ⅲ. Complete the following passage with words chosen from this unit. The initial letter of each is given.

Truth is a fact accepted as true, for which proof exists. Truth is a great principle, without which beauty may fade and love may w_____. Those who uphold truth have a strong s_____ of responsibility. Those who hold firmly to truth are f_____ to their duty and the people they serve. They c_____ themselves to the well-being of others. With a_____ to make a contribution to society, they are ready to correct their own mistakes, if any. It can be said that they are men of moral integrity who never ask for g_____ in return.

Truth d_____ upon us slowly but surely. In the long quest for truth, people have a_____ precious knowledge and experience. However, truth also needs n_____ just as plants need water, because many people are too p_____ with petty and sometimes even mean concerns to respond to the great beauty of truth when it f_____ or they frequently fail to appreciate truth when it is t_____.

In short, truth is an invaluable asset to the whole of humanity. Stick to the truth and we will w_____ a timeless pattern, and earn the respect and esteem of others, e_____ the world today above its present imperfections and place ourselves in the proud position of promoting the good of the humanity.

Ⅳ. Translate the following sentences into English, using the words and expressions given in brackets.

1. 這位駐聯合國大使被授權代表本國政府，處理與該國相關的所有外交事務。(invest with)

_____

2. 在火車上我一直在想期末考試的結果，直到乘務員提醒我目的地已經到了。(all the way; preoccupied with)

_____

3. 雖然車禍死亡名單中沒有她丈夫的名字，但她仍不停地在屋內走來走去，急切地盼望他早點回到家裡。（to and fro）

4. 我正準備把合同翻譯成英語，突然意識到合同涉及的雙方都是中國公司。（set out to do; dawn upon）

5. 聚會上人們盡情地唱歌跳舞，把生活中的煩惱拋到了九霄雲外。（wit abandon）

6. 懷著做一名宇航員的強烈願望，杰克遜全身心地投入到長達兩年的艱苦體能訓練之中。（aspiration; commit oneself to; strenuous constitution training）

7. 他的油畫取材於亙古永存的神話故事，反應了那個時期歐洲人的鑒賞趣味。（timeless fairy story; exemplify; taste）

8. 那個公共汽車司機不想承擔事故責任，所以千方百計把責任推到車上的乘客身上。（put the blame on）

9. 他不僅冒著生命危險把老人從熊熊燃燒的房子裡救了出來，還騰出自家屋子讓老人住下。（make room）

10. 她從小就努力按照父母的教導去生活，形成了一整套為人處世的行為準則。（live by; accumulate）

Text B

On Idleness
by *Samuel Johnson*

Many moralists have remarked, that Pride has of all human vices the widest dominion, appears in the greatest multiplicity of forms, and lies hide under the greatest variety of disguises; of disguises, which, like the moon's veil of brightness, are both its luster and its shade, and betray it to others, though they hide it from ourselves.

It is not my intention to degrade Pride from this preeminence of mischief, yet I know not whether Idleness may not maintain a very doubtful and obstinate competition.

There are some that profess Idleness in its full dignity, who call themselves the Idle, as Busiris in the play ⌈calls himself the Proud⌋, who boast that they do nothing, and thank their stars that they have nothing to do; who sleep every night till they can sleep no longer, and rise only that exercise may enable them to sleep again; who prolong the reign of darkness by double curtains, and never see the sun but to ⌈tell him how they hate his beams⌋: whose whole labor is to vary the postures of indulgence, and whose day differs from their night but as a couch or chair differs from a bed.

These are the true and open votaries of idleness, for whom she weaves the garlands of poppies, and into whose cup she pours the waters of oblivion; who exist in a state of unruffled stupidity, forgetting and forgotten; who have long ceased to live, and at whose death the survivors can only say, that they have ceased to breathe.

But Idleness predominates in many lives where it is not suspected; for being a vice which terminates in itself, it may be enjoyed without injury to others; and it therefore not watched like Fraud, which endangers property, or like Pride, which naturally seeks its gratifications in another's inferiority. Idleness is a silent and peaceful quality, that neither raises envy by ostentation, nor hatred by opposition; and therefore nobody is busy to censure or detect it.

As Pride sometimes is hid under humility, Idleness is often covered by turbulence and hurry. He that neglects his known duty and real employment, naturally endeavors to crowd his mind with something that may bar out the remembrance of his own folly, and does any thing but what he ought to do with eager diligence, that he may keep himself in his own favor.

Some are always in a state of preparation, occupied in previous measures, forming plans, accumulating materials, and providing for the main affair. These are certainly under the secret power of Idleness. Nothing is to be expected from the workman whose tools are forever to be sought. I was once told by a great master, that no man ever excelled in painting, who was eminently curious about pencils and colors.

There are others to whom Idleness dictates another expedient, by which life may be passed unprofitably away without the tediousness of many vacant hours. The art is, to fill the day with petty business, to have always something in hand which may raise curiosity, but not solicitude, and keep the mind in a state of action, but not of labor.

This art has for many years been practiced by my old friend Sober, with wonderful success. Sober is a man of strong desires and quick imagination, so exactly balanced by the love of ease, that they can seldom stimulate him to any difficult undertaking; they have, however, so much power, that they will not suffer him to lie quite at rest, and though they do not make him sufficiently useful to others, they make him at least weary of himself.

Mr. Sober's chief pleasure is conversation; there is no end of his talk or his attention; to speak or to hear is equally pleasing; for he still fancies that he is teaching or learning something, and is free for the time from his own reproaches.

But there is one time at night when he must go home, that his friends may sleep; and another time in the morning, when all the world agrees to shut out interruption. These are the moments of which poor Sober trembles at the thought. But the misery of these tiresome intervals, he has many means of alleviating. He has persuaded himself that the manual arts are undeservedly overlooked: he has observed in many trades the effects of close thought, and just ratiocination. From speculation he proceeded to practice, and supplied himself with the tools of a carpenter, with which he mended his coalbox very successfully, and which he still continues to employ, as he finds occasion.

He has attempted at other times the crafts of the shoemaker, tinman, plumber, and potter; in all these arts he has failed, and resolves to qualify himself for them by better information. But his daily amusement is chemistry. He has a small furnace, which he employs in distillation, and which has long been the solace of his life. He draws oils and waters, and essences and spirits, which he knows to be of no use; sits and counts the drops as they come from his retort, and forgets that, whilst a drop is falling, a moment flies away.

Poor Sober! I have often teased him with reproof, and he has often promised reformation: for no man is so much open to conviction as the Idler, but there is none on whom it operates so little. What will be the effect of this paper I know not; perhaps he will read it and laugh, and light the fire in his furnace; but my hope is that he will quit his trifles, and betake himself to rational and useful diligence.

Words

1. dominion n. 統治權；領土，疆土；版圖
2. multiplicity n. 多樣性
3. preeminence n. 卓越，傑出
4. votary n. 信徒，追隨者
5. garland n. 花環，花冠
6. unruffled adj. 安詳；鎮定的；平靜的（水面等）
7. terminate vi. & vt. 結束；使終結；解雇；到達終點站
8. gratification n. 滿足；滿意；喜悅；使人滿意之事
9. inferiority n. 劣勢；下等；次級
10. ostentation n. 炫耀；賣弄；擺闊；講排場
11. expedient n. 應急辦法，權宜之計
12. solicitude n. 關心，掛念，渴望
13. alleviate vt. 減輕，緩和
15. reproof n. 責備，責難，指責
14. ratiocination n. 推論，推理

Notes

1. Samuel Johnson（18 September 1709-13 December 1784）, often referred to as Dr. Johnson, was an English author who made lasting contributions to English literature as a poet, essayist, moralist, literary critic, biographer, editor and lexicographer. Johnson was a devout Anglican and committed Tory, and has been described as「arguably the most distinguished man of letters in English history」.

2. ... that Pride has of all human vices the widest dominion... →among all human vices, Pride enjoys the widest influence...

「dominion」原意為「統治、管轄、主權」，這裡指的是「作用、影響」。

3. ... appears in the greatest multiplicity of forms, and lies hid under the greatest variety of disguises... →... has the most forms of appearance, and hides itself in the largest number of disguises...

4. It is not my intention to degrade Pride from this preeminence of mischief, yet I know not whether Idleness may not maintain a very doubtful and obstinate competition. →I do not intend to reduce Pride in the severity of mischief, but I do not know whether or not Idleness may be a doubtful and tenacious competitor of Pride.

5. There are some that profess Idleness in its full dignity, who call themselves the Idle... →Some people affirm openly the loftiness of Idleness; they call themselves the Idle...

6. Busiris：愛德華・楊（Edward Young, 英國詩人、劇作家兼文藝評論家）在 1719 年的作品，其中 Busiris 是該悲劇中的埃及國王。

7. votaries→A person who is filled with enthusiasm, as for a pursuit or hobby; an enthusiast.

8. ... the waters of oblivion... →... the waters which make people totally forgetful...

9. ... predominates in many lives... →... has many lives under its control...

predominate：to have or gain controlling power or influence.

e.g. Good predominates over evil in many works of literature.

10. ... that neither raises envy by ostentation, nor hatred by opposition→Idleness is neither envied for showing off, nor is it hated for objection.

11. ... Idleness is often covered by turbulence and hurry. →... Idleness is often under the disguise of agitation and hurry.

12. ... something that may bar out the remembrance of his own folly... →... something that makes him forget his own stupidity...

13. with eager diligence→eagerly and industriously.

14. keep himself in his own favor→always be appreciative of himself

15. Some are always in a state of preparation, occupied in previous measures, forming plans, accumulating materials, and providing for the main affair. →Some are perpetually making preparations, busy with previous measures, setting up plans, collecting materials, and getting themselves ready for the main affair.

16. ... Idleness dictates another expedient... →... Idleness imposes another temporary means to approach some urgent need...

17. without the tediousness of many vacant hours→without the tiresome dullness of much unoccupied time

18. ... fill the day with petty business... →... have the day full of insignificant occupations...

19. to have always something in hand which may raise curiosity, but not solicitude... →to be busy with something that may cause curiosity instead of care...

20. Sober is a man of strong desires and quick imagination, so exactly balanced by the love of ease, that they can seldom stimulate him to any difficult undertaking... →Sober is a man enjoying such a precise balance between the love of ease and the strong desires and quick imagination, that he can rarely be spurred to take up any difficult task...

21. the misery of these tiresome intervals→the distress emerging during these boring intervals.

22. ... he has many means of alleviating. →... he has many ways to reduce (the distress).

alleviate: to lessen the effect of.

e.g. The drug alleviate cold symptoms.

23. undeservedly overlooked→unfairly neglected.

24. He has attempted at other times the crafts of the shoemaker, tinman, plumber, and potter... →He has tried his hand at the techniques of the shoemaker, tinman, plumber, and potter...

25. ... for no man is so much open to conviction as the Idler... →... for the Idler is the readiest to acknowledge his guilt...

Content Awareness

Ⅰ. Idleness may be an embodiment of laziness, but sometimes idleness is under the disguise of hustle and bustle. What's your understanding about idleness? Is there a time when you find it difficult to fill the leisure time in a satisfactory way?

Ⅱ. Paraphrase the following sentences in your own words.

1. Idleness is often covered by turbulence and hurry.

2. Nothing is to be expected from the workman whose tools are forever to be sought.

3. Sober is a man of strong desires and quick imagination, so exactly balanced by the love of ease, that they can seldom stimulate him to any difficult undertaking

4. But the misery of these tiresome intervals. He has many means of alleviating.

5. What will be the effect of this paper I know not.

Language Focus

Ⅰ. For each blank in the following passage, choose the most suitable word from the following list of words. Each word can be used only once.

withstand   continued   associated   unusual   conduct
motivation   however   prime   performance   difference
remove   established

Stress is a natural part of everyday life and there is no way to avoid it. In fact, it is not the bad thing that is often supposed to be. A certain amount of stress is vital to provide _____ and give purpose to life. It is only when the stress gets out of control that it can lead to poor _____ and ill health.

The amount of stress a person can _____ depends very much on the individual. Some people are not afraid of stress, and such characters are obviously _____ material for managerial responsibilities. Others lose heart at the first signs of _____ difficulties. When exposed to stress, in whatever form, we react both chemically and physically. In fact we make choice between 「flight」 or 「fight」 and in more primitive days the choices made the _____ between life and death. The crises we meet today are unlikely to be so extreme, but _____ little the stress, it involves the same response. It is when such a reaction lasts long, through _____ exposure to stress, that health becomes endangered. Such serious conditions as high blood pressure and heart disease have _____ links with stress. Since we cannot _____ stress from our lives we need to find ways to deal with it.

Ⅱ. For each of the sentences below, write a new sentence as similar as possible in meaning to the original sentence. You are required to use the word given in capital letters without any alteration.

Example: He didn't turn up for the meeting yesterday. (FAILED)

Answer: He failed to turn up for the meeting yesterday.

1. I'm sorry I was rude to you. (APOLOGIZE)

Unit 6 Attitudes to Life

149

2. Never before have I seen such a good performance. (FIRST)

3. He hardly ever drinks wine with his meals. (USED)

4. You'd better not answer that letter. (IF)

5. The detective went into the house and immediately switched on the lights. (MOMENT)

Ⅲ. Translate the following passage into English.

真理是什麼？真理是人們對客觀世界及其規律的正確反應。真理讓人們充滿希望，讓人生充滿光彩，所以許多人把追求真理作為人生的最終目標。人類歷史上有許多人為了追求真理，獻出了自己寶貴的生命，對人類做出了傑出的貢獻。

真理是絕對的，又是相對的。我們說真理是絕對的，是因為真理能夠客觀地反應事物的本質。但是，任何真理都只是人們對事物發展在一定階段的正確認識，所以它又是相對的、不斷發展的。

真理的光芒有時可能會黯淡，但永遠不會熄滅。對某些人來說，真理也許太遙遠，實際上真理就在我們身邊，只要我們用心去尋找，就一定會追求到真理。

6.3 Practical Translation

語篇的翻譯方法——摘譯

在英漢翻譯中，主要有兩種翻譯方法：全譯和變譯。全譯是將原文幾乎沒有遺漏地翻譯成另一種文字，主要用於文學作品和社科哲學類作品，其目的在於把原文全面地展現給譯文讀者。變譯是對原文採用擴充、取捨、濃縮、補充等方法傳達信息的中心內容或部分內容的一類宏觀方法，包括摘譯、編譯、改譯等。

摘譯是摘錄和翻譯的結合，即摘取原文的精華加以翻譯，主要用於新聞或科技文體的翻譯。摘譯必須遵循以下原則：（1）整體性原則，即保持原文宏觀結構上的完整性。（2）針對性原則，即選擇原文中重要的或讀者感興趣的內容進行翻譯。（3）簡要性原則，即譯文傳達的信息必須簡潔明瞭。（4）客觀性原則，即譯文中不可加入譯者的個人觀點。

摘譯應該先摘後譯，在通讀並充分理解原文的基礎上，摘取該文獻的主要內容或譯文讀者感興趣的內容進行翻譯。摘取的單位可以是詞語、句子、段落或者章節。一旦選取了擬翻譯的信息，就要遵循全譯原則，將其完整地翻譯出來。

例1：Apple expects to have a fix this month for a vulnerability in the iPhone that could allow an attacker to gain control of the device remotely via SMS, according to CNET NEWS. com.

An attacker could exploit a weakness in the way iPhones handle SMS messages to do things like use GPS to track the phone's location, turn on the microphone for eavesdropping, or take control of the device and add it to a botnet, Charlie Miller, co-author of The Mac Hacker's Handbook and principal security analyst at Independent Security Evaluators, said in a presentation at the SyScan conference in Singapore. The presentation was covered by IDG News Service.

Miller said that under an agreement with Apple, he was barred from providing too much detail on the vulnerability. He plans to give a more detailed presentation on the hole at the Black Hat conference in Las Vegas at the end of the month.

Despite the SMS hole, the iPhone is more secure than OS X on computers, Miller said. That is because the iPhone doesn't support Adobe Flash and Java, only runs software digitally signed by Apple, includes hardware protection for data stored in memory, and runs applications in a sandbox, he said.

Apple representatives did not immediately respond to an email request for comment.

譯文：據美國CNET科技資訊網報導，蘋果公司預計將於本月修復iPhone中存在的一個安全漏洞，這一漏洞使黑客能夠通過發送短信遙控手機。獨立安全評估公司的首席安全分析師查理·米勒聲稱，黑客能夠利用iPhone處理短信服務中存在的漏洞，採用全球定位系統來跟蹤iPhone的位置，打開手機麥克風竊聽用戶通話，或者控制手機，把手機變成「僵屍網絡」中的一員。米勒指出，儘管存在這一短信服務漏洞，不過相對於電腦上的OS X系統，iPhone還是比較安全的。

解析：譯文中保留了原文的主要信息：iPhone的短信服務功能存在安全漏洞，這一漏洞的潛在危害，以及蘋果公司預計何時修復該漏洞。第四段的第一句雖然和全文關係不是非常緊密，但很可能是讀者非常關心的信息，所以也包含在譯文中。

例2：A 36-year-old Swiss amateur parachutist made a successful 650-metre drop using a replica of a parachute designed more than 500 years ago by Leonardo da Vinci.「I came down... smack in the middle of the tarmac at Payerne military airport,」said Olivier Vietti-Teppa.「A perfect jump.」Vietti-Teppa is the first person to have made it safely to the ground with the Leonardo model. In 2000, Britain's Adrian Nicholas tried it but had to pull the ripcord on a modem backup parachute to complete his descent safely.

Vietti-Teppa jumped from a hovering helicopter and the Leonardo parachute opened at 600 meters, he reported. The parachute he used was made using modem fabric along lines designed by the Renaissance genius. The specifications were found in a text dating from 1485. The parachute consists of four equilateral triangles, seven meters on each side, made of parachute fabric, Vietti-Teppa explained. The base of the pyramid is a square of mosquito net, which enables the parachute to open. A wooden frame originally conceived by da Vinci was not used on the model in action on Saturday. One drawback: it is impossible to maneuver or steer the Leonardo parachute.「You come down at the whim of the wind,」said Vietti-Teppa, who carried out advance tests using a scale dummy model launched from a remote, controlled model helicopter.

譯文：瑞士一名 36 歲的跳傘愛好者成功地從 650 米的高空降落，而他用的降落傘可是 500 多年前萊昂納多・達・芬奇設計的降落傘的複製品。維耶提—特帕是第一個用達・芬奇設計的這款降落傘安全降落到地面的人。他解釋說，降落傘是由 4 個邊長為 7 米的等邊三角形構成，由降落傘綢製作而成。

解析：摘譯中包含了原文的主要信息：該跳傘者用達・芬奇設計的降落傘的複製品成功地完成了高空跳傘，成為完成這一嘗試的史上第一人；該降落傘的構造。其他未翻譯的句子中，有些是對主要信息的重複，比如第二段的前兩句；有些則是與主旨關係不緊密，故刪去不譯。

Translation Practice

Translate the following passage into Chinese using the translation method you've learned above.

Prime Minister Gordon Brown of Britain disclosed Saturday that an eye examination showed two tears in his right retina—a revelation that could embolden critics who want him to step down before a national election.

Downing Street moved quickly to quash speculation over Brown's health, issuing the statement only one day after a regular examination at a London eye hospital. Brown's office said his eyesight remained unchanged and that no operations were planned to address the situation.

「Were there to be any change? he would of course make a further statement,」Brown's office said in a statement.

Brown, who lost the use of his left eye in a sporting accident when he was a teenager and had surgery to save the sight in the other one, has been dogged by questions about his eyesight in recent months.

During a visit to the United States for the Group of 20 summit, he was forced to deny that he was slowly going blind.

NBC Nightly News anchor Brian Williams had questioned Brown over reports that he was using larger and larger text sizes as his remaining vision declined.

「I had all sorts of operations,」Brown said during the September interview.「I then had one operation on the other eye and that was very successful, so my sight is not at all deteriorating,」he said.

The same month he told the BBC that「it would be a terrible, terrible indictment of our political system if you thought that because someone had this medical issue they couldn't do their job」.

The September comments came as former Home Secretary Charles Clarke told the *London Evening Standard* newspaper that he hoped rumors Brown would quit—perhaps on health grounds—would come true.

Brown must call a general election by June 2010. Recent polls overwhelmingly suggest that the opposition Conservative Party will win after 13 years out of power.

British prime ministers rarely disclose details about their health unless they need to take time off work—as in 2004, when Brown's predecessor Tony Blair had a surgical procedure to correct an irregular heartbeat.

Som Prasad, a consultant ophthalmologist at Arrowe Park Hospital in northwest England, said retinal tears affect 3% of people over 40 in Britain, and only occasionally cause serious problems.

6.4 Focused Writing

Personal Statements

When you are applying for scholarships, for graduate schools, or for a number of post-graduate positions, you are usually required to write a personal statement (also called Statement of Purpose or Personal Goals Statement), as an introduction to the selection committee. This document requires you to indicate what type of person you are, and why you would be a suitable candidate for the program. You should outline your strengths as confidently and concisely as possible, a task that requires thought, takes time and can prove quite challenging.

What is a personal statement?

Though the requirements differ from application to application, the purpose of a personal statement is to represent your goals, experiences and qualifications in the best possible light, and to demonstrate your writing ability. Put it simply, a personal statement is a picture of you as a person, a student and a potential scholarship winner and gives an indication of your academic abilities, priorities and judgment.

How is a personal statement organized?

As mentioned above, the requirements for personal statements differ, but in general a personal statement includes the following information.

Introduction

Mention the specific name of the program, the position and/or the title of the degree you are seeking, in the first paragraph.

Detailed Supporting Paragraphs

Subsequent paragraphs should explain clearly:

1. Why you are interested in your subject. Give as specific reasons as you can. 「It seems interesting」 is not sufficient!

2. Why you want to study at that specific institution. You should have done your research and be able to show that you know about the university and what it has to offer in specific terms. For example, what are the professors in the Department where you want to study publishing? Be able to show that you know and have read their recent work and how or where it relates to your field of interest.

3. Information about your academic achievements and levels to date. Flesh out what is on your CV by including any awards or honors you have received.

4. A paragraph indicating your background, interests and any accomplishments outside of your studies along with mention of any long-term goals to help show what type of person you are. Universities usually like to know that their students are well-rounded and interesting people.

5. Address any specific questions relating to the application that may have arisen. Each paragraph should be focused and should have a topic sen-

tence that informs the reader of the paragraph's emphasis.

Conclusion

Tie together the various issues that you have raised in your personal statement, and reiterate your interest in the specific program or position. You might also mention how the job or degree is a step toward a long-term goal in the closing paragraph.

Sample

As a senior student currently majoring in finance at Zhejiang University, I believe that my solid academic background in mathematics, economics and finance makes me an excellent candidate for the distinguished doctoral program in Economics at Duke University. I am particularly interested in econometrics and financial economics, and I am determined to return to China and to be a professor of economics at a university after graduation.	Introduction: mentioning the name of the program, the title of the degree, and above all, her interest in it.
During my undergraduate years, I had an outstanding academic track record. For the past three and a half years, my GPA has been the highest among the 160 students of my major, which has ensured me the First Prize of Excellent Achievement Scholarship for three consecutive years. Besides courses listed in my transcript, I have also audited Advanced Econometrics for Finance and presently I am taking Advanced Financial Economics as my elective in order to be well prepared for advanced research.	Supporting Paragraph 1: a brief description of her educational assets.
My interest in economics was initially cultivated by my participation in a student-organized economics discussion group in my freshman year. Our informal meetings often started with a student's presentation on a pre-chosen topic, followed by a discussion. Our readings were diversified, ranging from The Nature of the Firm by Ronald Coase to Portfolio Selection by Harry Markowitz. Although our discussion was not in-depth, this informal group did ignite my interest in economics and exposed me to a variety of economic materials.	Supporting Paragraph 2: How her interest in economics was fueled.
Thecourses I took during my sophomore year on theories of Probability, Mathematical Statistics, and Econometrics triggered my interests in the field of econometrics. I enjoyed the Intermediate Econometrics course and the textbook Econometric Analysis by William Greene, for they offered me both basic techniques in applied econometrics and a general insight into econometric theories. Also at that time, I enrolled in a mathematical modeling team and participated in the Mathematical Modeling Competition, which was indeed a perfect opportunity for me to integrate my mathematics knowledge, financial economics knowledge, and econometric techniques and put them into practice. Quite by accident, the problem to be solved that time was a financial one, mainly focusing on the optimum decision in subscribing new shares in the Chinese stock market. We collected relevant data such as the	Supporting Paragraph 3: How her interest in economics was enhanced.

new share returns ratio and the lot winning rate, developed a mathematical model based on the optimization method, and later applied it to the practical problem. Our team won Second Prize From this experience, I learned the importance of 「digitalizing」 economic theories so as to link the economic theory to tangible economic data, as well as empirical analysis which aims to ensure the consistency of economic theories and data. What's more, the combination of analytical rigor and applied focus attracted me so much that I was determined to further my education in this field.	
Currently, I am involved in a Student Research Training Program focusing on the growing environment and macro-policy influence for small and medium sized enterprises (SMEs) in Zhejiang Province. I have collated literature, designed questionnaires, and I am now conducting field work in Zhejiang under the guidance of my professor in order to gain first-hand data before performing a quantitative analysis. During the reading collation period, I was surprised to find that in much Chinese economic literature, econometric methods are misused without consideration of the conditions or assumptions required for them to be valid. For example, some literature even neglected the sample size requirement when conducting time series analysis. These findings, though disappointing, further spurred me to go abroad and pursue a rigorous econometrics training.	Supporting Paragraph 4: Her current participation in a program helped crystallize her reasons for pursuing her doctoral degree in the United States.
I really hope to be able to attend the economics doctoral program at Duke because this program satisfies my needs and Interests perfectly by its dedication to anchor all teaching and research firmly in core disciplines and the diversity of its professors' specialities. The program not only would help consolidate my foundation in econometrics, but also would offer me another opportunity to find out what field truly interests me. Since I have a firm econometrics background and currently major in finance, I would like to find a held which combines the theories and applications of the two. Duke's system just provides me with such an opportunity. I am interested in both theoretical research in time series and its application in financial markets. Also, since my mentor in China has just decided to start a project on the application of extreme value theory in the Chinese stock market and I am in charge of data collection, I would also like to further my research in that area. Besides what I have mentioned above, I am willing to conduct rigorous research in other fields as well.	Supporting Paragraph 5: How she is eligible for further study and her interest in research.
In conclusion, I firmly believe that I have the intellectual aptitude, perseverance, and motivation to succeed in my study in econometrics at Duke and future academic career. I am confident that my solid economics and mathematics foundation and my rich research experience, will make me a valuable member of your program. I Sincerely hope that you will feel the same.	Conclusion: reiterating the reason for choosing the program, and concluding the essay positively.

Sample 2

  My interest in science dates back to my early childhood. I have always excelled in physical sciences and have received numerous awards in mathematics in high school. At age 18, I attended Beijing Normal University, majoring in physics. Four years of extensive study on physics and my current work in surface science inspire me to undertake a greater challenge in pursuing a doctorate degree in physics. My aspiration to be a research scientist also makes the graduate study an absolute necessity for me.

  As an undergraduate student, I specialized in Physics, mathematics, and computer science. And in my Junior year study I studied computational physics in Applied mathematics III, during which I developed a 2-dimensional model with the finite size effect as a course project. In addition to being elated (歡欣鼓舞的) by my computer simulated phase transition phenomena, I was also pleased with the computed values of the critical exponents which closely agree with theoretical values. During the two-year course on the fundamentals of experimental physics, I diligently studied the techniques of operating experimental equipment, such as the epitaxy systems, lithography, and computer controlled data acquisition interfaces. I enjoyed these hand-on experiences. My current duty, as a research assistant, is to set up diamond film growth kinetics experiments which is designed to verify whether the mechanism of H atoms destroying C-H bonds in diamond film growth is the bottleneck reaction to diamond film formation. The results will give valuable insights and better enhance the research efforts of another group here. In the meantime, I am learning about the scanning probe microscopy, charged particle optics, energy analyzers and instruments used in surface science through the seminars held in my group.

  In order to be knowledgeable in the breadth of physics, I have attended workshops and symposiums in different fields. In the symposium on Symmetries in Subatomic Physics held in 1995 in Beijing, I worked as an interpreter and edited the article「Conceptual Beginnings of Various Symmetries in the Twentieth Century Physics」from Prof. C. N. Frank Yang's speech and translated it into Chinese. Not only did I keep an open mind to get experiences in academics, I also actively participated in extracurricular activities in my university years. In the senior year, I was a part-time teaching assistant grading exams and answering questions in the courses, A Journey to Subatomic World and From Quarks to Black Holes. I also had a part-time position as the bulletin board system administrator for the Physical Society of PRC. I am currently constructing their WWW home page to improve information exchange and science education in China.

  Accumulating these valuable experiences, I am preparing myself for a career in scientific research. Being exposed to surface science, I am interested in mesoscopic systems and nanostructure materials. I plan to concentrate on condensed matter physics. Having carefully read the content of the graduate studies and on-going research programs at University of Washington at Seattle, I believe that UW is the best place for me to be. I am confident in that my diverse research experiences together with a firm commitment to physics have merited me to be qualified to undertake graduate study at the University of Washington at Seattle.

  Applicant * * * *
  mm/dd/yy

Writing Assignment

Suppose you are applying for a place on a doctoral degree program at a foreign university. Choose a university and write your Personal Statement. Base it on your real situation.

Unit 7 Travel Around the World

7.1 Get Started

Ⅰ. Read the following questions and share your answers with your partner.

1. Which do you prefer, a package tour or a tour you plan for yourself?

2. Which do you prefer, to travel alone or to travel with friends? How about with your family? Why?

3. Which means of transport do you prefer when traveling, train, bus, plane, ship or car?

4. What is the most interesting souvenir that you have ever bought on one of your holidays?

5. What is the most interesting place you have ever visited?

6. What difficult situation have you ever been in while traveling?

7. Have you ever been to a foreign country? Which countries have you traveled to?

8. Describe your worst trip.

Ⅱ. The travelers who are mindful of local culture will be welcomed wherever they go. The following questionnaire is designed to discover whether you are a culturally sensitive traveler. Simply answer 「yes」 or 「no」 to the following questions and total the answers.

1. Do you research your destinations prior to travel in order to learn about local history and culture?

2. Do you ask an expert rather than risk an embarrassing or offensive incident if you have questions about local customs?

3. Do you respect cultural guidelines regarding dress rather than impose your own style on a community when traveling?

4. Do you enjoy people's pride in their communities instead of arguing that yours is better?

5. When you visit places of worship, do you respect the rules even if you are not a follower of that religion?

6. Do your photographs attempt to capture the context of the subject rather than make a show of the subject?

7. Are you mindful of your body language and eye contact when you travel?

8. Do you attempt to speak the local language when you travel rather than start out in your mother tongue?

9. Do you seek to bolster, rather than deplete, resources in the areas to which you travel?

10. Do you conform to all laws in the countries to which you travel, even if you do not agree with them?

11. When you arrive home from a trip do you attempt to implement what you've learned into your daily life?

Interpretation

If you answered 「yes」 to between one to four questions then you are probably not a culturally sensitive traveler. While it is only human who travel to new places with some preconceived ideas, trying to research the areas to which you will travel before you take off for them. Don't believe urban myths or stereotypes and use your travels to shape your own informed opinions. If you like to travel with others who won't allow you the freedom to explore new cultures and discover new customs then consider a solo trip in the near future.

If you answered 「yes」 to between five to eight questions then you might be a culturally sensitive traveler. The next time you travel, be aware of what you expect from new cultures and how you interact with them. Make an effort to speak the local language, eat local foods and observe local customs. If you feel you need direction in how to become a more culturally sensitive traveler, then consider joining a tour group that places great emphasis on this type of travel.

If you answered 「yes」 to nine or more questions, then you are most likely a culturally sensitive traveler. You attach great importance to showing respect to the people and places you visit and benefit from these efforts undoubtedly. You can also consider helping family and friends with their pre-travel plans or travel with them so that others may benefit from your sensitive style of travel.

Ⅲ. The following are some benefits of traveling. Do you agree or not? Explain your reasons and give examples to each point.

· Traveling gives us the opportunity to disconnect from our regular life.

· Another great benefit of traveling is the relaxation you get from it.

· Traveling increases our knowledge and widens our perspective.

· New experiences from traveling enrich our live.

· Traveling with friends or family creates memories that can be treasured for a lifetime.

7.2　Read and Explore

Text A

Oslo

I remember on my first trip to Europe going alone to a movie in Copenhagen. In Denmark you are given a ticket for an assigned seat. I went into the cinema and discovered that my ticket directed me to sit beside the only other people in the place, a young couple locked in the sort of passionate embrace associated with dockside reunions at the end of long wars. I could no more have sat beside them than I could have asked to join in—it would have come to much the same thing—so I took a place a few discreet seats away.

People came into the cinema, consulted their tickets and filled the seats around us. By the time: the film started there were about 30 of us sitting together in a tight pack in the middle of a vast and otherwise empty auditorium. Two minutes into the movie, a woman laden with shopping made her way with difficulty down my row, stopped beside my seat and told me in a stem voice, full of glottal stops and indignation, that I was in her place. This caused much play of flashlights among the usherettes and fretful re-examining of tickets by everyone in the vicinity until word got around that I was an American tourist and therefore unable to follow simple seating instructions and I was escorted in some shame back to my assigned place.

So we sat together and watched the movie, 30 of us crowded together like refugees in an overloaded lifeboat, rubbing shoulders and sharing small noises, and it occurred to me then that there are certain things that some nations do better than everyone else and certain things that they do far worse and I began to wonder why that should be.

Sometimes a nation's little contrivances are so singular and clever that we associate them with that country alone—double-decker buses in Britain, windmills in Holland (what an inspired addition to a flat landscape: think how they would transform Nebraska), sidewalk cafés in Paris. And yet there are some things that most countries do without difficulty that others cannot get a grasp of at all.

The French, for instance, cannot get the hang of queuing. They try and try, but it is beyond them. Wherever you go in Paris, you see orderly lines waiting at bus stops, but as soon as the bus pulls up the line instantly disintegrates into something like a fire drill at a lunatic asylum as everyone scrambles to be the first aboard, quite unaware that this defeats the whole purpose of queuing.

The British, on the other hand, do not understand certain of the fundamentals of eating, as evidenced by their instinct to consume hamburgers with a knife and fork. To my continuing amazement, many of them also turn their fork upside-down and balance the food on the back of it. I've lived in England for a decade and a half and I still have to quell an impulse to go up to strangers in pubs and restaurants and say, 「Excuse me, can I give you a tip that'll help stop those peas bouncing all over the table?」

Germans are flummoxed by humor, the Swiss have no concept of fun, the Spanish think there is nothing at all ridiculous about eating dinner at midnight, and the Italian should never, ever have been let in on the invention of the motor car.

One Of the small marvels of my first trip to Europe was the discovery that the world could be so full of variety, that there were so many different ways of doing essentially identical things, like eating and drinking and buying cinema tickets. It fascinated me that Europeans could at once be so alike—that they could be so universally bookish and cerebral, and drive small cars, and live in little houses in ancient towns, and love soccer, and be relatively unmaterialistic and law-abiding, and have chilly hotel rooms and cosy and inviting places to eat and drink—and yet be so endlessly, unpredictably different from each other as well. I loved the idea that you could never be sure of anything in Europe.

I still enjoy that sense of never knowing quite what's going on. In my hotel in Oslo, where I spent four days after returning from Hammerfest, the chambermaid each morning left me a packet of something called Bio Tex Blå, a 「minipakke for ferie, hybel og weekend」, according to the instructions. I spent many happy hours sniffing it and experimenting with it, uncertain whether it was for washing out clothes or gargling or cleaning the toilet bowl. In the end I decided it was for washing out clothes—it worked a treat—but for all I know for the rest of the week everywhere I went in Oslo people were saying to each other, 「You know, that man smelled like toilet-bowl cleaner.」

When I told my friends in London thatI was going to travel around Europe and write a book about it, they said, 「Oh, you must speak a lot of languages.」

「Why, no.」 I would reply with a certain pride, 「only English,」 and they would look at me as if I were crazy. But that's the glory of foreign travel, as far as I am concerned. I don't want to know what people are talking about. I can't think of anything that excites a greater sense of childlike wonder than to be in a country where you are ignorant of almost everything. Suddenly you are five years old again. You can't read anything, you have only the most rudimentary sense of how things work, you can't even reliably cross a street without endangering your life. Your whole existence becomes a series of interesting guesses.

After Hammerfest, Oslo was simply wonderful. It was still cold and dusted with greyish snow, but it seemed positively tropical after Hammerfest, and I abandoned all thought of buying a furry hat. I went to the museums and for a day-long way out around the Bygdøy peninsula, where the city's finest houses stand on the wooded hillsides, with fetching views across the icy water of the harbour to the downtown. But mostly I hung around the city center, wandering back and forth between the railway station and the royal palace, peering in the store windows along Karl Johans Gate, the long and handsome main pedestrian street, cheered by the bright lights, mingling with the happy, healthy, relentlessly youthful Norwegians, very pleased to be alive and out of Hammerfest and in a world of daylight. When I grew cold, I sat in cafés and bars and eavesdropped on conversations that I could not understand or brought out my *Thomas Cook European Timetable* and studied it with a kind of humble reverence, planning the rest of my trip.

Thomas Cook European Timetable is possibly the finest book ever produced. It is impossible to leaf through its 500 pages of densely printed timetables without wanting to dump a double armload of clothes into an old Gladstone and just take off. Every page whispers romance:「Montreux—Zweisimmen—Spiez—Interlaken」,「Beograd—Trieste—Venezia—Verona—Milano」,「Göteborg—Laxå—(Hallsberg)—Stockholm」,「Ventimiglia—Marseille—Lyon—Paris」. Who could recite these names without experiencing a tug of excitement, without seeing in his mind's eye a steamy platform full of expectant travelers and piles of luggage standing beside a sleek, quarter-mile-long train with a list of exotic locations slotted into every carriage? Who could read the names「Moskva—Warszawa—Berlin—Basel—Genève」and not feel a melancholy envy for all those lucky people who get to make a grand journey across a storied continent? Who could glance at such an itinerary and not want to climb aboard? Well, Sunny von Bülow for a start. But as for me, I could spend hours just poring over the tables, each one a magical thicket of times, numbers, distances, mysterious little pictograms showing crossed knives and forks, wine glasses, daggers, miner's pickaxes (whatever could they be for?), ferry boats and buses, and bewilderingly abstruse footnotes.

Words and Expressions

1. abstruse adj. 深奧的，高深的
2. asylum n. 精神病院
3. auditorium n. 聽眾席，觀眾席
4. bookish adj. 嗜書的；好讀書的；喜歡學習的

5. cerebral adj. 要運用智力的；訴諸理性的

6. chambermaid n.（尤指旅館裡的）打掃臥室的女服務員

7. contrivance n. 發明物，新裝置

8. dagger n. 匕首，短劍

9. disintegrate v.（使）粉碎；崩裂；分崩離析

e.g. The whole plane just disintegrated in mid-air.

10. double-decker n. 雙層公共汽車

11. eavesdrop v. 偷聽

12. fetching adj.（尤指因著裝得體而）動人的，迷人的，吸引人的

13. flummox v. 使（某人）徹底不知所措（困惑不解）

14. fretful adj.（尤指為無足輕重的小事）煩躁的；發牢騷的

e.g. Don't assume your baby automatically needs feeding if she's fretful.

15. gargle v. 漱口，漱

16. glottal stop n. 喉塞音，聲門塞音

17. itinerary n. 旅行計劃；預訂行程

18. laden adj. 裝滿的，滿載的

e.g. He always comes back from France laden with presents for everyone.

19. law-abiding adj. 守法的；安分守己的

20. lemming n. 旅鼠

21. lunatic asylum n. 精神病院，瘋人院

22. materialistic adj. 實利主義的，物質主義的

23. unmaterialistic adj. 非實利主義的

24. passionate adj. 情欲強烈的，多情的

25. pickax n. 鎬，鶴嘴鋤

26. pictogram n. 象形文字

27. porcupine n. 豪豬，箭豬

28. pore v.（長時間）仔細閱讀；凝視，注視

29. quell v. 減輕，消除（疑慮）

e.g.「Jerry?」she called, trying to quell the panic inside her.

30. relentless adj. 嚴厲的；無情的；堅決的

31. relentlessly adv. 無情地；殘酷地

32. reverence n. 尊敬，崇敬

33. rodent n. 嚙齒動物（如老鼠、兔子等）

34. rudimentary adj. (有關某學科的知識或理解）基本的，初步的，粗淺的

35. sleek adj. (頭髮，皮毛）平直光滑的，有健康光澤的

36. thicket n. 灌木叢，小樹叢

37. usherette n. (影院的）女引座員，女服務員

38. windmill n. 風車；風力磨坊

39. get the hang of sth.：to learn how to do something or use something

e.g. Using the computer isn't difficult once you get the hang of it.

40. let sb. in on sth.：to tell someone about a secret plan, idea etc., and trust them not to tell other people.

e.g. If you promise not to tell, I'll let you in on a secret.

41. out of this world：so good, enjoyable, etc. it is unlike anything else you have ever experienced.

e.g. Tracy's new apartment is just out of this world.

42. pore over：to read or look at something very carefully for a long time.

e.g. They expected to find him poring over his notes the night before the exam.

43. work a treat：to work very well.

e.g. Our new system is working a treat.

44. word gets around：people hear about something.

e.g. If word of the Royal visit gets around, we'll have the press here ill force.

Proper Names

1. Basel 巴塞爾（瑞士西北部城市，在萊茵河畔）
2. Beograd 貝爾格萊德（塞爾維亞首都）
3. Copenhagen 哥本哈根（丹麥首都）
4. Hammerfest 哈默菲斯特（挪威北部港市）
5. Lyon 里昂（法國東南部城市）
6. Marseilles 馬賽（法國東南部港市）
7. Oslo 奧斯陸（挪威首都）
8. Stockholm 斯德哥爾摩（瑞典首都）
9. Trieste 的里雅斯特（義大利東北港市）

10. Verona 維羅納（義大利北部城市）

Notes

1. Bygdøy is a peninsula on the western side of Oslo, Norway.

2. Karl Johans Gate (Karl Johan Street), named after King Karl Johan, is the main street of the city of Oslo. The street includes many of Oslo's tourist attractions: Royal Palace, Oslo Cathedral, Central Station and Stortinget, the National Theater, the old University Buildings, the Palace Park and the pond 「Spikersuppa」(「the nail soup」), which is a skating rink in winter.

3. Thomas Cook is a British travel agent, born in Melbourne, England. He became a missionary in 1828 and later was an active temperance worker. In 1841 he chartered a special train to carry passengers from Leicester to Loughborough for a temperance meeting. The success of the guided excursion led to the formation of a travel agency bearing his name. Cook organized personally conducted tours throughout Europe and procured traveling and hotel accommodations for tourists making independent trips. He also provided travel services for the British government on several occasions.

4. Gladstone is the same as Gladstone bag, a small suitcase or portmanteau consisting of a rigid flame on which two compartments of the same size are hinged together.

5. Montreux（蒙特勒）is the French name for a resort town in Southwest Switzerland, on the northeast shore of Lake Geneva. Zweisimmen（茨韋西門）is a municipality in the district of Obersimmental in the canton of Berne in Switzerland. Spiez（施皮茨）is a city in the district of Niedersimmental in the canton of Bem in Switzerland. Interlaken（因特雷肯）is the German for the chief town of the Bernese Alps in Central Switzerland. Venezia is the Italian name for Venice（威尼斯）. Milano is Italian name for Milan（米蘭）. Göteborg is Swedish name for Gothenburg（歌德堡）. Laxå Municipality (Laxå kommun) is a municipality in Örebro County in central Sweden. Hallsberg（哈爾斯貝里）is a bimunicipal locality and the seat of Hallsberg Municipality, Örebro County, Sweden. Ventimiglia（文堤米利亞）is a town in northern Italy.

6. Moskva is the Russian name for Moscow. Warszawa is the Polish name

for Warsaw. Genève is the French name for Geneva.

7. A storied continent refers to a continent being the subject of many stories, namely, quite famous.

8. Martha Sharp Crawford von Bülow (1932 – 2008), known as Sunny von Bülow, was an American heiress, socialite, and philanthropist. Her husband, Claus von Bülow, was convicted of attempting her murder by insulin overdose, but the conviction was overturned on appeal. A second trial found him not guilty, after experts opined that there was no insulin injection and that her symptoms were attributable to over-use of prescription drugs. The story was dramatized in the book and movie, *Reversal of Fortune*. Sunny von Bülow lived almost 28 years in a persistent vegetative state until her death in a New York nursing home on December 6th. 2008.

Content Awareness

Ⅰ. Work in pairs to complete the outline of the text.

The author's experience in the cinema	A. His experience in the cinema: A small group of people _____
	B. His feelings: Some countries _____
Some interesting things about different nations in Europe	A. Some inventions are associated with a particular country. a. The British: _____ b. The Dutch: _____ c. The French: _____ B. Some strange things done by people from a particular nation. a. The French: _____ b. The British: _____ c. The German: _____ d. The Swiss: _____ e. The Spanish: _____ f. The Italian: _____

表(續)

Benefits of traveling to Europe	A. One can never be sure of anything in Europe since they alike in certain ways but different in others. a. Similarities: bookish and cerebral, and drive _____, and live in _____, and love soccer, and be relatively _____, and have chilly hotel rooms and _____. b. Differences: even eating and drinking and buying cinema tickets can be different. Example: a packet of something called _____. B. One can only know the basic things in life which results in a series of interesting guesses. Example: _____ C. _____. Example: the author's activities in Oslo.
Attractions of *Thomas Cook European Timetable*	One would feel excited and couldn't wait to take the trip.

Ⅱ. Read the following statements and decide whether they are true or false according to the text. Put 「T」before a true statement and 「F」before a false one.

1. The author didn't sit beside the young couple because he didn't like the discreet atmosphere.

2. All the other audience thought the author didn't follow the seat instruction simply because he was a foreigner.

3. In the author's opinion, the windmills in Holland help add variety to the landscape.

4. The author found it ridiculous to tell the British not to eat hamburgers with a fork and knife.

5. One can never be sure of what's going on in Europe since Europeans are from different nations.

6. The packet of something called Bio Tex Bla is mainly used for washing the toilet bowl.

7. The author's friends in Britain assume that one has to speak a lot of languages in order to travel around Europe.

8. Being in a different and unfamiliar country can bring a lot of problems,

which displeases the author.

9. The author wandered in the main street of Oslo in order to learn more about the history and culture of the city.

10. It is impossible to look through Thomas Cook European Timetable since it has 500 pages.

11. The author would spend time reading Thomas Cook European Timetable to plan his trip.

Language Focus

Ⅰ. Choose the answer that is closest in meaning to the underlined word in the sentence.

1. After the first visit, I came home laden with flats and pots and cardboard boxes.

  A. filled   B. loaded
  C. charged   D. left

2. The boy appeared fretful and disappointed that he couldn't join the others on their excursions.

  A. annoyed   B. restless
  C. relentless   D. anxious

3. The project disintegrated owing to lack of financial backing.

  A. broke up   B. turned up
  C. used up   D. torn up

4. This latest setback will have done nothing to quell the growing doubts about the future of the club.

  A. cast   B. express
  C. reduce   D. avoid

5. The tools that the ancient Egyptians used to build their temples were extremely rudimentary.

  A. simple   B. imperative
  C. obscure   D. periodic

6. In most cases, it is difficult to detect that someone is eavesdropping.

  A. peeping   B. overhearing
  C. cheating   D. whispering

7. Most patients derive enjoyment from leafing through old picture albums.

  A. turning   B. coming

  C. skimming   D. seeing

8. Kids these days are very materialistic. They only seem to be interested in expensive toys and computer games.

  A. concerned with money   B. interested in materials

  C. enthusiastic about substance   D. keen on information

9. We dumped our bags at the nearby Grand Hotel and hurried towards the market.

  A. threw away   B. put down

  C. took back   D. packed up

10. The only sounds were the distant, melancholy cries of the sheep.

  A. dissatisfied   B. painful

  C. unhappy   D. sharp

II. Fill in each of the blanks with an appropriate word from each group. Change the form if necessary.

  discreet discretion discrete

1. These small companies now have their own _____ identity.

2. We were all pretty open with each other but very _____ outside.

3. You can trust her to keep your secret—she's the soul of _____.

  audit auditor auditory auditorium

4. The external _____ come in once a year.

5. We gathered in an _____ and watched a videotape.

6. The yearly _____ takes place each December.

7. It's an artificial device which stimulates the _____ areas of the brain.

8. The fund is _____ annually by an accountant.

  conceive contrive conception contrivance

9. The _____ of the book took five minutes, but writing it took a year.

10. This was a steam-driven _____ used in the 19th century clothing factories.

11. Miraculously, he managed to _____ a supper out of what was left in the cupboard.

12. He was immensely ambitious but unable to _____ of winning power for himself.

gargle   giggle   gasp   gossip

13. Once one child starts _____ it starts the whole class off.

14. The circus audience _____ with amazement as she put her head in the lion's mouth.

15. The advertisement promises that _____ mouthwash will freshen your breath and kill germs.

16. There has been much _____ about the possible reasons for his absence.

passion   passionate   affection   affectionate

17. She gave her daughter a (n) _____ kiss and put her to bed.

18. He spoke with considerable _____ about the importance of art and literature.

19. Their father never showed them much _____.

20. I remember many _____ arguments taking place around this table.

relevant   relentless   reluctant

21. Many parents feel _____ to talk openly with their children.

22. Ridge's success is due to a _____ pursuit of perfection.

23. For further information, please refer to the _____ leaflet.

revere   reverence   reverent

24. I stood there, gazing down, and feeling a _____ for these spectacles of the natural world.

25. The Bishop's sermon was received in _____ silence.

26. Most of us _____ *Hamlet*, but few of us read it regularly.

pore   peer   peep   perceive

27. I saw her _____ through the curtains into the room.

28. She _____ through the mist, trying to find the right path.

29. A key task is to get pupils to _____ for themselves the relationship between success and effort.

30. Aunt Bella sat at the table, _____ over catalogs, surveying the accounts, calculating.

III. Fill in each of the blanks with an appropriate word from the box. Change the form if necessary.

> adventure   challenging   discover   diverse   enlighten
> enrich   gain   joyful   memory   opportunity
> outweigh   perspective   similarity   span   specific

Traveling provides tremendous opportunities for fun, adventure and discovery. When we visit places in other countries, we _____ a better understanding of the people living there. We learn their cultures, history and background. We discover the _____ they have with us, as well as their differences from us. It is interesting to learn from people with _____ backgrounds. Traveling helps to _____ our lives. It increases our knowledge and widens our _____. When we visit interesting places, we discover and learn many things. We _____ new people, surroundings, plants and animals. If we want to make our travels more exciting and _____, we can choose to plan our own tour and select the _____ places we want to visit. Traveling not only provides us fun and _____, it also provides us marvelous insights and _____ our minds. Traveling provides _____ for us to share our happiness with our friends and family. When we travel with our friends and family, we create _____ that would last a lifetime. It is indeed a(n) _____ thing to share the experience of a special trip with those we love. Giving them a wonderful traveling experience far _____ the benefit of buying presents for them. Goods have a limited life _____, whereas memories last forever.

Text B

A Russian Experience

It was almost midnight, yet the streets were bathed in a soft, shimmering light. The sun had just gone down and twilight would soon give way to night. We were strolling along the Nevsky Prospekt, a wide avenue stretching four kilometres and filled with people, music and street entertainers. This was St. Petersburg in August and it seemed the city was out to celebrate the long summer nights. We had just left the home of newly found Russian friends and after a wonderful traditional dinner decided to have some exercise before going to bed.

It has always been my dream to visit St. Petersburg. Absorbed by Russian history since childhood, I wanted to see it all for myself. Now, thanks to Perestroika, tourists are welcomed into Russia and St. Petersburg with its rich, cultural history is a popular choice.

We flew in from Stockholm and from the air immediately noticed a well-planned city with apartment blocks built in semi-circles with central courtyards and gardens. Not only did this seem practical, but the idea behind the design was to shelter residents from the fierce winter winds. The city was built by European architects in the 18th and 19th centuries and remains one of Europe's most beautiful cities. Straddling the wide River Neva, the city is made up of almost 50 islands connected by some 310 bridges. No wonder the sight of elegant buildings along the canals reminded me of Paris, Amsterdam and Venice.

I hadn't met many Russian people but I had an intense love for their country and traditions and was passionate about art and literature. Russian writers such as Pushkin, Tolstoy and Dostoevsky reach the very soul of ordinary Russians. and this I find intriguing. It was no different when I finally found myself in Russia. People were openly friendly and eager to discuss any aspect of their lives in their beloved Motherland. No matter how bad the economy, somehow these people have the ability to see the positive aspects of their lives, whatever their circumstances. We met an attractive woman from Moscow, and we fast became friends and it was she who invited us into the home of some dear friends of hers.

The apartment block was in an elegant area of St. Petersburg and was probably a palace in the past but now converted into apartments of four floors. The entrance through a narrow hallway was dark and dull and there was an old fashioned lift on the ground floor with steel folding gates that clanged shut, after which the lift moved very slowly upwards. It was quicker to walk up the staircase.

Our host, Yuri Petrochenkov, himself an artist, warmly greeted us at the door. He was tall with gray hair pulled into a tail. His open, friendly manner and twinkling eyes showed a sense of humor and his English with a thick accent made him an entertaining host. Nelly, his wife, spoke little English but understood a great deal more.

We were ushered into their main room, which served as a living-room, dining room and TV area. There was an air of intimacy in the room, as though it was the core part of this family. Many parties, social and political discussions and family gatherings take place here. We were honored to be there and I felt ashamed that I had absolutely no Russian language to attempt to communicate in. Why is it that people of the English-speaking world take for granted that the rest of the world should speak English? I had always meant to learn Russian and had enrolled for courses in the past but they never started because of lack of numbers.

Our meal was a feast in itself. We weren't offered wine, just vodka in little shot glasses and before drinking there is always a toast. Some nine vodkas later, Yuri was in fine form and had found a drinking partner in my husband!

Wandering along the river, we agreed that not only had we found new friends, but we had just spent probably the most enjoyable experience of our trip to Russia. This is what travel is all about—to get to the heart and soul of the people and to try to understand and experience a little of what makes others tick.

Words

1. shimmer vi. 閃爍，發微光
2. absorb vt. 吸引
3. straddle v. 跨越
4. passionate adj. 熱烈的；激昂的；易怒的
5. intriguing adj. 有趣的，迷人的
6. elegant adj. 優美的（人或其舉止）；漂亮的
7. clang v. 叮當地響
8. intimacy n. 親密；親近

9. enroll v. 招收；加入

Notes

1. shot glass: a tiny drinking glass, usually for strong alcoholic drinks.

Content Awareness

Ⅰ. Choose the best answer to each question with the information from the passage.

1. According to the author, the attraction of St. Petersburg to tourists is mainly its _____.

  A. elegant buildings   B. cultural history
  C. street entertainers   D. wonderful food

2. The author believes the significance of traveling lies in _____.

  A. seeing the wonderful world with its attractions
  B. understanding people and sharing their life experiences
  C. appreciating the culture and history of a strange land
  D. making friends with people from all walks of life

3. St. Petersburg reminded the author of Paris, Amsterdam and Venice because _____.

  A. it was also a city with a crisscross network of canals
  B. it resembled them in its rich culture and long history
  C. various styles of architecture in those places could be found in St. Petersburg
  D. it also ranked among the most beautiful cities in Europe

4. The author appreciates the Russians' positive attitudes toward life as _____.

  A. they are all friendly to foreign visitors
  B. they always treat their guests with great courtesy
  C. they love to exchange opinions on arts and literature
  D. they have the ability to handle whatever circumstances they are in

5. It can be inferred from the passage that _____.

  A. the author could speak Russian, a little awkwardly though
  B. it is popular to learn Russian in English-speaking countries

C. not many people in the author's country are interested in Russian

D. English-speaking people never care to learn a foreign language

Language Focus

I . Complete the crossword with the words from the passage.

Across

3. to behave in a particular way

7. to stretch across a river, gap, etc.

8. to shine with an unsteady light that changes constantly from bright to faint

9. to extend for a distance

11. a proposal for a drink in honor of or to sb. or sth.

13. close or warm friendship

14. very intense or strong

Down

1. a national, local or individual way of pronunciation

2. a large and special meal

4. the people who live in a particular place

5. a strong alcoholic drink originally from Russia

6. to invite people to one's home for a meal, party, etc., or to amuse people

7. to provide a place where sb. or sth. is protected

10. a long and narrow strip of waterway made for boats or for irrigation

12. the time when day is about to become night

II. Choose the word or expression that is closest in meaning to the underlined part in each sentence below.

1. The survey on the publishing market concludes that two thirds of print books will give way to digital ones in three years.

  A. pave the way for   B. get along with

  C. be replaced by   D. be reduced by

2. Thanks to the joint efforts of the international community, great progress has been made in the prevention and treatment of MDS.

  A. Because of   B. Being grateful for

  C. Just as   D. Being sorry for

3. You really need to prepare something to shelter yourself from the sunburn in the summer of Tibet.

  A. prevent from   B. protect from

  C. fight against   D. deal with

4. No wonder he has got promoted, as he puts all his heart into his work.

  A. It is not surprising   B. It is no doubt

  C. It is understandable   D. It is wonderful

5. Paul was in fine form at the wedding and kept everyone entertained.

  A. sober   B. drunk

  C. dizzy   D. cheerful

6. His survival from the air crash is a miracle in itself.

  A. considered alone   B. handled independently

  C. by all means   D. in this case

7. His songs seek to reach the very soul of the listeners.

  A. convey the real intention   B. touch the bottom of the heart

  C. express the feelings   D. get to the mind of

Ⅲ. Translate the following paragraphs into English.

1. 當我還是一個小女孩的時候，我就被中國的語言文字和歷史深深吸引，有朝一日能去中國遊覽一直是我的夢想。多虧了中國的改革開放政策，歡迎外國遊客來到這個具有 5,000 年歷史的神祕國度。當我終於夢想成真來到了中國，我注意到的第一件事，就是這裡人們的穿著主要是灰、藍兩種顏色的服裝，這讓我感到十分好奇。為了能觸摸到中國文化的精髓，我決定在中國多待一段時間。結果，我對中國的第一次造訪竟長達 3 年之久。

2. 巴黎迪士尼樂園是巴黎的主要旅遊景點之一，距離巴黎市中心約 32 千米。巴黎迪士尼由歐洲迪士尼公司營運，它是在美國本土以外開辦的第二個迪士尼主題公園，以其開放性及家庭遊樂性而聞名。難怪巴黎迪士尼樂園是世界上游覽人數最多的主題公園之一。

7.3　Practical Translation

英語新聞的翻譯

由於記者寫作風格的不同，英語新聞的文體結構無固定模式，但大體上說，它的主體結構由標題（headline）、導語（lead or introduction）和正文（body）三部分構成。

新聞的主要目的是為了吸引和打動讀者，因此標題起著非常重要的作用，它濃縮和概括了全文的中心問題，常被稱為「新聞報導的眼睛」。英語新聞導語，通常為文章的第一段，點出新聞的主題。就其構成要素來說，就是五個 W 和一個 H，即 who，what，when，where，why，how。正文是在導語的基礎上，引入更多的與主題相關的事實，使之更加詳實、具體，並展開一定的評論，進而得出結論。

英語新聞採取的最普遍的形式是「倒金字塔結構」（The Inverted Pyramid Form），即新聞事實的闡述按照重要性遞減的順序展開（in the order of descending importance）。它的優勢在於可以使讀者很快看到新聞的精華部分，讀到他們所需要的內容。這種「倒金字塔結構」在導語中體現得最為明顯。

英語新聞翻譯的難點在於標題和導語的翻譯，以下分標題和導語兩部分來講述英語新聞的翻譯。

一、英語新聞標題的翻譯

為了吸引讀者的眼球，英語新聞標題總是力求用有限的字數來表達新聞的內容，增強新聞的簡潔性和可讀性，因此它最主要的一個特點就是用詞經濟達意、簡短明了。

例 1：Oil to hit $100 by end of year and keep rising (*China Daily*)

譯文：油價年末將達每桶 100 美元，並將繼續上漲

解析：在這個標題中，由於 hit 字母相對較少，用它代替 reach，使得標題更加簡潔明瞭。

例 2：Hummer deal nod likely soon (*China Daily*)

譯文：「悍馬」收購協議即將正式達成

解析：這個標題中，由於 deal 字母相對較少，用它代替 agreement，使得標題更加簡短、醒目。

英語新聞標題的第二個特點是使用縮略語，這樣可以使語言簡潔明快，節省篇幅，避免標題過長。常用的縮略語形式是多個單詞的首字母縮略語（acronym）和某個單詞的縮略形式。

例 3：Hackers' attack on MOD site fail (CCTV 9)

譯文：黑客攻擊國防部網站失敗

解析：這個標題中，MOD 是 Ministry of National Defense（國防部）的縮略語。翻譯時應譯出 MOD 指代的意思，這樣標題的意義才完整、有效。

例 4：Hu-Obama talks attract int'l media attention（CCTV 9）

譯文：胡錦濤和奧巴馬的會談引起世界關注

解析：這個標題中，Hu 代表的是中國國家主席胡錦濤，int'l 是 international 的縮略語，翻譯時應譯出完整的人名和縮略語代表的意思。

英語新聞標題的第三個特點是省略。一般而言，省略以虛詞為多，而省略的虛詞有冠詞、助動詞和連詞等。

例 5：Cops say girl, 9, was stabbed（CNN）

譯文：警方說一個九歲女孩被刺

解析：完整的標題應該是 Cops say a girl of 9 years old was stabbed。為使語言簡練，a girl of 9 years old 被省略為 girl, 9，在翻譯成漢語時應把意思清楚完整地表達出來。

例 6：2 dead, 21 hurt in tour bus wreck（CNN）

譯文：旅遊大巴失事，2 人死亡，21 人受傷

解析：完整的標題應該是 Two people were dead and 21 were hurt in the wreck of a tour bus。英語中，為使語言簡潔明瞭，只保留了關鍵字眼，翻譯時需把被省略的內容補譯出來。

有時，有些標題綜合地體現以上提到的特點。

例 7：16 killed in blast in NW Pakistan's Peshawar（CNN）

譯文：巴基斯坦西北部城市白沙瓦發生爆炸，16 人死亡

解析：完整的標題應該是 Sixteen people were killed in a blast in the Northwestern Pakistan's Peshawar。

二、英語新聞導語和正文的翻譯

前面講過，英語新聞採取的最普遍的形式是「倒金字塔結構」，新聞事實按重要性呈現遞減順序。也就是說，把最重要的新聞事實放在最前面，次要的信息放在後面，起到補充說明的作用。而漢語句子常以「流水句」形式出現，闡述新聞事即時，按照新聞事實的重要性以遞增順序展開。這種重要性遞減和重要性遞增順序在導語的翻譯中體現得最為明顯，因此在翻譯英語新聞的導語時，譯者要清楚地把握這個特點，使譯文符合漢語表達習慣和漢語新聞文體的特點。

例 8：Four people, including a 12-year-old, died when an Amtrak train hit their car in Hardeeville, South Carolina, an official said Tuesday.（CNN）

譯文：周二，一位官員說，在美國南卡羅來納州哈迪威爾市，一輛

美國鐵路客運公司的列車和一輛汽車相撞，造成四人死亡，其中包括一名十二歲兒童。

解析：原文中，這則新聞的要點 Four people, including a 12-year-old, died 放在句子前面，突出體現讀者想要獲得的信息，吸引了讀者的注意力，並引起了他們的好奇心，使他們急切地想知道這次事故為什麼會發生。然後 when all Amtrak train hit theft car 講述了這件事情發生的原因，滿足了讀者的好奇心。最後一些次要信息，如地點 in Hardeeville, South Carolina，事件陳述人 an official 和時間 Tuesday 被一一提到。這種處理方式充分體現了英語新聞的闡述按照重要性遞減的順序來展開的特點，句子重心採取「前置式」。而漢語譯文則體現出兩大特點。一是漢語句子的「流水句」結構。英語句子嚴謹的「樹干」結構被完全打破，整個句子被拆分成幾個形式鬆散，邏輯關係不甚明確的幾個分句。二是漢語新聞事實的闡述是按照重要性遞增的順序來展開的。先提到一些次要信息，如時間、事件陳述人、地點，然後講出事件發生的原因「一輛美國鐵路客運公司的列車撞上了一輛汽車」，最後再講述新聞的要點「四個人，包括一名十二歲的兒童死亡」，句子重心採取「後置式」。

例9：Operating revenue of China's State-owned enterprises (SOEs) grew 0.5 percent year-on-year to 17,873.77 billion yuan ($2,617.91 billion) during the first 10 months of 2009 marking the first year-on-year growth this year, the Ministry of Finance (MOF) said in a statement on its website yesterday. (*China Daily*)

譯文：昨天財政部在其網站上公布的一份報告顯示，2009年1月到10月，國有企業累計實現營業收入17,873.77億元（相當於2,617.91億美元），首次出現0.5%的同比增長率。

解析：原文中，這則新聞的要點 Operating revenue of China's State-owned enterprises (SOEs) grew 0.5 percent year-on-year to 17,873.77 billion yuan ($2,617.91 billion) during the first 10 months of 2009 放在句子前面，非常清楚地告知讀者新聞的要點，吸引了讀者的注意，並讓讀者即刻獲得所需信息。然後一些細節，如新聞發布的單位、地址和時間：「the Ministry of Finance, on its website, yesterday」作為新聞要點的支撐信息一一展開，體現了英語新聞的闡述是按照新聞事實的重要性遞減的順序展開的，句子重心採取「前置式」。漢語譯文也充分體現出漢

語的句式特點，一個帶獨立主格結構的完整的「樹干式」英語句式被拆分成幾個不注重形式結構的嚴密性，少用關聯詞語，句子結構鬆散的漢語分句。而新聞事實的闡述按照重要性遞增的順序展開。先提到一些細節，然後新聞的要點被放在句子的後半部分，句子重心為「後置式」。

Translation Practice

Translate the following headlines and leads into Chinese.

1. S Korea sets emission-cut target (*China Daily*)

2. Firms vie for bigger share of car market (*China Daily*)

3. Spanish PM: Somali pirates free fishermen (CNN)

4. China receives 94m overseas tourists in Jan – Sept, down 3.45% (*China Daily*)

5. US, Russian leaders say nations closer to deal to cut nuclear arms (CNN)

6. South African runner Caster Semenya will be allowed to keep the gold medal she won in the women's 800-meters at the World Athletics Championships in Berlin, Germany, in August, the country's sports ministry announced Thursday (CNN)

7. After complaining of feeling badly for days, Nicole Richie was hospitalized for pneumonia at Cedars-Sinai Medical Center in Los Angeles and was 「doing well」, her rep said Wednesday

7.4　Focused Writing

Notices

A notice is used to inform people. This may include instructions, warnings or change to a plan. They are typically written on behalf of people in authority within a company or organization but may also be for the general public from government or other institutions. Notices may be posted in many different ways—on a notice or bulletin board, published in the mass media or sent as a letter or an e-mail.

Notices take various forms, thus involving different formats. To gain a better understanding, let us take a look at the following samples.

Sample 1

Retail Sales Department
Temporary Move, 15-22 November 2009

We regret that the Retail Sales Department will be closed from 15-22 November for re-wiring. Customers can still buy from our normal stock at a temporary location in a heated greenhouse 30 yards down Farm Lane, near the gate of the Wholesale Flower's Department.
We apologize to customers for any inconvenience caused.

John Wallace
Managing Director
November 9th, 2009

Note: The above notice is a business notice. Typically such notices have a clear heading, which is often in bold and in large letters. All the information in a notice is laid out clearly and the tone of the notice is typically formal. The information in a notice is brief but accurate and sufficient for readers to understand; in this case mat they can shop as normal but in a different place. The name and the position of the person who wrote the notice and the date is usually included.

Sample 2

Asian Finance Association-Nippon Finance Association Joint International Conference
Tokyo
6-9 July 2008

The Nippon Finance Association (NFA) and the Asian Finance Association (AsianFA) are jointly organizing a conference at the Pacifico Yokohama International Convention Center, Tokyo, Japan.
Eighty hundred finance scholars and professionals from around the world are expected to participate. There will be a special session on 「Corporate Governance Around the World」 with Professor Ralph Walkling (President of Financial Management Association) in the chair.
Keynote speakers include Eduardo Schwartz (UCLA), Kenneth Singleton (Stanford), and George Constantinides (University of Chicago).
Interested participants should book attendance and accommodation before July 4th 2008 through the web site <http://www.pacifico.co.jp/english/index.html>.

Note: This is a notice concerning an international academic conference. Such notices, will include the time and venue of the conference and may also indicate the expected number of participants, highlight the main event and provide the names of keynote speakers in order to capture attention.

Sample 3

Call for Papers

Nature Methods is now accepting submissions of papers for the life sciences and the areas of chemistry relevant to the life sciences.

Specific areas of interest include, but are not limited to:
· Recombinant DNA and protein technologies
· Construction and screening of libraries and arrays of nucleic acids, proteins and chemical compounds

Microarrays, display techniques, combinatorial chemistry, lab-on-a-chip technologies
· Isolation, purification and detection of biological molecules

Separation techniques, chromatography, chiral separation, labeling, epitope tagging, amplification of nucleic acids, single molecule detection and characterization
· Methods for analysis of structure and function of biological molecules

Molecular structure determination, mass spectrometry, binding assays, sequencing, detection of post-translational modifications, mutagenesis, chemical tagging of biomolecules
· Electrophysiology
· Techniques of analysis and manipulation of gene expression

Gene targeting, transduction, RNA interference
· Cell culture methodology
· Imaging and probing technologies

Microscopy, optical spectroscopy, histology, labeling, hybridization techniques, probe scanning, chemical tagging of molecules, single cell manipulation
· Immunological techniques

Production of antibodies, antibody-based assays, immunolabeling
· Animal studies methodology

Pharmacology, physiology, behavior

Papers should be submitted complete with abstract before February 30th, 2010.

Note: This is a notice asking for papers for an academic journal called Nature Methods. This type of notice has a very clear purpose which is to invite contributions from readers. The notice clarifies the purpose, and indicates exactly which topics will be relevant. Contributors are not expected to present papers that are not relevant to these topics.

Writing Assignment

Write a notice of a regional conference to be held in your nearest city.

Unit 8 Living a Full Life

8.1 Get Started

Ⅰ. Discuss with members of your group what is/are the most important element(s) for living a full life. You may choose one or more from the following list or provide your own answer. Then give reasons why you have made such a choice.

- a good appearance
- a happy mindset
- perfect health
- a good job
- a happy family
- close friends
- a good neighborhood
- an absorbing hobby
- lottery winnings

Ⅱ. Read the letter from John Doe and, with your partner, discuss how you could help him.

Dear Abby,

I feel like I almost can't breathe now. I work a ridiculous amount of hours and I don't have time to relax. My parents live 1,400 miles away and I am here all by myself. I have no time to make friends. Sometimes I feel I don't even have a life. What should I do?

Kind regards,

John

8.2　Read and Explore

Text A

Pleasure only gets you so far. A rich, rewarding life often requires a messy battle with adversity.

The Hidden Side of Happiness
by *Kathleen McGowan*

Hurricanes, house fires, cancer, whitewater rafting accidents, plane crashes, vicious attacks in dark alleyways. Nobody asks for any of it. But to their surprise, many people find that enduring such a harrowing ordeal ultimately changes them for the better. Their refrain might go something like this: 「I wish it hadn't happened, but I'm a better person for it.」

We love to hear the stories of people who have been transformed by their tribulations, perhaps because they testify to a bona fide type of psychological truth, one that sometimes gets lost amid endless reports of disaster: There seems to be a built-in human capacity to flourish under the most difficult circumstances. Positive responses to profoundly disturbing experiences are not limited to the toughest or the bravest. In fact, roughly half the people who struggle with adversity say that their lives have subsequently in some ways improved.

This and other promising findings about the life-changing effects of crises are the province of the new science of post-traumatic growth. This fledgling field has already proved the truth of what once passed as bromide: What doesn't kill you can actually make you stronger. Post-traumatic stress is far from the only possible outcome. In the wake of even the most terrifying experiences, only a small proportion of adults become chronically trouble. More commonly, people rebound—or even eventually thrive.

Those who weather adversity well are living proof of the paradoxes of happiness. We need more than pleasure to live the best possible life. Our contemporary quest for happiness has shriveled to a hunt for bliss—a life protected from bad feelings, free from pain and confusion.

This anodyne definition of well-being leaves out the better half of the story, the rich, full joy that comes from a meaningful life. It is the dark matter of happiness, the ineffable quality we admire in wise men and women and aspire to cultivate in our own lives. It turns out that some of the people who have suffered the most, who have been forced to contend with shocks they never anticipated and to rethink the meaning of their lives, may have the most to tell us about that profound and intensely fulfilling journey that philosophers used to call the search for「the good life」.

This broader definition of good living blends deep satisfaction and a profound connection to others through empathy. It is dominated by happy feelings but seasoned also with nostalgia and regret.「Happiness is only one among many values in human life,」contends Laura King, a psychologist at the University of Missouri in Columbia. Compassion, wisdom, altruism, insight, creativity—sometimes only the trials of adversity can foster these qualities, because sometimes only drastic situations can force us to take on the painful process of change. To live a full human life, a tranquil, carefree existence is not enough. We also need to grow—and sometimes growing hurts.

In a dark room in Queens, New York, 31-year-old fashion designer Tracy Cyr believed she was dying. A few months before, she had stopped taking the powerful immune-suppressing drugs that kept her arthritis in check. She never anticipated what would happen: a withdrawal reaction that eventually left her in total body agony and neurological meltdown. The slightest movement—trying to swallow, for example—was excruciating. Even the pressure of her cheek on the pillow was almost unbearable.

Cyr is no wimp—diagnosed with juvenile rheumatoid arthritis at the age of two, she had endured the symptoms and the treatments (drugs, surgery) her whole life. But this time, she was way past her limits, and nothing her doctors did seemed to help. Either the disease was going to kill her or, pretty soon, she felt she might have to kill herself.

As her sleepless nights wore on, though, her suicidal thoughts began to be interrupted by new feelings of gratitude. She was still in agony, but a new consciousness grew stronger each night: an awesome sense of liberation, combined with an all-encompassing feeling of sympathy and compassion. 「I felt stripped of everything I'd ever identified myself with.」she said six months later. 「Everything I thought I'd known or believed in was useless—time, money, self-image, perception. Recognizing that was so freeing.」

Within a few months, she began to be able to move more freely, thanks to a cocktail of steroids and other drugs. She says now there's no question that her life is better. 「I felt I had been shown the secret of life and why we're here: to be happy and to nurture other life. It's that simple.」

Her mind-blowing experience came as a total surprise. But that feeling of transformation is in some ways typical, says Rich Tedeschi, a professor of psychology at the University of North Carolina in Charlotte who coined the term「post-traumatic growth」. His studies of people who have endured extreme events, like combat, violent crime or sudden serious illness show that most feel dazed and anxious in the immediate aftermath; they are preoccupied with the idea that their lives have been shattered. A few are haunted long afterward by memory problems, sleep trouble and similar symptoms of post-traumatic stress disorder. But Tedeschi and others have found that for many people—perhaps even the majority—life ultimately becomes richer and more gratifying.

Something similar happens to many people who experience a terrifying physical threat. In that moment, our sense of invulnerability is pierced, and the self-protective mental armor that normally stands between us and our perceptions of the world is torn away. Our everyday life scripts—our habits, self-perceptions and assumptions—go out the window, and we are left with a raw experience of the world.

Still, actually implementing these changes, as well as fully coming to terms with a new reality, usually takes conscious effort. Being willing and able to take on this process is one of the major differences between those who grow through adversity and those who are destroyed by it. The people who find value in adversity aren't the toughest or the most rational. What makes them different is that they are able to incorporate what happened into the story of their own life.

Eventually, they may find themselves freed in ways they never imagined. Survivors often say they have become more tolerant and forgiving of others, capable of bringing peace to formerly troubled relationships. They say that material ambitions suddenly seem silly and the pleasures of friends and family paramount—and that the crisis allowed them to recognize life in line with their new priorities.

People who have grown from adversity often feel much less fear, despite the frightening things they've been through. They are surprised by their own strength, confident that they can handle whatever else life throws at them. 「People don't say that what they went through was wonderful,」 says Tedeschi. 「They weren't meaning to grow from it. They were just trying to survive. But in retrospect, what they gained was more than they ever anticipated.」

In his recent book *Satisfaction*, Emory University psychiatrist Gregory Berns points to extreme endurance athletes who push themselves to their physical limits for days at a time. They cycle through the same sequence of sensations as do trauma survivors: self-loss, confusion and, finally, a new sense of mastery. For ultramarathoners, who regularly run 100-mile races that last more than 24 hours, vomiting and hallucinating are normal. After a day and night of running without stopping or sleeping, competitors sometimes forget who they are and what they are doing.

For a more common example of growth through adversity, look to one of life's biggest challenges: parenting. Having a baby has been shown to decrease levels of happiness. The sleep deprivation and the necessity of putting aside personal pleasure in order to care for an infant mean that people with newborns are more likely to be depressed and find their marriage on the rocks. Nonetheless, over the long haul, raising a child is one of the most rewarding and meaningful of all human undertakings. The short-term sacrifice of happiness is outweighed by other benefits, like fulfillment, altruism and the chance to leave a meaningful legacy.

Ultimately, the emotional reward can compensate for the pain and difficulty of adversity. This perspective does not cancel out what happened, but it puts it all in a different context: that it's possible to live an extraordinary rewarding life even within the constraints and struggles we face. In some form or other, says King, we all must go through this realization. 「You're not going to be the person you thought you were, but here's who you are going to be instead—and that turns out to be a pretty great life.」

Words and Expressions

1. adversity n. 逆境, 不幸, 厄運

e.g. But out of this adversity has sprung a surprisingly fine vintage. （酒的釀造年份）

She somehow manages to keep laughing in the face of adversity.

2. aftermath n. 後果, 餘殃, 餘波

3. alleyway n. 小巷, 胡同

4. altruism n. 利他主義, 無私

5. anodyne adj. 不冒犯他人的, 四平八穩的

6. aspire v. 追求, 渴望, 有志於

7. bliss n. 極樂, 無上幸福, 福佑, 至福

e.g. I didn't have to get up till 11—it was sheer bliss.

8. bona fide adj. 真正的; 真實的; 真誠的

e.g. Only bona fide members are allowed to use the club pool.

9. bromide n. 意在使人消氣卻沒有效果的話

10. dazed adj. （尤指因震驚、意外事故等而）茫然的, 迷亂的, 恍惚的

e.g. Her face was very pale and she wore a dazed expression.

11. encompass v. 覆蓋, 圍住

e.g. The fog soon encompassed the whole valley.

12. excruciating adj. 劇烈疼痛的

13. gratifying adj. 令人高興的, 使人滿足的

e.g. It's gratifying to note that already much has been achieved.

He felt a gratifying sense of being respected and appreciated.

14. hallucinate v. 產生幻覺

15. harrowing adj. 折磨人的, 可怕的, 令人痛苦的

16. ineffable adj. （好或美得）難以名狀的, 不可言喻的

17. legacy n. 遺留下來的狀況

e.g. The invasion left a legacy of hatred and fear.

18. mind-blowing adj. 令人極度興奮（震驚）的；非常奇怪

e.g. Astronauts have mind-blowing views of planet Earth.

19. neurological adj. 神經的

20. nostalgia n. 對往昔事物的留戀，懷舊情緒

e.g. Her work is pervaded by nostalgia for a bygone age.

He looked back on his university days with a certain amount of nostalgia.

21. ordeal n. 可怕的經歷，痛苦的折磨

22. paramount adj. 至高無上的，最重要的

e.g. A woman's role as a mother is of paramount importance to society.

23. province n.（知識、研究的）範圍、領域；職責範圍

e.g. Sales forecasts are outside my province—talk to the Sales Manager.

24. preoccupied adj. 全神貫注的，入神的

e.g. Rod's completely preoccupied with all the wedding preparations at the moment.

25. refrain n.【正式】一再重複的話（想法）

e.g. Their proposal met with constant refrain that it was impractical.

26. rheumatoid arthritis n. 類風濕性關節炎

27. shrivel v.（使）皺縮；（使）干枯；（使）干癟

28. steroid n. 類固醇，甾族化合物

29. tranquil adj. 平靜的，寧靜的，安謐的

e.g. In summer, the normally calm, tranquil streets fill with crowds of tourists.

30. trauma n. 痛苦的經歷

31. traumatic adj.（經歷）痛苦難忘的；造成精神創傷的

32. tribulation n. 苦難，艱難

33. ultramarathoner n. 超級馬拉松運動員

34. vomit v. 嘔吐，嘔出，吐出

35. wimp n. 懦弱無用的人

36. (be) on the rocks：困難重重，瀕臨失敗

e.g. I'm afraid Tim's marriage is on the rocks.

37. cancel out：抵消

e.g. Recent losses have cancelled out any profits made at the start of the year.

38. come to terms with：妥協，接受

e.g. Counseling helps her come to terms with her grief.

39. for the better：好轉

e.g. The weather has taken a turn for the better.

40. in line with：與……一致（符合）

e.g. Annual pay increases will be in line with inflation.

41. in the wake of sth.：（尤指不好的事）緊隨……而來；作為……的後果

e.g. Outbreaks of disease occurred in the wake of the drought.

42. keep... in check：控制某人（物）

e. g You must learn to keep your emotions in check.

Proper Names

1. Emory University 埃默里大學（位於美國城市亞特蘭大）
2. Gregory Berns 格列高利·伯恩斯
3. Kathleen McGowan 凱思琳·麥克高恩
4. Laura King 勞拉·金
5. Rich Tedeschi 單奇·特德斯基
6. Tracy Cyr 特蕾西·塞爾

Notes

1. Rafting or whitewater rafting is a challenging recreational activity using an inflatable（可充氣的）raft to navigate a river or other bodies of water. This is usually done through whitewater rapids or different degrees of rough water, in order to thrill and excite the raft passengers. The development of this activity as a leisure sport has gained popularity since the mid-1970s.

2. People who are chronically troubled are suffering from an ailment that has continued for a long time and cannot be cured.

3. The word「weather」is used here as a verb, meaning「to come through a very difficult situation safely」.

4. The verb「season」originally means「adding salt, pepper, etc. to food being cooked」. Here, it is used in a figurative sense, meaning「mixing with」.

5. A withdrawal reaction is what happens to someone during the period after they have given up a drug that they were dependent on, including the unpleasant mental and physical effects that causes.

6. The word 「way」 in this sentence is an adverb, meaning 「by a large amount」.

7. Post-traumatic stress disorder is a mental illness that can develop after a very bad experience, such as a plane crash.

Content Awareness

I. Choose the sentences that best expresses the meaning of the sentences from the text.

1. Positive responses to profoundly disturbing experiences are not limited to the toughest or the bravest.
   A. Positive responses only happen to the toughest and the bravest people.
   B. Anyone could obtain positive outcomes from difficult experiences.
   C. Only the toughest and the bravest people will undergo disturbing circumstances.
   D. The toughest and the bravest people are more likely to encounter profoundly disturbing experiences.

2. What doesn't kill you can actually make you stronger.
   A. You are lucky not to be killed.
   B. You could become stronger after experiencing an attempted murder.
   C. You could become stronger after going through a hard experience.
   D. The strong people have a better chance of survival.

3. Post-traumatic stress is far from the only possible outcome.
   A. One could experience much more than post-traumatic stress.
   B. The only thing to get from a hard experience is post. traumatic stress.
   C. Post-traumatic stress is a much stronger reaction than others.
   D. Everyone who has gone through a profoundly disturbing experience will have post-traumatic stress.

4. Those who weather adversity well are living proof of the paradoxes of happiness.
   A. Those who experience different weather conditions can find happiness.
   B. Weathermen are most likely to experience the paradoxes of happiness.
   C. Those who come out of a difficult situation soundly are the best examples of the paradoxes of happiness.
   D. People gain happiness and sorrow if they handle adversity well.
5. We need more than pleasure to live the best possible life.
   A. The best possible life of humans depends on whether they are happy
   B. The best possible life comes from pleasure.
   C. The best possible life needs more pleasure.
   D. Pleasure is not the only thing that contributes to the best life.
6. It is dominated by happy feelings but seasoned also with nostalgia and regret.
   A. good life is made up of a greater part of happiness with some nostalgia and regret.
   B. Nostalgia and regret may ruin a happy life.
   C. Nostalgia and regret is common in average people's feelings.
   D. Happy feelings may drive out nostalgia and regret.
7. But this time, she was way past her limits, and nothing her doctors did seemed to help.
   A. This time her doctors couldn't set a limit for her.
   B. This time she went beyond her doctors' demands.
   C. This time her doctors couldn't help her go over her limits.
   D. This time the pain was too much for her and couldn't be controlled.
8. Still, actually implementing these changes, as well as fully coming to terms with a new reality, usually takes conscious effort.
   A. Changes do not come by themselves without action being taken.
   B. It is not easy for people to accept a new reality and make these changes.

C. Reality and changes may come together.

D. Many people have made conscious effort for changes but they failed.

9. What makes them different is that they are able to incorporate what happened into the story of their own life.

A. They are different because they have their own business and life.

B. They have become special by making their experience a part of their life.

C. They become good story-tellers once they put their own experience into the stories.

D. They are able to distinguish stories from real life.

10. The short-term sacrifices of happiness is outweighed by other benefits, like fulfillment, altruism and the chance to leave a meaningful legacy.

A. It is more meaningful to have a child than enjoying life as a couple.

B. Giving birth to a child brings more happiness than enough sleep.

C. A family with children has more financial benefits.

D. Other valuable benefits are more important than the loss of some happiness for a short period.

Language Focus

Ⅰ. Choose a word to complete each of the sentences below. Every word can be used twice. Change the form if necessary.

season   weather   refrain   province   haunt

value   coin   promise   wake   prize

1. The show will tour the _____ after it closes in London.

2. Nancy _____ to the sound of birds outside her window.

3. The stigma of being a bankrupt is likely to _____ him for the rest of his life.

4. We've never had much _____ with vandals (故意破壞公共財物者) around here.

5. Unpainted wooden furniture _____ to a gray color.

6. There have been demonstrations in the streets in the _____ of

the recent bomb attack.

7. The term「cardboard city」was _____ to describe communities of homeless people living in cardboard boxes.

8. The _____ is that these restrictions have remained while other things have changed.

9. The company just managed to _____ the recession.

10. Renaissance art is not really his _____—he specializes in the modem period.

11. Let's toss a _____ to see who goes first.

12. The winner will receive a prize with a _____ of £1,000.

13. A headless rider _____ the country lanes.

14. The post office _____ to resume first-class mail delivery to the area on Friday.

15. Thank you for going to so much _____ to find what I was looking for.

16. On the other side of the _____, there'll be tax incentives for small businesses.

17. The day dawned bright and clear, with the _____ of warm, sunny weather.

18. The young have a completely different set of _____ and expectations.

19. The protest began with a small group, but then others took up the _____.

20. He _____ the house for me at £80,000.

Ⅱ. Complete the following sentences with an appropriate word or phrase from the box. Change the form if necessary.

adversity	ordeal	anticipate	drastic	suicidal
preoccupy	legacy	nostalgia	retrospect	tranquil
deprivation	aspire	aftermath	cancel out	ultimately

1. The _____ atmosphere of the inn allows guests to feel totally at home.

2. Technological advances might _____ lead to even more job los-

ses.

3. In the _____ of the shootings, there were calls for tighter controls on gun ownership.

4. Her kindness and generosity _____ her occasional flashes of temper.

5. He was beginning to wonder if he would survive the _____.

6. Foreign food aid has led to a _____ reduction in the numbers of people dying of starvation.

7. Perhaps her most important _____ was her program of educational reform.

8. There were food shortages and other _____ during the Civil War.

9. The new economic policies could prove _____ for the party.

10. The building will be completed around six months earlier than _____.

11. The experience was enough to keep him _____ for some time.

12. The road to happiness is paved with _____.

13. She _____ to nothing no less than the chairmanship of the company.

14. He might be influenced by _____ for the surroundings of his happy youth.

15. In _____, I wish that I had thought about alternative courses of action.

Ⅲ. Complete the following sentences by translating the Chinese in brackets into English. Try to use the expressions you have learned from the text.

1. Watching your baby being born is _____ (極其令人興奮的經歷).

2. There is _____ (內置儲存空間) in all bedrooms.

3. This handout focuses on _____ (自我保護措施) under difficult climatic conditions.

4. I'm sure we could offer you some _____ (短期的工作).

5. So, how is it that we all, or at least many of us, have such a

_____（歪曲的、否定的自我觀念）？

6. Helen Hunt stars as a character undergoing _____（改變了生活的事件）in *Then She Found Me*.

7. She has written a book that is beautiful because of the honesty and the raw emotion that is portrayed in _____（無所不包的細節）.

8. Having a decent job contributes to _____（一個好的自我形象）.

Text B

Returning to College

If I thought I'd live to be a hundred, I'd go back to college next fall. I was drafted into the Army at the end of my junior year and, after four years in the service, had no inclination to return to finish college. By then, it seemed, I knew everything.

Well, as it turns out? I don't know everything, and I'm ready to spend some time learning. I wouldn't want to pick up where I left off. I'd like to start all over again as a freshman. You see, it isn't just the education that appeals to me. I've visited a dozen colleges in the last two years, and college life looks extraordinarily pleasant.

The young people on campus are all gung ho to get out and get at life. They don't seem to understand they're having one of its best parts. Here they are with no responsibility to anyone but themselves, a hundred college next fall. I was drafted into the Army service, had no inclination to return to finish or a thousand ready-made friends, teachers trying to help them, families at home waiting for them to return for Christmas to tell all about their triumphs, three meals a day—so it isn't gourmet food—but you can't have everything.

Too many students don't really have much patience with the process of being educated. They think half the teachers are idiots, and I wouldn't deny this. They think the system stinks sometimes. I wouldn't deny that. They think there aren't any nice girls/boys around. I'd deny that. They just won't know what an idyllic time of life college can be until it's over.

The students are anxious to acquire the knowledge they think they need to make a buck, but they aren't really interested in education for education's sake. That's where they're wrong, and that's why I'd like to go back to college. I know now what a joy knowledge can be, independent of anything you do with it.

I'd take several courses in philosophy. I like the thinking process that goes with it. Philosophers are fairer than is absolutely necessary, but I like them, even the ones that I think are wrong. Too much of what I know of the great philosophers comes secondhand or from condensations. I'd like to take a course in which I actually had to read Plato, Aristotle, Hume, Spinoza, Locke, John Dewey and the other great thinkers.

I'd like to take some calculus, too. I have absolutely no ability in that direction and not much interest, either, but there's something going on in mathematics that I don't understand, and I'd like to find out what it is. My report cards won't be mailed to my father and mother, so I won't have to worry about marks. I bet I'll do better than when they were mailed.

There are some literary classics I ought to read and I never will, unless I'm forced to by a good professor, so I'll take a few courses in English literature. I took a course that featured George Gordon Byron, usually referred to now as 「Lord Byron」, and I'd like to take that over again. I did very well in it the first time. I actually read all of *Don Juan* and have never gotten over how great it was. I know I could get an A in that if I took it over. I'd like to have a few easy courses.

My history is very weak, and I'd want several history courses. I'm not going to break my back over them, but I'd like to be refreshed about the broad outline of history. When someone says sixteenth century to me, I'd like to be able to associate it with some names and events. This is just a little conversational conceit, but that's life.

If I canfind a good teacher, I'd certainly want to go back over English grammar and usage. He'd have to be good, because you might not think so sometimes, but I know a lot about using the language. Still, there are times when I'm stumped. I was wondering the other day what part of speech the word 「please」 is in the sentence, 「Please don't take me seriously.」

I've been asked to speak at several college graduation ceremonies. Maybe if I graduate, they'll ask me to speak at my own.

Words

1. gourmet n. 美食家，講究吃喝的人
2. stink vi. 招人厭惡；糟透
3. idyllic adj. 田園詩般的；牧歌的；質樸宜人的；平和歡暢的
4. philosophy n. 哲學；哲理；人生觀
5. condensation n. 冷凝；冷凝液
6. literary adj. 文學（上）的；精通文學的；愛好文學的；從事文學研究（或寫作）的
7. conceit n. 自負；幻想；思想，觀點；巧妙構思
8. stump vt. 使為難

Content Awareness

Ⅰ. Choose the best answer to each question with the information from the passage.

1. What does the author think of the students on campus?

    A. They lack a sense of responsibility.

    B. They are too willing to make friends.

    C. They make their families worry about them.

    D. They fail to realize that college life is precious.

2. What do you think is a ready-made friend, as mentioned in Line 15?

    A. A friend who offers you help when you are in real need.

    B. A friend who is always ready to help you.

    C. A friend who is easily and immediately available.

    D. A friend who will make everything ready for you.

3. The author thinks that the college students' attitude toward college education is _____.

    A. realistic   B. pessimistic

    C. unfair   D. objective

4. For what reason does the author want to return to college?

    A. He wants to make some ready-made friends.

B. He intends to acquire knowledge to make more money.

C. He wants to live an independent life.

D. He finds it is a joy to get better educated.

5. The author wants to take calculus because _____.

A. he has a special talent for it

B. he is curious about mathematics

C. he can bring home a good report

D. he is interested in it

Language Focus

Ⅰ. Pair each word in the left column with a word in the right column to form a collocation, and then complete the following sentences with the paired words.

Model　1. gourmet — a. card
　　　　2. mail — b. food
(gourmet—food, mail—card)

1. idyllic adj.　　　　a. youngster
2. appeal to v.　　　 b. knowledge
3. deny v.　　　　　 c. stump
4. acquire v.　　　　d. inclination
5. refresh v.　　　　 e. conceit
6. question n.　　　 f. scene
7. lose v.　　　　　 g. claim
8. show v.　　　　　h. memory

1. It seemed even the _____ mountain _____ couldn't take his mind off his work.

2. I'm not sure whether the topic on fashion will _____ all the _____.

3. Both countries have firmly _____ Japan's _____ to the island.

4. A smart learner knows how to make best use of his time to _____ the _____ he is here for.

5. Perhaps this photograph will _____ your _____?

204

6. The _____ about the inefficient measures to deal with the nuclear leakage _____ the spokesman of the government.

7. After many setbacks, Peterson _____ his _____ but not ambition.

8. In his report the economist stressed that the market _____ no _____ of recovery.

II. Study the following sentences taken from the passage and then paraphrase the underlined part in each sentence.

1. I'd like to start all over again as a freshman. (Lines 6–7)

2. I actually read all of *Don Juan* and have never gotten over how great it was. (Line 42)

3. I know I could get an A in that if I took it over. (Line 43)

4. I'm not going to break my back over them. (Lines 46)

5. I'd certainly want to go back over English grammar and usage. (Line 50)

1. I'd like to _____ as a freshman.

2. I actually read all of *Don Juan* and _____ how great it was.

3. I know I could get an A in that if I _____.

4. I'm not going to _____ over them.

5. I'd certainly want to _____ English grammar and usage.

III. Translate the following paragraphs into English.

1. 大學生活格外愉快。校園裡的年輕人們都在全力以赴地獲取知識。他們除了自己的學習，對其他事情無需負責。他們應該耐心地體會接受教育的過程，而不要急於去掙錢。他們應該知道，校園生活是在為他們走出校園去追求成功做準備。

_____

_____

_____

_____

2. 在一個不斷創新的世界，學位不能保證你擁有成功的事業。因此，發奮學習是人們普遍的做法。他們對終身學習態度積極。他們有些人回到學校，在那裡他們可以利用學習資源。有些人調換工作，以豐富

自己的工作閱歷。甚至在退休以後他們還會投入時間進行學習。

8.3 Practical Translation

科技英語的翻譯

　　科技英語是用來陳述自然界、科技界所發生或出現的事情，描述其規律、特點、過程等的語言，多採用客觀性的描述方式，要求概念準確、判斷嚴密、推理周密、結構嚴謹。它在詞法、語法、句法和修辭角度上都體現出自己的特點。

　　第一，在詞法上，科技英語強調語言的簡練和專業性，大量使用複合詞、縮略語和屬於某一專業領域的專業化詞彙。

　　例1：Space technology should be combined with civilian life to develop various high-tech products.

　　譯文：要將航天技術與民用生活相結合，開發出多種高科技含量的產品。

　　例2：DNA has a double helix structure, which was discovered by Francis Crick and James Watson in the Cavendish lab at Cambridge in 1953.

　　譯文：DNA（脫氧核糖核酸）的雙螺旋結構是由弗朗西斯·克里克和唐姆斯·沃森於1953年在劍橋的卡文迪許實驗室裡發現的。

　　解析：例1中，原語為了語言的簡練，high-technological 縮略成了 high-tech。在目標語中，為了強調客觀事實，原文的被動句譯成了漢語的無主句，符合漢語的句式特點。例2中，DNA 是專業詞彙，lab 是 laboratory 的縮略語，為了讓目標讀者看懂，在譯文中，DNA 要譯出完整的意思，而且被動句譯成了漢語的主動句，行文更流暢。

　　第二，在語法上，科技英語中的名詞化結構（nominalization）、一般現在時和被動語態用得較多。使用名詞化結構和一般現在時是因為科

技文體要求行文簡潔、表達客觀、內容確切、信息量大，強調已存在的事實，而非某一行為。運用被動語態是因為科技文章側重敘事推理，強調客觀準確性。第一、二人稱使用過多，會造成主觀臆斷的印象，因此盡量使用第三人稱敘述，採用被動語態。

例3：The greatest source of worry at the moment is the disposal of radioactive wastes. Until now these wastes have been packed in containers and buried in remote areas or dumped in the ocean.

譯文：現在最令人擔心的問題是放射性廢物的處理。到目前為止，這些廢物是用容器裝好，埋在邊遠地區或沉入海裡。

例4：The blood sugar level represents a balance between the amount of carbohydrate ingested or formed from protein and lipid, on the other hand, and the storage or utilization of carbohydrate, on the other.

譯文：攝入的或由蛋白質及脂肪轉化來的糖類與體內糖類貯存或利用這兩者之間的數量平衡，便是血糖水準的標志。

解析：例3和例4的兩個句子都符合科技英語的語法特點。為了表達客觀、內容確切，兩個句子都用了一些名詞化結構的詞彙，如例3的source of worry，disposal，例4的balance，storage，utilization。為了避免造成主觀推理和臆斷，強調客觀事實，兩個句子都採用了一般現在時和被動語態。而科技漢語最明顯的特點是多用無主句，語言平實，多採用客觀性描述方法，因此例3的譯文採用了直譯的翻譯方法，翻譯出了原文的內容，語言平實、客觀。例4譯文中，為了符合漢語的習慣，被動語態處理成漢語的無主句，而且英語句子多採用重心前置式，但漢語句子應採取重心後置式，因此在譯文中，把「血糖水準的標志」放在句子最後，從前面的分析出發，最後形成一個結論，句子結構銜接、連貫、合理。

第三，在句法上，科技英語使用大量的長句和複雜句，修飾、限定及附加成分多；注重銜接和連貫，注重邏輯的嚴密，以達到句子連貫、行文流暢的目的。

例5：We do not realize how much we depend on the earth's gravity until we are deprived of it, when our feet no longer stay on the ground, we float around in the air and the slightest touch may send us drifting off in the opposite direction.

譯文：我們只有在失去地球引力的時候，才意識到它對我們是多麼

的必不可少。那時候，我們將無法立足於地面，全都漂浮在半空中，哪怕是被輕輕一碰，我們都會朝著相反的方向飄移。

例6：Aluminum remained unknown until the 19th century, because nowhere in nature is it found free, owing to its always being combined with other elements, most commonly with oxygen, for which it has a strong affinity.

譯文：鋁總是和其他元素結合在一起，因為鋁對氧有很強的親和力，最常見的就是和氧結合在一起。因此，在自然界任何地方都找不到處於遊離狀態的鋁。由於這個原因，直到19世紀，鋁才為人們所知。

解析：例5和例6都是典型的英語長句和複雜句。為使句子邏輯嚴密、銜接連貫，在主幹結構SV（主語+謂語）之外，添加了很多修飾、限定和附加的成分。例5中有時間狀語從句、定語從句。例6中有時間狀語從句、原因狀語從句、定語從句。為了符合漢語行文的習慣，譯文作了兩個方面的調整。一是英語的長句，按照時間先後、先因後果的關係，切分成了漢語的兩個短句，句子短小，意思清楚，陳述客觀合理，漢語句子的「意合」特徵也更明顯。二是符合了漢語句子重心後置式的特點。在例6中，英語原文中的重心Aluminum remained unknown出現在句子開頭；而在譯文中，它被放在句子末尾，句式更加連貫、銜接和地道。

Translation Practice

Translate the following paragraphs into Chinese.

1. The heart is about the size of a fist, weighs about 9-11 ounces and is placed snugly between the lungs, a little more to the left than to the right.

2. The successful launching of China's first experimental communication satellite, which was propelled by a three-stage rocket and has been in operation ever since, indicates that our nation has entered a new stage in the development of carrier rockets and electronics.

3. Since the joint gap between a piston and a cylinder has great influence on the service life of an engine, and the primary factor influencing the joint gap is the deformation of piston under working condition, it is important to show up the actual deformation of piston and for this purpose the finite element has been widely applied to analyze it numerically in China.

8.4　Focused Writing

Memos

What is a memo?

Memo (short for memorandum) writing is something of an art form. A letter is not a memo, nor is a memo a letter. Memos vary in large measure in formality and complexity and have quite wide applications for both internal and external communication.

Companies use memos to announce policies, spread information, delegate responsibilities, instruct employees, and report the findings of a research or an investigation. Companies also rely on memos to keep employees informed about company goals, to persuade employees to take an action, or to build employee morale.

How is a memo laid out?

As with alt writing, memo writing needs a structure. Because they are short, rambling meanderings (閒聊) will soon destroy the memo's effectiveness and become a waste of productive time to those that read it and to the person who writes it. A memo should include the following information:

—A「To」section containing the name of the receiver. For informal memos, the receiver's given name. e. g.「To: Andy」is enough. For more formal memos, use the receiver's full name. If the receiver is in another department, use the full name and the department name. It is usually not necessary to use Mr., Mrs., Miss or Ms. unless the memo is very formal.

—A「From」section containing the name of the sender. Rear to the rule in the「To」section.

—A「Subject Heading」containing the subject of the memo. In other words, it tells the reader about what the memo is about in a few words.

—A「Date」section. To avoid confusion between the British and American date systems, write the month as a word or an abbreviation. e. g.「January」or「Jan.」.

—The message.

Unless the memo is a brief note, a well-organized memo message should contain the following sections.

* Situation—an introduction or the purpose of the memo.

* Problem (optional) —e. g. Since the move to the new office in Kowloon Bay, staff members have difficulty in finding a nearby place to buy lunch.

* Solution (optional) —e. g. Providing a microwave oven in the pantry (餐具室或食品儲藏室) would enable staff to bring in their own lunchboxes and reheat their food.

* Action—this may be the same as the solution, or be the part of the solution that the receiver needs to carry out. e. g. we would appreciate it if you could authorize up to $3,000.

These components should be positioned as below:

Memo

To:
From:
Subject:
Date:

_____
_____
_____
_____
_____

Writing Assignment

A professor of physics in your college has asked for the shifting of the physics laboratory to the ground floor of the building. The governing board of the college has agreed to this proposal. As president of the college, write a memo to the professor, giving details of the new laboratory: area, facilities, staff and funds sanctioned for the shifting.

Unit 9 Psychological Health

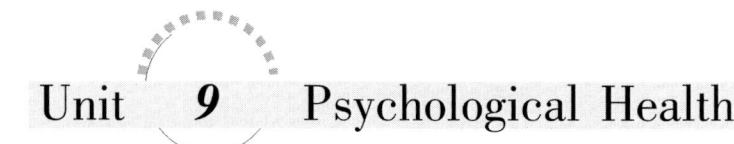

9.1 Get Started

Ⅰ. Your best friend has recently been in low spirits ever since she was diagnosed with COPD (慢性阻塞性肺病). She stays in bed most of the time and misses a lot of classes. She has nothing to do, and moreover wants to do nothing. How would you encourage her to cope with the disease with a positive attitude?

Ⅱ. Discuss the following questions with members of your group.

1. What kind of person do you think is a healthy person?

2. Where does pressure usually come from? Give examples.

3. Do you think that a working man is a happier, healthier man? Why or why not?

9.2 Read and Explore

Text A

A Working Man Is a Healthy Man

OK, you're only 30-year-old—or maybe even 40 or 50—and are already fantasizing about retiring. You've got the _____ (fill in the blank: stock options, trust fund, rich wife) in place and now the only question is when. What's the best time to devote yourself full-time to golf?

A dreadful thought, perhaps—particularly if working for a living has never agreed with you—but epidemiological analyses of every variety have long concluded that men who retire early don't live as long as men who keep working late into geezerhood. Given the opportunity to fill our days with nothing but recreational activity, we get in trouble—get beaned by a shanked golf ball, fall off a fishing boat after a beer, too many, that kind of thing.

Anything that removes us too much from the nurturing world of women is simply bad for our health. That's not to say that we don't suffer some ill effects from work. Men are the victims of more than 90 percent of all job-related accidents. Our highly competitive instincts also propel us to advance in our professions and climbing the ladder can be stressful (although interestingly, most CEO's are in excellent health; they're highly resilient, born leaders).

Any job in which the tasks are slightly beyond our reach is going to cause stress—along with the high blood pressure, depressed immunity and increased risk of cardiovascular disease. But, then, raising children is stressful. Unemployment is really stressful. Vacations can be stressful. Driving in Milan is even a nightmare.

The point is that, in terms of the picture? not working, whether by choice or not, is worse for us than working. This has always been true, but now there are some modern wrinkles on this truism that reflect changing gender roles.

Rewards of Success

Work is good for men—especially if the proper conditions are in place. For instance—and this is not likely to sit well with social egalitarians—men who are married to 「homemaker」 wives are more likely to have upwardly mobile careers. That's the conclusion of the Cornell University Retirement and Well-Being Study, which also found the converse to be true: Men married to women who work full-time are more likely to have downwardly mobile careers. From other data, we know that a successful and accomplished man is a healthy and happy man.

A recent Scottish study also points to the effects changing gender roles are having on men's working life. The increased number of women in both part-time and full-time work, the researchers say, may indirectly be responsible for rising rates of suicide and depression in men, at least in the British Isles. For men, the resultant loss of status as sole financial provider for the family and the perceived loss of social status could all be risk factors for depression.

Family life also affects the benefits a man obtains from work. After having a baby, American men work longer hours, particularly if the child is a boy.

「We can only guess that having a son increases the value of marriage and family for men,」says Shelly Lundberg, a psychologist at the University of Washington, an economics professor who did the research. Using data from the US Panel Study of Income Dynamics, he found that the birth of a first son generated an average increase in a man's work time of 84 hours every year after the boy's 40 birth—the equivalent of more than two additional weeks on the job. Men added only 31 hours after having a daughter. They also discovered a 「fatherhood premium」that raised men's hourly wages by about 5 percent every time they fathered a child.

Retirement

Research repeatedly has shown that a working family man with more disposable income is a happier, healthier man.

Still not convinced? The findings of people who study retirement suggest some good reasons not to retire. For one thing, newly retired men experience more marital conflict than non-retired men. Your wife simply finds it stressful to wonder whether you've been beaned by a golf ball or bobbing in the ocean next to your empty beer can.

The good news is that you can regain whatever you may have lost by retiring—and then going back to work. Psychologists Jungmeen E. Kim and Phyllis Moen of Cornell found that men who retire often gain a new lease on life when they decide to go back to work.

「Post-retirement employment appears to be beneficial for their psychological well-being,」says Kim. Those who are retired and re-employed report the highest morale and lowest depression. And men who are retired and not re-employed experience the lowest morale and most depression.

Their study of 534 married men and women between 50 and 74 found the work. status links to morale and depression were regardless of age, income and health.

So suck it up, buddy, and plan to work until you drop. It's one prescription for longevity that is known to work.

Words and Expressions

1. fantasize v. 幻想，想像
2. epidemiological adj. 流行病學的
3. longevity n. 長壽；壽命
4. propel vt. 推進；推動；驅動；驅使
5. resilient adj. 能復原的；彈回的，有彈性的
6. immunity n. 免疫力
7. cardiovascular adj. 心血管的
8. egalitarian n. 平等主義；平等主義者
9. suicide n. & vt. 自殺
10. premium n. 保險費；額外費用；附加費
11. convince vt. 使相信，說服，使承認
12. marital adj. 婚姻的，夫妻（間）的
13. bobbing vt. 使上下（或來回）快速擺動
14. morale n. 士氣；精神面貌
15. prescription n. 處方藥

Notes

1. The US Panel Study of Income Dynamics (PSID): A longitudinal survey of a representative sample of US individuals and families. It has been ongoing since 1968. The data were collected annually through 1997, and biennially starting in 1999. The data files contain the flail span of information collected over the course of the study. PSID data can be used for cross-sectional, longitudinal, and intergenerational analysis and for studying both individuals and families.

Content Awareness

Ⅰ. Choose the best answer to each question with information from the passage.

1. In the sentence (Para. 1)「… now the only question is when」, here「when」means ＿＿＿＿＿.

   A. when to devote yourself full-time to golf

B. when to marry a rich wife

C. when to retire

D. when to have a vacation

2. Men who keep working late into geezerhood _____.

    A. usually work for a living

    B. usually don't like recreational activities

    C. usually get into trouble

    D. can live longer than men who retire early

3. Work is good for men because _____.

    A. all working men are healthy and happy

    B. men who are married to 「homemaker」 wives are more likely to have upwardly mobile careers

    C. more women coming to work may lead to the rising rates of suicide and depression in men

    D. raising children and housekeeping are stressful for men

4. Which of the following statements isn't the good reason for not to retire?

    A. Family life affects the benefits a man obtains from work.

    B. You can regain whatever you may have lost by retiring.

    C. You can devote yourself to golf.

    D. Men should work to support the family.

5. Which statement is not true according to the passage?

    A. We don't suffer any ill effects from work.

    B. A successful and accomplished man is a healthy and happy man.

    C. Newly retired men experience more marital conflict than non-retired men.

    D. Men who retired early experience the lowest morale and most depression.

II. Answer the following questions with information from the passage.

1. What thought is dreadful according to the author?

_____

_____

2. What will happen if we fill our days with nothing but recreational ac-

tivities?

3. In what way do we suffer some ill effects from work?

4. What other things also cause stress besides work?

5. What kind of men are more likely to have downwardly mobile careers?

6. Can you give us an example about「A working man is a healthy man」?

Language Focus

Ⅰ. Fill in the blanks with the words given below. Change the form where necessary.

| recreation | victim | propel | depress | finance |
| devote | nothing | conclude | regardless | benefit |

1. Black is a cunning man, but he has finally become a(n) _____ of his own behavior.

2. They feared that rising inflation would further _____ the economy.

3. We should _____ ourselves assiduously and faithfully to the duties of our profession.

4. The jury _____, from the evidence, that she was guilty.

5. In the Mediterranean, there is a temperate climate _____ to health.

6. You can't accept _____ drug use and expect to control the drug problem.

7. John is a person _____ by ambition.

8. Many computer software corporations are experiencing _____ reverses.

9. Don't worry about my illness; what I need is _____ but a day's rest.

10. We will persevere _____ of past failures.

Ⅱ. Complete the following sentences with words or expressions from the passage. Change the form where necessary.

1. Inventors are now working on new devices that would be fully placed, _____ a tiny power pack, in the patient's chest.

2. I quite _____ what you said, though I don't believe that you can put it into practice.

3. Which sport has the most expenses _____ training equipment, players' personal equipment and uniforms?

4. The doctor was asked to _____ the hospital because of an emergency case.

5. Beverage companies should _____ collecting and recycling discarded plastic bottles and cans.

Ⅲ. Each of the verbs and nouns in the following lists occurs in Passage A. Choose the noun that you think collocates with the verb and write it down in the blank.

Verbs	Nouns
1. raise _____	wages
2. increase _____	roles
3. experience _____	an opportunity
4. give _____	children
5. climb _____	stress
6. cause _____	value
7. change _____	conflict
	a ladder

Ⅳ. Translate the following paragraph into Chinese.

Psychological health and well-being should not be confused with the question of whether or not you suffer from mental or emotional disorder. The research on well-being concerns itself with the feelings of normal individuals, or subjects from the general population. When we talk about psychological health, we are referring to how ordinary people are doing in life. In other words, if you are feeling distressed, that doesn't necessarily mean that you are mentally ill. Psychological health concerns itself with how you cope, how you are doing in response and whether you find life to be interesting and enjoyable.

_____

_____

_____

_____

_____

Text B

Spiritual Laws
by *Ralph Waldo Emerson*

When the act of reflection takes place in the mind—when we look at ourselves in the light of thought, we discover that our life is embosomed in beauty. Behind us, as we go, all things assume pleasing forms, as clouds do far off. Not only things familiar and stale, but even the tragic and terrible, are comely, as they take their place in the pictures of memory. The river-bank, the weed at the water-side, the old house, the foolish person, —however neglected in the passing—have a grace in the past. Even the corpse that has lain in the chambers has added a solemn ornament to the house. The soul will not know either deformity or pain. If, in the hours of clear reason, we should speak the severest truth, we should say, that we had never made a sacrifice. In these hours the mind seems so great, that nothing can be taken from us that seems much. All loss, all pain, is particular; the universe remains to the heart unhurt. Neither vexations nor calamities abate our trust. No man ever stated his grieves as lightly as he might. Allow for exaggeration in the most patient and sorely ridden hack that ever was driven. For it is only the finite that has wrought and suffered; the infinite lies stretched in smiling repose.

The intellectual life may be kept clean and healthful, if man will live the life of nature, and not import into his mind difficulties which are none of his. No man need be perplexed in his speculations. Let him do and say what strictly belongs to him, and, though very ignorant of books, his nature shall not yield him any intellectual obstructions and doubts. Our young people are diseased with the theological problems of original sin, origin of evil, predestination, and the like. These never presented a practical difficulty to any man, — never darkened across any man's roa, who did not go out of his way to seek them. These are the soul's mumps, and measles, and whooping-coughs, and those who have not caught them cannot describe their health or prescribe the cure. A simple mind will not know these enemies. It is quite another thing that he should be able to give account of his faith, and expound to another the theory of his self-union and freedom. This requires rare gifts. Yet, without this self-knowledge, there may be a sylvan strength and integrity in that which he is. ⌈A few strong instincts and a few plain rules⌋ suffice us.

My will never gave the images in my mind the rank they now take. The regular course of studies, the years of academic and professional education, have not yielded me better facts than some idle books under the bench at the Latin School. What we do not call education is more precious than that which we call so. We form no guess, at the time of receiving a thought, of its comparative value. And education often wastes its effort in attempts to thwart and balk this natural magnetism, which is sure to select what belongs to it.

In like manner, our moral nature is vitiated by any interference of our will. People represent virtue as a struggle, and take to themselves great airs upon their attainments, and the question is everywhere vexed, when a noble nature is commended, whether the man is not better who strives with temptation. But there is no merit in the matter. Either God is there, or he is not there. We love characters in proportion as they are impulsive and spontaneous. The less a man thinks or knows about his virtues, the better we like him. Timoleon's victories are the best victories: which ran and flowed like Homer's verses, Plutarch said. When we see graceful, and pleasant as roses, we must thank a soul whose acts are all regal, God that such things can be and are, and not turn sourly on the angel, and say, 「Crump is a better man with his grunting resistance to all his native devils.」

Not less conspicuous is the preponderance of nature over will in all practical life. There is less intention in history than we ascribe to it. We impute deep-laid, far-sighted plans to Caesar and Napoleon; but the best of their power was in nature, not in them. Men of an extraordinary success, in their honest moments, have always sung, 「Not unto us, not unto us.」 According to the faith of their times, they have built altars to Fortune, or to Destiny. Their success lay in their parallelism to the course of thought, which found in them an unobstructed channel; and the wonders of which they were the visible conductors seemed to the eye their deed. Did the wires generate the galvanism? It is even true that there was less in them on which they could reflect, than in another; as the virtue of a pipe is to be smooth and hollow. That which externally seemed will and immovableness was willingness and self-annihilation. Could Shakespeare give a theory of Shakespeare? Could ever a man of prodigious mathematical genius convey to others any insight into his methods? If he could communicate that secret, it would instantly lose its exaggerated value, blending with the daylight and the vital energy the power to stand and to go.

The lesson is forcibly taught by these observations, that our life might be much easier and simpler than we make it; that the world might be a happier place than it is; that there is no need of struggles, convulsions, and despairs, of the wringing of the hands and the gnashing of the teeth; that we miscreate our own evils. We interfere with the optimism of nature; for, whenever we get this vantage-ground of the past, or of a wiser mind in the present, we are able to discern that we are begirt with laws which execute themselves.

Words

1. comely adj. <文>英俊的，好看的
2. deformity n. 缺陷（道德等方面的）；畸形的人（或物）
3. abate v. 減少，減輕
4. expound vt. 解釋，詳細講解
5. sylvan adj. 森林的，林木的；鄉村的
6. thwart vt. 阻撓；挫敗；使受挫折

7. vitiate v.（使）削弱；（使）破壞；（使）損害

8. preponderance n. 數量上的優勢

9. impute vt. 把（錯誤等）歸咎於

10. self-annihilation n. 自我消滅（在對神默禱中的）

11. prodigious adj. 異常的，驚人的；巨大的，龐大的；奇異的；非常的

12. conspicuous adj. 明顯的；顯而易見的；惹人注意的；顯目

13. galvanism n. 流電，電療法，流電學

14. immovableness n. immovable 的變形，不動的事物

16. begirt v. 圍繞，縛，以帶子纏繞（begird 的過去式和過去分詞）

17. gnash v. 磨咬（牙）

18. convulsion n.［醫］抽搐；大笑；震動；動亂

19. wring n. 緊緊握手；劇痛

20. execute vt. 執行；完成；履行

Notes

1. When the act of reflection takes place in the mind, when we look at ourselves in the light of thought, we discover that our life is embosomed in beauty. →When we reflect, when we think over ourselves, we find that our life is filled with beauty.

2. Not only things familiar and stale, but even the tragic and terrible, are comely, as they take their place in the pictures of memory. →When we vision the things in our mind's eye, not only the familiar old things but also the tragic and terrible things are pleasing and attractive.

3. in the hours of clear reason→when we are clear-minded.

4. . All loss, all pain, is particular; the universe remains to the heart unhurt. →All loss, all pain, is a single case; the universe remains intact in our hearts.

5. For it is only the finite that has wrought and suffered; the infinite lies stretched in smiling repose. →For work and suffering are limited; tranquility with smiles extends without bounds.

6. The intellectual life may be kept clean and healthful, if man will live the life of nature, and not import into his mind difficulties which are none of

his. →The intellectual life may be kept pure and healthful, if man will live the natural life, and will not bother his mind with difficulties that do not involve him.

7. Let him do and say what strictly belongs to him, and, though very ignorant of books, his nature shall not yield him any intellectual obstructions and doubts. →Let him do and say what is literally his, and, though having no idea of books, his nature will not produce him any obstacle or doubt in thoughts.

8. These never presented a practical difficulty to any man, —never darkened across any man's road, who did not go out of his way to seek them. →If a man did not make special efforts to seek the theological problems, the problems would never be a practical difficulty to him, and would never cast shadows over his road.

9. These are the soul's mumps, and measles, and whooping-coughs, and those who have not caught them cannot describe their health or prescribe the cure. → The theological problems are soul's mumps, and measles, and whooping-coughs, and those who have not ever been down with these soul's diseases cannot describe their health or make a prescription.

10. The regular course of studies, the years of academic and professional education, have not yielded me better facts than some idle books under the bench at the Latin School. →The regular course of studies, the years of formal and professional education, have not given me better facts than what I have learned from some insignificant books at the Latin School.

11. We form no guess, at the time of receiving a thought, of its comparative value. →When receiving a thought, we do not guess about its comparative value.

12. ... in attempt to thwart and balk this natural magnetism... →... in making every effort to prevent and stop this natural magnetism...

13. In like manner, our moral nature is vitiated by any interference of our will. →In the same way, our moral nature is impaired by any bother of our will. vitiate: weak; undermine.

14. People represent virtue as a struggle, and take to themselves great airs upon their attainments... →People describe virtue as a struggle, and ac-

quire a haughty pose for their accomplishments...

15. ... and the question is everywhere vexed, when a noble nature is commended, whether the man is not better who strives with temptation. →... and the question is debated here and there, that is, when a man with noble nature is approved, whether a man who is distracted by temptation is not better.

16. We love characters in proportion as they are impulsive and spontaneous. →The more passionate and unaffected people are, the more we love them.

17. Timoleon：提摩勒昂，希臘政治家和將軍。

Homer：荷馬，希臘史詩作者，創作了西方文學最偉大的兩部作品《伊利亞特》(The Iliad) 和《奧德賽》(The Odyssey)。

Plutarch：普盧塔克，古希臘傳記作家、散文家，最著名的作品是《希臘羅馬名人傳》(The Live of the Noble Grecians and Romans)。

18. Not less conspicuous is the preponderance of nature over will in all practical life. →The superiority of nature over will is also obvious in all practical life.

19. Their Success lay in their parallelism to the course of thought... → They succeeded because they acted in accordance with the course of thought...

20. ... which found in them an unobstructed channel... →They became smooth channels for the course of thought.

21. ... as the virtue of a pipe is to be smooth and hollow. →... as the property of a pipe is to be free from roughness and obstruction.

22. The lesson is forcibly taught by these observations, that our life might be much easier and simpler than we make it; that the world might be a happier place than it is: that there is no need of struggles, convulsions, and despairs, of the wringing of the hands and the gnashing of the teeth; that we miscreate our own evils. →The lesson is convincingly taught by these observations. The observations are that our life might be much easier and simpler than we make it; that the world might be a happier place than it is; that there is no need of struggles, paroxysms, and despairs; that there is no need of sorrow and anger; that we create our own evils by mistake.

gnash one's teeth：咬牙切齒，指人非常憤怒。

wring one's hands：緊握別人雙手，指人很抱歉、難過。

23. ... for, whenever we get this vantage-ground of the past, or of a wiser mind in the present, we are able to discern that we are begirt with laws which execute themselves. →... because, when we get the vantage of the past or get the vantage of a wiser mind in the present, we are able to perceive with intellect that we are encircled with laws that function by themselves.

24. Ralph Waldo Emerson (May 25, 1803—April 27, 1882) was an American essayist, philosopher, and poet, best remembered for leading the Transcendentalist movement of the mid 19th century. His teachings directly influenced the growing New Thought movement of the mid 1800s. He was seen as a champion of individualism and a prescient critic of the countervailing pressures of society.

Content Awareness

Ⅰ. People differ in their tastes for the flavors of life: some enjoy dynamic pace to find an exit of ambition in the social world and some tend to find stability and harmony in the tranquil nature. What kind of life do you like to have, a life full of struggles and successes, or a life lavished with peace and purity?

Ⅱ. Paraphrase the following sentences in your own words.

1. When the act of reflection takes place in the mind, when we look at ourselves in the light of thought, we discover that our life is embosomed in beauty.

2. These never presented a practical difficulty to any man, —never darkened across any man's road, who did not go out of his way to seek them.

3. We form no guess, at the time of receiving a thought, of its comparative value.

_____

4. We love characters in proportion as they are impulsive and spontaneous.

_____

5. Not less conspicuous is the preponderance of nature over will in all practical life.

_____

Language Focus

Ⅰ. For each blank in the following passage, choose the most suitable word from the following list of words. Each word can be used only once.

received   followed   means   contained   follows   arose

participate   elaborated   seasonal   feared   separated   accepted

There are many theories about the beginning of drama in ancient Greece. The one most widely _____ theory is that drama came out of ritual. The argument for this view goes as _____. In the beginning, human beings thought that the natural forces of the world, even the _____ changes, were not predictable, and they sought through various _____ to control these unknown and _____ powers. Those measures which appeared to bring good results were then kept and repeated until they became fixed rituals. Finally stories _____ which explained the mysteries of the rituals. As time passed some rituals were given up, but the stories, later called myths, remained and provided material for art and drama.

Those who believe that drama came out of ritual also argue that those rites _____ the seed of theater because music, dance, masks, and costumes were almost always used. Furthermore, a suitable place had to be provided for performances, and when the entire community did not _____, a clear division was usually made between the ⌈acting area⌋ and the ⌈auditorium⌋. In addition, there were performers, which were usually given by religious leaders. Wearing masks and costumes, they often performed as an actor might. Finally such dramatic representations were _____ from religious activities.

Another theory thought that drama came from the human interest in story telling. According to this view, tales are gradually _____. A closely related theory traces theater to those dances that are rhythmical and gymnastic or that are imitations of animal movements and sounds.

Ⅱ. Sentence Recasting: For each of the sentences below, write a new sentence as similar as possible in meaning to the original sentence. You are required to use the word given in capital letters without any alteration.

Example: He didn't turn up for the meeting yesterday. (FAILED)

Answer: He failed to turn up for the meeting yesterday.

1. The burglar alarm rang as soon as he climbed through the window. (HARDLY)

_____

2. If you had told me earlier, I would have avoided that date. (GIVEN)

_____

3. I haven't enjoyed myself so much for years. (SINCE)

_____

4. Whenever I go to that bank, there is a long line. (NEVER)

_____

5. He was going to join the local golf club. (INTENTION)

_____

9.3　Practical Translation

商務合同的翻譯

商務合同是一種特殊的應用文體，其文體屬於莊嚴文體（the frozen style），在用詞、句法結構、文體和行文方式方面都有其自身的特點和要求。

一、用詞準確明晰、嚴謹統一

商務合同需要將合同雙方的意願清晰地表達出來，首先要考慮語言的明晰性。合同文本中的詞語是合同文本最基本的單位，對某些關鍵詞

的疏忽或望文生義，可能會對合同的履行造成重大法律責任或經濟損失，所以為了盡可能把一切都寫得準確無疑，作者往往會不惜筆墨重複名詞或修飾詞，盡量避免代詞或省略手段的使用，而且盡可能考慮到同義詞和近義詞之間的細微差異。

例1：Nothing herein contained shall prevent a carrier or a shipper from entering into any agreement, stipulation, condition, reservation or exemption as to the responsibility and liability of the carrier or the ship for the loss or damage to, or in connection with, the custody and care and handling of the goods prior to the loading on, and subsequent to, the discharge from the ship on which the goods are carried by sea.

譯文：本公約中的任何規定，都不禁止承運人或托運人就承運人或船舶對海運貨物在裝船前或卸貨後的保管、照料和搬運或與之有關的義務，以及貨物的丟失或損害的責任，訂立任何協議、規定、條件、保留或免責條款。（中國翻譯：2006.11）

解析：這裡的 agreement, stipulation, condition, reservation or exemption 都有「協議條款」的意思，responsibility 和 liability 是同義詞，都有「責任」的意思，但它們的含義都有細微差別。翻譯時，要充分發掘和窮盡它們之間的細微差別，不惜重複，翻譯出每一個詞的意思，使譯文沒有遺漏。

二、文體正式，多古體慣用詞、拉丁語詞語及拉丁詞源詞語

商務合同的權威性和規範性要求它的文體要莊嚴、行文要嚴肅，不可使用俚語、俗語等鬆散拖沓的句子。而許多古體慣用詞、拉丁語詞語及拉丁詞源詞語的使用能夠表明商務合同文中的先後順序、因果關係，能使語言顯得更加莊嚴和明確。

例2：This Agreement is made by and entered into between China National Import & Export Corporation (hereinafter referred to as Party A) and American Smith Wells Corporation (hereinafter referred to as Party B), whereby Party A agrees to appoint Party B to act as its sole distributor for the under-mentioned commodity (ies) in the designated territory on the terms and conditions set forth below.

譯文：本協議由中國進出口公司（以下簡稱甲方）與美國斯密斯·威爾斯公司（以下簡稱乙方）擬定並訂立。據此甲方同意委託乙方在指定的地區內按如下條例任甲方為下述商品的獨家經銷商。

解析：在原文中，hereinafter，whereby 都是英文古體詞，這種古體詞頻繁出現在商務合同中，顯示出商務合同的正式性和規範性。這些古體詞都能在漢語中找到相對應的詞，如 hereinafter 譯為「以下」或「在下文中」，whereby 譯為「據此」或「憑那個」，具體翻譯成哪個就要根據上下文的邏輯關係確定了。這些古體詞通常是一些合成詞，由 here，there，where 加介詞構成，如：herein（於此，在這裡），hereof（於此，關於這點），thereof（關於，在其中），thereon（在其上，關於），whereupon（於是，因此），wherewith（以其）等。

例 3：No party or anyone acting on its behalf shall have any ex parte communication relating to the case with any candidate for presiding arbitrator.

譯文：當事人或當事人的任何代理人不得就案件與任何首席仲裁員候選人進行單方聯繫。

解析：因為拉丁詞語具有言簡意賅、約定俗成、表達更準確的特點，商務合同中經常出現拉丁語。在這個例子中，ex parte 就是一個拉丁詞語，表示「單方的，片面的」的意思，體現了嚴謹準確的含義。出現在商務合同中的拉丁語還有 bona fide（真正的，現任的），ex officio（依職權的，由於其職權地），inter alia（尤其，特別），per se（本身，就本身而論）。

三、格式化結構和表達方式

商務合同作為一種應用文體，有一些格式化的可套用的句式或結構。

例 4：It shall be subject to ratification or acceptance by the signatory States.

譯文：本公約須經簽字國批准或接受。

例 5：Each Contracting State undertakes to adopt, in accordance with its Constitution, such measures as are necessary to ensure the application of this Convention.

譯文：各成員國均有義務按照其憲法採取確保本公約實行的必要措施。

例 6：Provided that the enterprises are still able to repay the debts, *Measures for Liquidation of Enterprise with Foreign Investment* shall govern.

譯文：如企業仍有債務償還能力，應按《外商投資企業清算辦法》進行非破產清算。

解析：例 4 中的 be subject to（以……為條件，受……制約），例 5 中的 in accordance with（依據，按照），例 6 中的 provided that（倘若，假如）都為合同中約定俗成的格式化的表達結構，體現了商務合同的正式性。而例 4 中的 shall 是商務合同中使用頻率最高的特殊表達方式，它含有「本條款具有法律規定的指令性和強制性」之意，其含義相當於 must，但合同中不使用 must 一詞，都用 shall 代替。

商務合同具有很強的專業性，為了避免產生歧義，避免產生不必要的糾紛，商務合同的翻譯必須把「準確嚴謹」（faithfulness & accuracy）作為首要原則，因此商務合同的翻譯不同於其他文體的翻譯，不講究文採韻味，只要求準確嚴謹地反應當事人的意思和合同雙方所限定的責任、權利及義務。

商務合同翻譯的第二個標準是「通順和完整」（smoothness & wholeness）。合同文本是一種法律文件，屬於莊嚴性文體，經雙方當事人簽字後就對雙方當事人形成法律約束力，成為有效的合同。因此為了保證文本的有效性和真實性，商務合同的翻譯強調通順和完整的原則，不僅在詞語翻譯方面，而且在句式處理方面都要滿足這些要求，並充分符合漢語的行文習慣。

例 7：Should one of the parties to the contract be prevented from executing contract by force majeure, such as earthquake, typhoon, flood, fire, and war and other unforeseen events, and their happening and consequences are unpreventable and unavoidable, the prevented party shall notify the other party by cable or fax without any delay, and within fifteen days thereafter provide the detailed information of the events and a valid document for evidence issued by the relevant public notary organization for explaining the reason of its inability to execute or delay the execution of all or part of the contract.

譯文：由於地震、臺風、水災、火災、戰爭以及其他不能預見並且對其發生和後果不能防止或避免的不可抗力事件，影響任何一方履行合同時，遇有上述不可抗力的一方，應立即用電報、傳真通知對方，並應在十五天內提供不可抗拒力詳情及合同不能履行或者部分不能履行，或者需要延期履行的理由的有效證明文件，此項證明文件應由不可抗拒力發生地區的公證機關出具。

解析：這個例子的原文很長，共 97 個字，是一個完整的長句。長句中不僅出現了法語詞 force majeure，古體詞 thereafter，而且出現了商

務合同中的特殊表述方式 shall，體現了文本內容的先後關係和語言的莊嚴和明確，用詞準確、嚴謹，而且為了明確反應合同雙方的責任、權利及義務，不惜筆墨地採用了繁復和冗長的句式結構。翻譯時，文本中的每一個詞都得到了準確和完整的翻譯，沒有疏忽和遺漏之處。句式結構方面，為了符合漢語的行文需要，一個長句被處理成了幾個意思完整、句式連貫的句子，並運用了「並」「或者」等連接詞，做到了譯文的嚴謹、準確、通順以及完整。

Translation Practice

Translate the following paragraph into Chinese.

1. In accordance with the Law of the People's Republic of China on Joint Venture Using Chinese and Foreign Investment and other relevant Chinese laws and regulations, both parties agree to set up a joint venture limited liability company (hereinafter called the joint venture company).

2. A member shall, ex officio if its legislation so permits or at the request of an interested party, refuse or invalidate the registration of a trademark which contains or consists of a geographical indication with respect to goods not originating in the territory indicated, if use of the indication in the trademark for such goods in that Member is of such nature as to mislead the public as to the true place of origin.

9.4　Focused Writing

Meeting Minutes

What are the minutes of a meeting?

The minutes of a meeting are the official written record of the proceedings of a business meeting or any formal meeting. The minutes provide a written record of the decisions made during the meeting, evidence of the decision-making process and also usually indicate who is responsible for ensuring that the decisions are carried out. Over a period of time they provide a history of the company's actions and can therefore be a guide for further actions.

What is included in the minutes of a meeting?

In general, the minutes should provide the following information:

· the name of the group or committee holding the meeting;

· the time, date and venue of the meeting;

· the people present (The number of the attendees and their names, usually only when the number is fewer than 10);

· absentees (The names of people who would normally attend but are absent on this occasion);

· the name of the chairperson (You may write: 「The meeting was called to order by Mr. (or Ms.) X at Y o'clock.」);

· minutes of last meeting (Indicate whether the minutes of the previous meeting were read and approved as a true record or amended and whether they were accepted);

· reports (Summarize any reports delivered and any key action taken on them, e. g. acceptance, approval, endorsement, referral, etc.);

· discussions (Record the main discussion of each item on the agenda of the meeting along with the names of people speaking);

· decisions (Write down any decisions made at the meeting and the name of the person responsible for carrying out each decision and the deadlines set for each action. For example, 「Tina Brown agreed to investigate the cost of double glazing the offices and will report by May 30th, 2009.」);

· record of any announcements including the date of the next meeting (For example, 「The next meeting was scheduled to be held at 9:00 a. m. on January 12th.」);

· adjournment (Indicate at what time the meeting ended: 「The meeting was adjourned at 11:30 a. m.」).

Which points should be noted when writing the minutes of a meeting?

There are a number of points to note when writing the minutes of a meeting.

1. Use the past tense because minutes are a record of a meeting that has already taken place. The only exception to this rule is when recording resolutions: They are written in the present tense because they have not happened

yet but will in the future.

2. Use indirect speech when recording attendees' words.

3. The words 「to move」 and 「a motion」 are sometimes used in minutes to refer to 「to propose」 and 「a proposal」 respectively. For example, you may write, 「*He moved that...*」 or 「*X proposed the motion that...*」 when an attendee proposes a new idea.

4. After a policy has been discussed and formally proposed, another attendee may second or question the motion. When the decision has been made, you may write: 「*The motion was proposed by X seconded by Y and passed unanimously*」 「*... passed with a majority vote of 7 to 4*」 「*... defeated*」 「*... tabled.*」

5. The word 「minutes」 is a noun in its plural form. For example, you could write 「*The minutes of the last meeting were approved as submitted.*」

6. Use formal language in a clear, concise and simple way without using pompous or stuffy vocabulary. Use the passive voice to describe events.

7. Do not attempt to write down every word that has been said. It is necessary to summarize what the attendees say but to do it honestly and not to include your own ideas, even if you disagree with the speaker.

8. The writer of the minutes should not make personal comments about the attendees.

9. The notes taken at the meeting should be written up formally as soon as possible after the meeting and are usually circulated to all attendees and interested parties.

10. The minutestaker's job is important and should not just be passed off to junior staff.

Sample

Lincoln Community Council
December 10th, 2009 Minutes
Bachman Hall

Present: George Bird, Dan Little, Tina Mabey, Marilyn Terry, Kathy Campbell, Jolene Denny, Larry Elder, Paula Williams

Call to Order

The meeting was called to order by Chair Marilyn Terry at 9:30 a.m.

Minutes of Last Meeting

The November 8th, 2009 minutes were amended and approved.

Report on Hall of Fame

    The committee reported back on assignments from the November 8th meeting for the Hall of Fame induction during Homecoming. Dan Little contacted Richard Ellis, George Bird contacted Danny Valentine and Jolene Denny contacted Richard Chase. All nominees agreed to be inducted and to attend the assembly, make a short speech and attend the football game on Homecoming Day, December 27th.

    Tina Mabey and Principal Campbell have talked with the students who will be preparing the videos of the inductees. They will need five or six pictures of each inductee to prepare the videos (including one recent photo for the plaque) and a narration introducing the inductees. The assigned committee members agreed to follow-up in getting pictures to the students and preparing a one-minute introduction. Tina will continue working with the students to be sure the videos are ready.

    George Bird reported that Brent Willey, formerly of the committee, agreed to prepare the certificates for framing and the plaques. Marilyn Terry will get the certificates from Brent and get them framed for presentation.

New Officer Elections

    MOTION: To elect Tina Mabey to chair the council Proposed by George Bird and seconded by Larry Elder. Vote was unanimous.

    MOTION: To elect Paula Williams as vice-chair to take and prepare minutes. Proposed by Dan Little and seconded by Jolene Denny. Vote was unanimous.

School Improvement Plan

    Principal Campbell briefed the council on the current School Improvement Plan and implementation, including the applicable test results. The council will discuss the new plan at the next meeting and were encouraged to consider possible changes to the current goals.

Announcement

    The next meeting was scheduled for Tuesday, January 5th, 2010 at 9:30 a.m.

Adjournment.

    There being no other issue to be discussed on hand, the chairman adjourned the meeting at 11:00 am.

Minutes prepared by Monica Stitt-Bergh

Writing Assignment

Suppose you are asked to Write the minutes for a committee meeting. The meeting was held at 9:00 o'clock on Wednesday, January, 6th, 2010, in the Conference Room. Prof. Li Ming (Chairman), Prof. Wu Jun, Associate Prof. Dong Zheng, Dr Wang Hong, Mr. Fang Rui and you (as a secretary) attended the meeting. The meeting approved the minutes of the previous meeting and discussed the following questions: whether to build a gym or not; the proposal to set up a Career Service Center; the announcement of new department chairs, time and location of the next meeting. The meeting ended at 11:00 o'clock.

Unit 10 Conflicts in the World

10.1 Get Started

1. What are the two men in the picture doing? How do you think the conflict can be resolved?

2. What's going on in the picture? Do you think it is possible that the world conflict would be resolved by a star war?

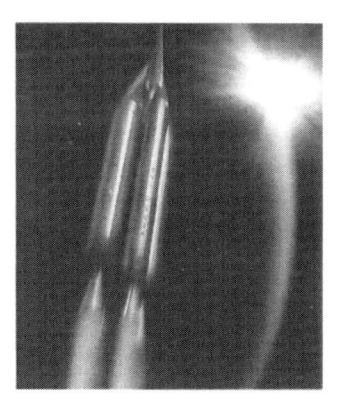

3. By what means do the masses express their opinions on the conflicts?

Ⅱ. Work with your partner and take turns to start the conversations.

Task 1

Situation: Two students are talking about the suicide bombings by Palestinians and Israel's retaliation they read about from the newspapers.

Role A: You find it difficult to understand the Palestinians' suicide attacks against Israeli civilians. Palestinians should stop such meaningless sacrifice of their own lives and the lives of innocent Israeli people.

Role B: You think that the Israeli government should also give up retaliating against innocent Palestinians because peace can only be brought about by reconciliation rather than retaliation.

Tips

Both sides are cutting off their own noses to spite their faces.

It's one thing to..., it's another to...

I can't understand why...

If only they could work together rather than...

suicide bombings, innocent civilians, come to terms with, peace talk...

Task 2

Situation: Two friends are talking about air travel after the September 11 incident.

Role A: You're scared by the terrorist attack and reluctant to fly in the future, believing that Similar incidents are certain to happen again if the root of terrorism is not eliminated.

Role B: You're not as pessimistic as your friend. You try to convince him/her that security against terrorists has been very tight, making air travel much safer now.

Tips:

I have to admit...

I'm kind of hesitant about

Their goal was to...

What are the chances of...

There's a big difference between... and...

terrorists' shadow of fear, hesitant, security measures, hijack...

10.2　Read and Explore

Text A

Yitzhak Rabin was elected Israel's prime minister in June 1992. He fought for peace and came into contact with states and politicians against whom he had fought numerous wars. The historic handshake between Yitzhak Rabin and Yasir Ararat marked the beginning of the peace process. Yitzhak Rabin's peace policy received broad support from the Israeli people, but it also enraged many who opposed compromise with the PLO. The following is Yitzhak Rabin's last speech, delivered at a peace rally in Tel Aviv on November 4, 1995. Moments later he was shot by a young Jewish student and died a martyr for peace.

Yes to Peace—No to Violence
by Yitzhak Rabin

Permit me to say that I am deeply moved.

I wish to thank each and every one of you who have come here today to take a stand against violence and for peace. This government, which I am privileged to head, together with my friend Shimon Peres, decided to give peace a chance—a peace that will solve most of Israel's problems.

I was a military man for 27 years. I fought as long as there was no chance for peace. I believe that there is now a chance for peace, a great chance. We must take advantage of it for the sake of those standing here, and for those who are not here—and they are many.

I have always believed that the majority of the people want peace and are ready to take risks for peace. In coming here today, you demonstrate, together with many others who did not come, that the people truly desire peace and oppose violence.

Violence erodes the basis of Israeli democracy. It must be condemned and isolated.

This is not the way of the State of Israel. In a democracy there can be differences, but the final decision will be taken in democratic elections, as the 1992 elections which gave us the mandate to do what we are doing, and to continue on this course.

I want to say that I am proud of the fact that representatives of the countries with whom we are living in peace are present with us here, and will continue to be here: Egypt, Jordan, and Morocco, which opened the road to peace for us. I want to thank the President of Egypt, the King of Jordan, and the King of Morocco, represented here today, for their partnership with us in our march toward peace.

But, more than anything, in the more than three years of this Government's existence, the Israeli people have proven that it is possible to make peace, that peace opens the door to a better economy and society; that peace is not just a prayer.

Peace is first of all in our prayers, but it is also the aspiration of the Jewish people, a genuine aspiration for peace.

There are enemies of peace who are trying to hurt US, in order to torpedo the peace process.

I want to say bluntly, that we have found a partner for peace among the Palestinians as well: the PLO, which was an enemy, and has ceased to engage in terrorism. Without partners for peace, there can be no peace.

We will demand that they do thei r part for peace, just as we will do our part for peace, in order to solve the most complicated, prolonged, and emotionally charged aspect of the Israeli-Arab conflict: the Palestinian-Israeli conflict.

This is a course which is fraught with difficulties and pain. For Israel, there is no path that is without pain.

But the path of peace is preferable to the path of war.

I say this to you as one who was a military man, someone who is today Minister of Defense and sees the pain of the families of the IDF soldiers. For them, for our children, in my case for our grandchildren, I want this Government to exhaust every opening, every possibility, to promote and achieve a comprehensive peace. Even with Syria, it will be possible to make peace.

This rally must send a message to the Israeli people, to the Jewish people around the world, to the many people in the Arab world, and indeed to the entire world, that the Israeli people want peace, support peace.

For this, I thank you.

Words and Expressions

1. enrage vt. 激怒，使暴怒
2. martyr n. 烈士，殉道者
3. privilege vt. 給予……特權，特免
4. military adj. 軍事的；軍用的；討厭的；好戰的
5. democracy n. 民主政治；民主主義；民主國家；民眾
6. condemn vt. 譴責
7. mandate n. 授權；命令；委任
8. torpedo vt. 破壞
9. cease vt. 停止，終止，結束
10. prolong vt. 延長，拖延

Notes

1. Yitzhak Rabin: Israeli military and political leader who served as IDF Chief of Staff, diplomat, Minister of Defense and Prime Minister (1974-1977; 1992-1995) of the State of Israel. He was awarded the Nobel Prize for Peace in December 1994, along with Foreign Minister Shimon Peres and PLO Chairman Yasir Arafat.

2. Yasir Arafat: Leader of Al Fatah, and Arab group, and the Palestine Liberation Organization, both of which advocate the establishment of an inde-

pendent Palestinian state.

3. Shimon Peres: parliamentarian, Prime Minister (1984-1986; 1995-1996) and Foreign Minister (1986-1988; 1992-1995; 2001-2022) of the States of Israel.

Content Awareness

Ⅰ. Choose the best answer to each question with the information from the passage.

1. The peace-making process between Israel and Palestine started with _____.

  A. the election of Yitzhak Rabin as Israel's Prime Minister

  B. the speech made by Yitzhak Rabin at a peace rally

  C. the death of Yitzhak Rabin after he delivered his speech

  D. the historic meeting between Yitzhak Rabin and Yasir Arafat

2. Which one of the following statements is TRUE according to the passage?

  A. Egypt, Jordan and Morocco sent their representatives to the peace rally.

  B. The President of Egypt was present at the peace rally.

  C. The PLO leader Yasir Ararat was present at the peace rally.

  D. Shimon Peres held different opinions with Yitzhak Rabin.

3. Yitzhak Rabin decided to give up military actions mainly because _____.

  A. they caused too many deaths

  B. they didn't lead to peace

  C. they couldn't defend Israel

  D. they torpedoed Israel's economy

4. At the peace rally, Yitzhak Rabin sent a message to people around the world that _____.

  A. he was heading the Israeli government

  B. he believed differences could co-exist in a democracy

  C. he was determined to promote and achieve a comprehensive peace

  D. he was ready to relieve the pain of the families of the IDF soldiers

5. From the passage we can conclude that _____.
   A. Yitzhak Rabin was quite sure that peace was close at hand
   B. Yitzhak Rabin still doubted that peace could be made
   C. Yitzhak Rabin thought that violence was emotionally charged
   D. Yitzhak Rabin believed that there was a chance for peace

Language Focus

Ⅰ. Tick the choice in which the underlined part is closest in meaning to that of the sentence taken from the passage.

1. This government, which I am privileged to head, decided to give peace a chance. (Line 3)
   A. She came from a privileged background.
   B. Only the privileged few can afford private education.
   C. Margaret felt privileged to make a speech at the conference.

2. Violence erodes the basis of Israeli democracy. (Line 11)
   A. Repeated exposure of quality problems of milk has eroded public confidence in China's milk products.
   B. Airlines are worried that the rising prices of fuel would erode much of their earnings.
   C. Without the protection of plants, soil will gradually erode away.

3. It (Violence) must be condemned and isolated. (Line 11)
   A. The murderer was condemned to death after a trial lasting a year and a half.
   B. Local authorities were condemned for failing to tackle the problem of homelessness.
   C. The meat was condemned as unfit for human consumption.

4. The 1992 elections which gave us the mandate to do what we are doing. (Line 13)
   A. If you want to recover, you've got to follow the doctor's mandate.
   B. What we have discussed at the meeting will not become a mandate automatically.
   C. The four-year mandate for the free use of the patent ends today.

5. I want to thank the President of Egypt, ... represented here today, for

their partnership with us in our march toward peace. (Line 18)

  A. You can't control the march of science and technology.

  B. I went on a lot of peace marches when I was a college student.

  C. She started work here last March.

6. Peace is not just a prayer. (Line 22)

  A. I went into the church and didn't see a prayer there.

  B. The trapped 33 miners, who didn't seem to have a prayer, were rescued after 69 days underground.

  C. The state governor started his speech with a prayer for rain.

7. It (Peace) is also the aspiration of the Jewish people, a genuine aspiration for peace. (Line 24)

  A. The campaign is motivated by a genuine concern for the disabled.

  B. The strap is made of genuine leather.

  C. She is the most genuine person I've ever met.

8. I want this Government to exhaust every opening, every possibility, to promote and achieve a comprehensive peace. (Line 41)

  A. Preparing for the wedding had exhausted my poor mother.

  B. Rescue workers will exhaust all means possible to rescue the people trapped by the fire.

  C. Use a pipe to exhaust the left gasoline in the tank before you check on it.

Ⅱ. Study the collocations with peace in the passage and paraphrase each of them. The first one has been done for you as an example.

1. to take a stand for *peace* (Line 2)

Paraphrase: to choose to defend peace

2. no chance for *peace* (Line 5)

Paraphrase: _____

3. to take risks for *peace* (Line 9)

Paraphrase: _____

4. to desire *peace* (Line 10)

Paraphrase: _____

5. to open the road to *peace* (Line 17)

Paraphrase: _____

6. our march toward *peace* (Line 19)

Paraphrase: _____

7. to make *peace* (Line 21)

Paraphrase: _____

8. a genuine aspiration for *peace* (Line 24)

Paraphrase: _____

9. to do their part for *peace* (Line 31)

Paraphrase: _____

10. the path of *peace* (Line 37)

Paraphrase: _____

Ⅲ. Translate the following paragraphs into English.

我衷心地感謝所有今天到場和因種種原因無法到場的人們，感謝你們堅決地反對恐怖主義和捍衛和平。當世界發展到今天這個階段，我們比以往任何時候都更渴望消除恐怖主義並擁有和平。為了我們自己，也為了我們的子孫和整個人類，讓我們盡一切可能來促進和實現全面和平。

_____

_____

_____

_____

Text B

The Need for Handgun Control

by *Edward M. Kennedy*

The wounding of President Reagan has stunned the world and stirred a vast reaction. Yet he is only the most famous casualty of an endless guerrilla war inside this country waged with a growing arsenal of handguns in the wrong hands. Every day others less famous are wounded or killed; their families worry and suffer. They weep and, too often, they mourn.

Every 50 minutes an American is killed by a handgun; 29 Americans who are alive today will be shot dead tomorrow. In the streets of our cities, the arms race of Saturday-night specials and cheap handguns will take 10,000 lives this year and will threaten or wound another 250, 000 citizens. In the past year alone, we have seen a 13 percent rise in violent crime, the greatest increase in a decade.

Today the clear and present danger to our society is the midnight mugger and the deranged assassin. And their weapons are as close as the nearest pawnshop. There are 55 million handguns in circulation. The lethal number rises by two and a half million each year.

The shooting of President Reagan was frightening, but not surprising. Are we now too accustomed to the repeated carnage of our national leaders? Are we ready to accept the neighborhoods of our cities as permanent free-fire zones? That sort of fatalism insures more fatalities.

But handgun control is hardly the whole answer to lawlessness. That is why we must adopt other measures as well.

We can, and we must, set more stringent conditions on bail, because no suspect charged with violent crime should be free to rape or to rob again. We can, and we must, demand that juveniles who shoot, stab and assault should not be allowed to misuse their youth as an automatic excuse for their offenses. We can, and we must, provide sufficient resources for law enforcement. No police officer should ever have to jeopardize his life for a subsistence salary that cannot support his family.

All of this is important—but none of it is enough. In the truest sense, law enforcement is part of our national defense. And in the effort to defend ourselves, we must not duck the question of gun control. No sane society should stand by while its enemies arm themselves—whether those enemies are adversaries abroad or criminals and assassins at home.

Crime control means gun control. This is not an easy issue for any officeholder or candidate. In 1980, in the presidential primaries. I constantly met voters who opposed me because they thought I favored confiscation of hunting rifles, shotguns and sporting pistols. It was not true, but it was believed—because the gun lobby had repeated it over and over.

Other senators and representatives faced a similar assault in 1980. The political action committees opposing gun control spent $2.2 million for their candidates, while those on the other side had less than a tenth as much to contribute. That is why we cannot control the plague of handguns, even though two-thirds of the American people have favored such control ever since 1963.

Perhaps this latest tragedy will challengeus to put away past apprehensions and appeals which have treated handgun control as a sinister plot or a subversion of civil liberties. I hope we can now agree that the first civil liberty of all citizens is freedom from fear of violence and sudden death on the streets of their communities.

In this session of congress, I will join again with Rep. Peter Rodino (D-N. J.) to introduce a bill to control handguns. It will be a moderate bill. It will be a sensible bill. It is all I will seek on this issue—and it is something all Americans should be able to support.

All Americans, including sportsmen and hunters, should be able to support a ban on Saturday-night specials and cheap handguns. Those guns are not accurate beyond a range of 10 or 15 feet. They are meant to maim or kill another human being. Saturday-night specials can be purchased now because of a loophole in the law that allows their lethal parts to be imported from abroad, to be assembled and sold in this country. And last week, one of those weapons almost killed our President.

All Americans, including all liberals, should be able to support a mandatory minimum prison sentence for any felon who commits a crime with a handgun. And all Americans, including the National Rifle Association, should be able to support a waiting period for the purchase of handguns to prevent them from falling into the hands of criminals and psychopaths.

The question is not whether we will disarm honest citizens, as some gun lobbyists have charged. The question is whether we will make it harder for those who break the law to arm themselves.

Gun control is not an easy issue. But, for me, it is a fundamental issue. My family has been touched by violence; too many others have felt the same terrible force. Too many children have been raised without a father or a mother. Too many widows have lived out their lives alone. Too many people have died.

We all know the toll that has been taken in this nation. We all know the leaders of our public life and of the human spirit who have been lost or wounded year after year: My brother, John Kennedy, and my brother, Robert Kennedy; Medgar Evers, who died so that others could live free; Martin Luther King, the apostle of nonviolence who became the victim of violence; George Wallace, who has been paralyzed for nearly nine years, and George Moscone, the mayor of San Francisco who was killed in his office. Last year alone, we lost Allard Lowenstein and we almost lost Vernon Jordan. Four months ago, we lost John Lennon, that gentle soul who challenged us in song to 「give peace a chance」. We had two attacks on President Ford and now the attack on President Reagan.

It is unacceptable that all these good men have been shot down. They all sought, each in their own way, to make ours a better world. And, too often, too soon, their own world came to an end.

It is unacceptable that a man who has been arrested before, who has been apprehended carrying loaded guns through an airport security check, who apparently has psychiatric problems as well as a criminal record should be able to go to a pawnshop and buy a cheap handgun imported because of a loophole in the law, and then use that gun to attempt murder against the President of the United States.

It is unacceptable that there are states in the American union where the accused attacker of President Reagan could today buy another Saturday night special.

The day after Martin Luther King's assassination, Robert Kennedy said: 「The victims of violence are black and white, rich and poor, young and old, famous and unknown. They are, most important of all, human beings whom other human beings loved and needed. No one, no matter where he lives or what he does, can be certain who next will suffer from some senseless act of bloodshed. And yet it goes on, and on, and on, in this country of ours. Why?」

Thirteen years later, that same tragic question must be raised again.

It is for us to answer it. We must resolve that the next generation of Americans will not have to witness the carnage next time and ask— 「Why?」

Words

1. guerrilla n. 遊擊隊；遊擊戰；遊擊隊員

2. carnage n. 大屠殺，殘殺

3. deranged adj. 瘋狂的；神經錯亂的；混亂的

4. fatalism n. 宿命論；天數

5. jeopardize vt. 危及，損害；使陷入險境或受傷；使……遇險

6. confiscation n. 沒收，充公，徵用

7. apprehension n. 不安，憂慮，憂懼；理解（力），領悟，瞭解；拘捕

8. mandatory adj. 強制的；命令的；受委託的

9. apostle n.（基督教的）使徒；（改革運動的）倡導者

10. apprehend vt. 理解；憂慮

11. psychiatric adj. 精神病學的；精神病治療

12. loophole n. 漏洞

13. assassination n. 暗殺

Notes

1. Edward M. Kennedy：（born in 1932）the senior senator from Massachusetts, he is the youngest and only surviving son of Joseph and Rose Kennedy. For many years he had been considered one of the leaders of the Democratic Party. He is a strong advocate of gun control, and he published this essay in 1981, shortly after John Hinkley tried to kill former U. S. President Reagan.

2. The wounding of President Reagan has stunned the world and stirred a vast reaction→The wounding of President Reagan has greatly shocked the whole world and has provoked strong feelings.

stun：to surprise or upset someone so much that they do not react immediately.

e.g. The football player stunned the crowd with a last-minute goal.

stir：to make someone have a strong feeling or reaction.

e.g. Looking at the photographs stirred childhood memories of the long hot summers.

3. the arias race of Saturday-night specials → the competition to have more weapons like the Saturday-night specials.

Saturday-night specials → Saturday-night pistol, colloquial American English expression for the cheap handguns that are easily hidden.

4. the midnight mugger and the deranged assassin → those who attack or rob others at night and those dangerous, crazy, and mentally-ill guys who murder important people.

5. their weapons are as close as the nearest pawnshop → they can buy their weapons in the nearest pawnshop.

6. the lethal number → the number of this lethal weapon.

lethal: fatal, causing death or able to cause death.

7. Are we now too accustomed to the repeated carnage of our national leaders? → Are we now too used to the constant killing of the leaders of our Country?

be accustomed to → be used to; accepting sth. as normal or usual.

e.g. My parents are not accustomed to the hustle and bustle of life in New York.

This is not the kind of treatment I am accustomed to.

8. That sort of fatalism insures more fatalities. → The belief that there is nothing we could do about these handgun events will lead to more deaths.

9. set more stringent conditions on bail → set more strict conditions on the temporary release of an accused person.

(out) on bail → free until one's trial after someone has given a guarantee to pay an amount of money.

e.g. The accused was released on bail of $1,000. Yet he committed another crime while he was out on bail.

10. not be allowed to misuse their youth as an automatic excuse for their offenses → not be allowed to use their young age conveniently as an excuse for the crime they have committed.

11. to jeopardize his life for a subsistence salary that cannot support his family → to put his life in danger because of a meager salary that cannot support his family.

jeopardize: to risk losing or spoiling something important.

e.g. The security of the whole operation has been jeopardized by their carelessness.

12. duck the question→avoid the question.

duck: dodge, or to avoid something, especially a difficult and unpleasant duty.

e.g. At the press conference, Jack ducked a question about his involvement in the bank scandal.

13. No sane society should stand by while its enemies arm themselves→If the people in a society are normal and sensible, they should not do nothing about the increasing number of handguns possessed by their enemies.

stand by: to be present while something bad is happening but not take any action to stop it.

e.g. How can you just stand by and let him treat the dog like that?

14. presidential primaries→the primary election of the president. In the U. S., it refers to an election in which people in certain states vote to select party candidates for a future major election.

15. ... they thought I favored confiscation of hunting rifles... → they thought I support the idea of confiscating hunting rifles...

confiscate: officially take private property away from someone, usually as a punishment.

e.g. If you are caught smuggling goods into the country, you will probably be confiscated.

Miss Smith confiscated all our sweets.

16. the gun lobby→a group of people who try to influence politicians on the issue of guns.

17. the plague of handguns→large numbers of handguns are being used in our society and have caused great trouble and damage to the safety of our life and our property.

18. The latest tragedy will challenge us to put away past apprehensions and appeals which have treated handgun control as a sinister plot or a subversion of civil liberties. →Although handgun control has been thought of as a dark scheme or a deprivation of freedom, the wounding of President Reagan will force us to discard our past worries and appeals about handgun control,

for freedom from fear of violence and sudden death on the streets is the first civil liberty.

19. Rep. Peter Rodino (D-N. J.) →representative Peter W. Rodino (D-N. J.), a member of the Watergate Committee.

20. beyond a range of 10 or 15 feet→farther than a distance of 10 or 15 feet.

21. They are meant to maim or kill another human being. →These guns are used with an evil intention of wounding someone permanently or killing him.

22. loophole in the law→a way of avoiding something because the words of the law are not clear or are badly chosen.

23. liberals: those who support gradual political or social changes, as opposed to conservatives.

24. psychopath: a person who suffers from a severe mental or emotional disorder, esp. one who behaves in a violently aggressive way.

25. disarm honest citizens→make the good, law-abiding citizens to give up guns.

26. We all know the toll that has been taken... →We all know the number of people killed or injured by handguns...

toll: the number of deaths, casualties or injuries.

e.g. The death toll in the earthquake has risen to an alarming number.

The bombings took a heavy toll, killing hundreds of innocent citizens.

27. Martin Luther King: He was the leader of American Civil Rights Movement against racial segregation and was awarded Nobel Peace Prize in 1964. He was shot to death in Memphis Tennessee in 1968.

28. Allard Lowenstein: (1929-1980) a liberal democratic politician. Lowenstein was murdered in his Manhattan office on March 14, 1980, at age 51 by a deranged gunman, Dennis Sweeney.

29. Vernon Jordan: (born in 1935) a lawyer and business executive in the United States. He served as a close adviser to Former President Bill Clinton and has become known as an influential figure in American politics. On May 29, 1980, he was shot and seriously wounded outside the Marriott Inn in Fort Wayne, Indiana.

30. John Lennon: (1940-1980) best known as a singer, songwriter, poet and guitarist for The Beatles. His creative career also included the roles of solo musician, political activist, artist, actor and author. As half of the legendary Lennon-McCartney songwriting team, he heavily influenced the development of rock music, leading it towards more serious and political messages. On the night of December 8, 1980, Lennon was shot four times in the back (the fifth shot missed) in the entrance hallway of the Dakota by Mark David Chapman. Lennon had autographed a copy of Double Fantasy for Chapman earlier that same night. Give Peace a Chance is one of his famous songs.

31. It is unacceptable that all these good men have been shot down. →It is hard to accept such a fact that all the above mentioned good citizens have been either killed or paralyzed by handguns.

32. They all sought, each in their own way, to make ours a better world. →They all made effort to make our world a better one in their own different ways.

33. the American union→the United States of America.

34. We must resolve that the next generation of Americans will not have to witness the carnage next time... →We must make a definite decision that our younger generation will not witness the killing of perfectly good citizens by handguns...

Content Awareness

Ⅰ. Handguns and other firearms have a long tradition in American civilization. The right to bear arms is an American right featured in the second Amendment of the Constitution. But the amount of death and injury caused by handguns has increased as the ownership of handguns has risen. Should the U. S. citizens possess a gun for self-protection, or sporting purpose? Or should the U. S. government place a stricter ban on handguns? Discuss the gun control controversy as a public security issue and from the victim's perspective.

Ⅱ. Paraphrase the following sentences in your own words.

1. The wounding of President Reagan has stunned the world and stirred a vast reaction.

2. And their weapons are as close as the nearest pawnshop.

3. And in the effort to defend ourselves, we must not duck the question of gun control.

4. Too many widows have lived out their lives alone.

5. We all know the toll that has been taken in this nation.

Language Focus

Ⅰ. For each blank in the following passage, choose the most suitable word from the following list of words. Each word can be used only once.

disadvantage	matter	advantage	philanthropic
display	convincing	behavior	evolutionary
obtain	desperate	biological	finer

Altruism is the performance of an unselfish act. As a pattern of _____ this act must have two properties: it must benefit someone else and it must do so to the _____ of the benefactor. It is not merely a _____ of being helpful, it is helpfulness at a cost to yourself. Since human beings are animals whose ancestors have won the long struggle for survival during their _____ history, they cannot be genetically programmed to _____ true altruism. Evolution theory suggests that they must, like all other animals, be entirely selfish in their actions, even when they appear to be at their most self-sacrificing and _____. This is the _____, evolutionary argument and it is completely _____ as far as it goes but it does not seem to explain many of mankind's 「_____ moments」. If a man sees a burning house and inside it his small daughter, an old friend, a complete stranger, or perhaps a screaming kitten, he may, without pausing to think, dash headlong into the building and be badly burned in a _____ attempt to save a life.

Ⅱ. Sentence Recasting: For each of the sentences below, write a new sentence as similar as possible in meaning to the original sentence. You are required to use the word given in capital fetters without any alteration.

Example: He didn't turn up for the meeting yesterday. (FAILED)

Answer: He failed to turn up for the meeting yesterday.

1. The book was going to be published in a matter of weeks. (DUE)

_____

2. Are these two rooms the same size? (DIFFERENCE)

_____

3. What do you think of the new boss? (STRIKE)

_____

4. He thought I was a newcomer. (TOOK)

_____

5. I feel sure you will be able to pass the test. (CONFIDENCE)

_____

Ⅲ. Translate the following paragraphs into English.

恐怖主義從未停止濫殺無辜，在世界各地造成重大傷亡。恐怖災難幾乎每一週都在世界的某個地方發生。我們絕不會放棄與企圖破壞世界平靜生活的人作鬥爭，並迫使他們停止從事恐怖活動。抵制這種暴力行為是所有國家的利益所在，也一直是幾十年來聯合國議程上的重要問題。

_____

_____

_____

10.3　Practical Translation

廣告英語的翻譯

廣告作為信息的載體，與人們的生活密切相關。它通過各種各樣的介質，如報紙、雜誌、電視、廣播、網絡等進行傳播。無論廣告語最終以何種語言形式出現，它都具有一個特點，那就是鮮明的目的性，即說服顧客進行購買。而這種目的需要借助語言來實現，廣告就是語言的買賣（Advertising is a business of words.）。廣告語具有很強的感染力和表現力，能讓人記憶猶新、回味良久。廣告英語必須簡潔、形象、富於感染力，為了達到這個目的，簡明、易懂易記的選詞，充滿創造力的新詞，短小精悍、構思巧妙的佳句，各種修辭手法的匠心獨用對廣告的效力至關重要。

一、廣告英語的特點
1. 簡明、易懂易記的選詞，充滿創造力的新詞。
例1：Nike, just do it.（耐克）
譯文：耐克，想做就做。
例2：A diamond lasts forever.（戴比爾斯鑽石）
譯文：鑽石恆久遠，一顆永流傳。
這兩個廣告的原文和漢語譯文都用大眾化的通俗易懂的詞彙，沒有任何晦澀、深奧的詞語，消費者看得明明白白、清清楚楚，廣告的號召力很強。
例3：Give a Timex to all, to all a good Time.（天美時手錶）
擁有一塊天美時表，擁有一段美好時光。
例4：It is not just a battery, it's Duracell.（金霸王電池）
這不僅僅是電池，這是金霸王。
廣告英語中有時會出現一些新造的詞彙，這些新詞由我們所熟知的詞加上前後綴或將兩個詞創造性地組合而成。這樣的新詞使廣告具有獨特之處，並準確地傳達產品的獨特性能。例3中，Timex = Time + Excellent，既表述了這則廣告的主題是計時的手錶，又充分強調了表的計時準確的特點，使消費者在不經意間記住了產品和產品的特點。例4中，

Duracell＝Durable＋cell 也有異曲同工之妙，既強調了該種電池能量非常強大，而且鮮明地指出了這則廣告的主題是電池。

2. 短小精悍、構思巧妙的佳句。

例5：We lead. Others copy.（理光複印機）

譯文：我們領先，他人仿效。

例6：Take time to indulge!（雀巢冰激凌）

譯文：盡情享受吧！

廣告面向全體消費者，要讓消費者一看即明、牢記於心，就要求語言簡練，在句式上盡量避免使用複雜句，多用簡單句。廣告還帶有一定的訴求目的，敦促消費者做出積極的反應，並採取行動，因此廣告中祈使句也頻繁出現。例5由兩個簡單句組成，句子乾脆利落，不加任何修飾詞，但該產品的作用和領先程度一覽無餘。例6是祈使句，希望人們在繁忙的生活中抽出時間來享受生活，享受一切，包括享受冰激凌，它充分滿足了現代人的情感需求，消費者的內心被感動，也就會採取行動來享受這種產品。譯文採用了簡單句和祈使句，在形式上和內容上都完全對等。

例7：Where there is a way, there is a Toyota.（風電汽車）

譯文：車到山前必有路，有路必有豐田車。

例8：We take no pride and prejudice.（美國《時代》週刊 Time 雜誌廣告）

譯文：我們既不驕傲，也無偏見。

巧妙使用英語和漢語中耳熟能詳的句子來創造出新的句子，這也是廣告中常用的方法，這些構思巧妙的佳句能讓人迅速地記住這個廣告，也記住廣告所承載的產品。例7的英文廣告別出心裁地套用了 Where there is a will, there is a way 的句子，傳達了一種樂觀積極、永不言敗的生活態度，而譯文也恰到好處地套用了中國的一句諺語「車到山前必有路」。雖然「有路必有豐田車」有點誇張，但這則廣告形象地闡述了豐田汽車所承載的理念和它的受歡迎程度，也就暗含了它的卓越品質。例8的英文廣告巧妙地借用了奧斯汀的名著《傲慢與偏見》（*Pride and Prejudice*）的篇名，表明該雜誌所作的報導是公正、毫無偏見的，以此表明自己的不偏不倚，主持正義和公道。

3. 各種修辭手法的匠心獨用

借助修辭，可以提高廣告的感染力，達到打動消費者的目的。廣告

中運用的修辭手法很多，常見的有排比、擬人、比喻、雙關等。

例9：Money doesn't grow on trees. But it blossoms at our branches.（英國勞埃得銀行 Lloyd Bank）

譯文：錢長在樹上不行，但在我們這「行」就行！

英語廣告中的 branch 和 blossom 兩詞是雙關語。branch 一為字面含義，承接上句中的 trees，指「樹枝」；而更深一層的含義則為「銀行的分行、支行」。blossom 一詞也有兩層意思，一方面表示開花、枝繁葉茂；另一方面表示錢的增值。這個廣告的真正意圖是號召人們將錢存到勞埃得銀行，在那裡錢會不斷增值。

例10：Apple Thinks Different.（蘋果電腦）

譯文：蘋果電腦，不同凡「想」。

這句英語廣告詞採用擬人的修辭手法，把蘋果電腦生動地擬化為一個會思考的人，而且它的思想還與眾不同。這句廣告詞充分展現了蘋果電腦卓爾不群的品質，讓消費者有了擁有蘋果電腦的念頭。而漢語譯文套用了「不同凡響」的四字成語，並按照原文 think 一詞的意思將「不同凡響」創造性地改譯成「不同凡想」。

例11：Take TOSHIBA, take the world.（東芝電子）

譯文：擁有東芝，擁有世界。

這句英語廣告詞採用了排比和重複的修辭手法。排比和重複的運用使句子更有氣勢，語言更有力量，廣告的作用也更為突出，能一下子吸引人的眼球。漢語句子也採用了排比和重複的修辭手法。

二、廣告英語的翻譯

廣告英語的翻譯，最常用的方法就是直譯和意譯。直譯是盡可能保留原文的語言結構，用目標語中最相近的語言結構來處理它，如前文例1、3、4、5、6、8、11 都採用了這種方法。意譯通常指目標語中保留原文所要傳達的基本信息，但為了語言表達生動活潑，提高廣告的吸引力，原文的形式允許有一定的創造性，如前文例2、9 都是採用這種方法。

在廣告英語翻譯中，我們還可以創造性地對原文的內容和意義進行深度挖掘，或完全摒棄原文的形式進行創造性的翻譯，使廣告語在目標讀者中引起更多、更美好的聯想。

例12：Connecting People.（諾基亞）

譯文：科技以人為本。

這句英文廣告語的字面意義為「聯繫大眾」,但如果漢語中用這句話來做廣告,顯得比較平淡,不易吸引人們的眼球並引起人們的購買慾望,而且也無法顯示諾基亞作為一個科技型企業的特點。漢語中用「科技以人為本」作為譯文,雖然形式上不對等,但從深層意思上來說,它不僅強調了諾基亞的企業特點,而且強調了諾基亞一貫以來信奉的理念,那就是從產品開發到人才管理都要體現以人為本的思想。也正是通過執行這一理念,諾基亞才有可能使全世界的人通過手機這種通信設備聯繫在一起。

為了使譯文更加出彩,更能被漢語讀者所接受,廣告英語的翻譯方法還有套譯法。英語和漢語兩種語言在傳播發展中已逐漸形成了某些固定模式或習慣表達方法。套譯即指套用這些已經約定俗成的模式,如漢語中的四字成語或諺語等對英語廣告進行翻譯。前文的例7、10都採用了這種方法。

Translation Practice

Translate the following advertisements into Chinese.
1. Start ahead.(飄柔)
2. Every time a good time.(麥當勞)
3. Everyone's invited.(三星數碼)
4. The world's local bank.(匯豐銀行)
5. Time is what you make of it.(斯沃奇手錶)

10.4　Focused Writing

Brochures

What is a brochure?

A brochure is a pamphlet or booklet, especially one that summarizes promotional information in printed or digital versions. Brochures are designed and used as a marketing tool to advertise services or products and to provide information to people about many different types of topics: such as the A (H1N1) flu, technical specifications of equipment, or tourist sites.

What points should be noted when writing a brochure?

The following aspects are worth our attention in writing brochures.

Layout:

—There are no particular rules regarding layout other than that the brochure should be user friendly. This means that the information should be clearly and concisely written and easy to read. Therefore, sentences should be short. The use of capital letters, bold type, sub-headings, pictures and diagrams are also common. An interesting aspect of brochures is that they are seldom read in what we have come to know as 「the right order」. Therefore, cross referencing to different sections may be necessary.

Content:

—Brochures normally provide information. However, it is important to think of the main purpose of the brochure: who will use it and how. If the purpose of the brochure is to advertise a product then it should merely pique the reader's interest (激起讀者的興趣). Saying too much could just be boring! However, do ensure that clients who may like to follow up on what the brochure is advertising can do so easily—ensure website addresses, telephone numbers or email addresses are clearly and accurately displayed. If the brochure provides instructions, then of course, all essential information should be provided logically and clearly.

Language:

—Language in brochures must be clear, easy to understand and persuasive. Full sentences are not necessary for the whole text; slogans may be useful when persuading people to buy a certain product or to use a certain service. Figures or statistics may also be employed to impart information briefly and clearly.

Sample 1   **A Product Brochure**

Go the Distance with Marathon
Marathon: No faults. No halts. No kidding.

What happens to your business if your servers go down? Don't want to even think about the answer? With Marathon Endurance solutions this is a question you will never need to ask.

Marathon Endurance protects your Intel/Windows—based servers from downtime due to component failures, hot swaps, and transient operating system faults. It provides the highest levels of fault and disaster tolerance so your business can continue to work at peak productivity, generate revenue, save money, and satisfy your customers.

The Endurance Product

It's Marathon's patented technology that makes the difference:
- Choice—available on leading server brands
- ComputeThru processing—no failure event will stop a transaction in progress
- Load'n Go^{TM}, No Touch Recovery^{TM}—any replaced component will automatically rejoin
- Continuous data access—data is available even through failures of OS or hardware
- Uninterrupted connectivity—duplicate network connections
. OS fault resilience—patented architecture provides extra level of OS fault resilience for off-the-shelf Windows OS
- No need for scripting or cluster API programming
. Disaster tolerance—optional SplitSite capability allows physical separation of redundant systems

For more information

Please contact your authorized Marathon Business Partner or Marathon directly:
Marathon Technologies Corporation
1300 Massachusetts Avenue
Boxborough, MA 01719 U. S. A.
Toll Free: 1-800-884-6425
Phone: 978-266-9999
Fax: 978-266-0023
Email: info@ marathontechnologies. com
www. marathontechnologies. com

Sample 2: A School Brochure

At Harvard, you can study Catalan, French, Italian, Portuguese or Spanish, as a total beginner or at whatever level you reached in high school. Through our many courses in language, literature, and culture, you can study the Romance world of the past or look into what is going on today in France, Spain, Latin America, Italy, Portugal and Brazil, as well as in other countries and regions where Romance languages are spoken. You will learn about these places and peoples by reading their literature, watching their films, studying their cultural history, reading the press, or watching television news programs transmitted by satellite or via the web Many of our courses use feature films, and a number include computer-based materials.

As you can see from the variety of offerings listed in the Courses of Instruction, we recognize that Harvard students are a diverse group, and have many different reasons for studying the language or literature of a given culture. In our department, whose languages are spoken on five continents, as well as in the South Pacific, you can read many of the classic authors who have defined Western thought and civilization as we know it, as well as those who are voicing the ideas and experience of emerging nations.

French

Regardless of your special interests or the concentration you choose, during your years at Harvard you will feel the influence of France. Historically, France and its culture have played a major role in areas as diverse as philosophy, sociology, political science, cuisine, dance, art and cinema, as well as literature and literary theory. Today, French studies encompass the literature and culture of the entire French-speaking world both inside and outside of France, including many countries in Africa and the Caribbean, Belgium and Switzerland in Europe, and our northern neighbor, the Canadian province of Quebec. Some students are attracted to French by the beauty of the language; others a re fascinated by the desire to study or live in France or in a francophone country and realize that to do so, they need to know the language Along with language, courses in French in the Department of Romance Languages and Literature, allow students to study intellectual currents in literature, including the canon (the classics of French literature), contemporary philosophy and criticism, feminist writings, contemporary civilization, and francophone novels, poetry and cinema.

Italian

Although you may not know it, you already speak Italian. Opera, piano, tempo, pasta, pizza, maestro and soprano are just a few examples of words that you use without realizing their Italian connection. But Italian is more than food and music. For you at Harvard, studying Italian will be like going beyond a few coastal resorts that you may know to explore a new and rich continent. There you will find that Italian is indeed the language of good things in life, but also the vehicle of a glorious tradition of master pieces and landmarks of our civilization from Dante and Machiavelli to Pirandello and Fellini.

(The introduction to other languages taught is omitted due to limited space here.)

The Office of International Programs (OIP), the Harvard Summer School and the David Rockefeller Center for Latin American Studies (DRCLAS) offer several opportunities for study and work in Spanish-speaking countries. In addition to its office in Cambridge, the David Rockefeller Center has overseas offices in Santiago, Chile and São Paulo, Brazil, and soon plans to open an office in Mexico City. These orifices help organize comprehensive academic and extracurricular/work experiences for Harvard students in many different Latin American countries. For specific information regarding programs and opportunities available to students, visit the David Rockefeller Center web site, the Office of International Programs website and the Harvard Summer School.

For further information

For information about the Department of Romance Languages and Literature and about language study, literature courses, or concentration in French, Italian, Portuguese, and Spanish, you can consult the department's website at http: //www. fas. harvard. edu/~rll or call (617) 495-2524. You are also welcome to visit us and to speak with our Undergraduate Advisers in Boylston Hall.

Writing Assignment

Write a brochure for the postgraduate program you are pursuing.

國家圖書館出版品預行編目（CIP）資料

大學英語綜合 / 梁虹, 王洋　主編. -- 第一版.
-- 臺北市：崧博出版：崧燁文化發行, 2019.04
　　面；　公分
POD版

ISBN 978-957-735-777-9(平裝)

1.英語教學 2.高等教育

805.103　　　　　　　　　　　108005441

書　　名：大學英語綜合
作　　者：梁虹、王洋 主編
發 行 人：黃振庭
出 版 者：崧博出版事業有限公司
發 行 者：崧燁文化事業有限公司
E - m a i l：sonbookservice@gmail.com
粉 絲 頁：　　　　　　網　址：
地　　址：台北市中正區重慶南路一段六十一號八樓815室
8F.-815, No.61, Sec. 1, Chongqing S. Rd., Zhongzheng Dist., Taipei City 100, Taiwan (R.O.C.)
電　　話：(02)2370-3310　傳　真：(02) 2370-3210
總 經 銷：紅螞蟻圖書有限公司
地　　址：台北市內湖區舊宗路二段121巷19號
電　　話：02-2795-3656 傳真:02-2795-4100　　網址：
印　　刷：京峯彩色印刷有限公司（京峰數位）

　　本書版權為西南財經大學出版社所有授權崧博出版事業股份有限公司獨家發行電子書及繁體書繁體字版。若有其他相關權利及授權需求請與本公司聯繫。

定　　價：330元
發行日期：2019年04月第一版
◎ 本書以POD印製發行